My Soul Then Sings:

Book Two of the Song of the Heart Series

My Soul Then Sings:

Book Two of the Song of the Heart Series

Michelle Lindo-Rice

Urban Books, LLC
97 N18th Street
Wyandanch, NY 11798

My Soul Then Sings: Book Two of the Song of the Heart
Series Copyright © 2015 Michelle Lindo-Rice

ISBN 13: 978-1-62286-812-4
ISBN 10: 1-62286-812-9

First Trade Paperback Printing September 2015
Printed in the United States of America

10 9 8 7 6 5 4 3 2 1

*This is a work of fiction. Any references or similarities
to actual events, real people, living or dead, or to real
locales are intended to give the novel a sense of reality.
Any similarity in other names, characters, places, and
incidents is entirely coincidental.*

Distributed by Kensington Publishing Corp.
Submit Orders to:
Customer Service
400 Hahn Road
Westminster, MD 21157-4627
Phone: 1-800-733-3000
Fax: 1-800-659-2436

My Soul Then Sings:

Book Two of the Song of the Heart Series

Michelle Lindo-Rice

What readers are saying about

My Soul Then Sings:
Book Two of the Song of the Heart Series

"Michelle Lindo-Rice really pushed herself to the next level of literary entertainment."
—Blessedselling author E. N. Joy of the *New Day Divas* series

What readers are saying about

Sing a New Song:
Book One of the Song of the Heart Series

"Ms. Lindo-Rice writes with heart, humor, and honesty."
—Shana Burton, author of *Flawless,* and *Flaws and All*

"Michelle Lindo-Rice has written a sweet story of the power of love despite the main character's (Tiffany's) sordid past."
—Michelle Stimpson, bestselling author of *Falling into Grace*

"The author's writing is crisp and her character's emotions are authentic."
—Pat Simmons, award-winning and bestselling author of the *Guilty* series.

"The author did a phenomenal job in drawing the reader's heart and spirit into the characters . . . Ms. Lindo-Rice developed an endearing, engaging, multilayered story with realism and redemption."

—Norma Jarrett, *Essence* bestselling author of *Sunday Brunch*

What readers are saying about

Walk a Straight Line

"The message of resilience in Colleen's story is powerful and important . . . as is the message of commitment, love, and friendship that come through."

—Rhonda McKnight, bestselling author of *An Inconvenient Friend* and *What Kind of Fool*

What readers are saying about

My Steps Are Ordered

"The author does a wonderful job expressing issues in marriage, how secrets affect a family, and how God can turn any situation around."

—Teresa Beasley, A&RBC Reviews

Dedication

To my sister, Zara Grace Nicola Anderson

Your smile lights up a room.
Your voice ushers in the presence of God.

Acknowledgments

I am very thankful to God. He is my all.
THANK YOU:
To my sons: Eric Michael Rice and Jordan Elijah Rice.

To my parents, family, and friends, who read, reread, and then purchase my books: Zara Anderson, Sobi-Dee Lindo, Margaret "Mommy" Anderson, Jane Adams, and Christine Reed.

Extra special mention to my young publicist: Angelicia Anderson. Thanks, Angie, for giving out bookmarks and telling everyone at school, even teachers, about my books.

To Velma Thompson: Thanks for the prayers and for putting a bookmark in every letter you put in the mail.

To the Urban Family: Mr. Weber, Natalie, Smiley, Karen, and all the others.

To Joylynn Ross, acquisitions editor and bestselling author of one of my all-time favorite reads: *I Ain't Me No More*. Yes, I have to mention it.

To J. J. and Amy. To bloggers and reviewers who journey with me through every novel: Teresa Beasley, Kiera Northington, Orsayor Simmons, Tiffany Tyler, Patricia Markham Woodside, and others.

To *all* my loyal readers: Your words of encouragement, reviews, and word-of-mouth praise are unequaled. Special mention to Leslie Hudson, the first person to write me as a new author. And, I must include April Gordon Buchanan.

A Note to My Readers

Friends, thank you so much for choosing to read my work. Welcome to my world. I am so blessed to bring you my fifth novel with Urban Books. When I started writing over twelve years ago, I never imagined that God would bless me with the opportunity to reach so many readers.

My Soul Then Sings is the second book of what I am calling, the "Song of the Heart" series. Though I love drama and all the complication and messiness that come with it, I want to tell you about something that is not complicated. In fact, it is quite simple.

Salvation. Salvation is a free gift from God to all who are willing to accept it. Even though we do not deserve it, Romans 5:8 says, "But God commendeth his love toward us, in that, while we were yet sinners, Christ died for us."

Yes. It's true. Jesus has paid for all our sins by shedding His blood. All those thousands of years ago, Jesus looked ahead in time. He saw me. He saw you. And Jesus decided we were worth Him giving His life. And, He did.

Now, please enjoy *My Soul Then Sings*. Strap on your seat belts and enjoy the ride!

Sincerely,
Michelle Lindo-Rice

Chapter One

Five years.

For five whole years Ryan Oakes had kept a secret, but he knew it was confession time.

"Today," he said, gripping the steering wheel, "I'm telling Patti the truth, today."

Ryan pulled his cream-colored Lincoln Navigator in the driveway of his five thousand square foot Brick Georgian Colonial home in Garden City, Long Island. He put the car into park but kept the motor running.

Ryan tapped the wheel. He had been saved for all of six months now, and someone had forgotten to tell him that salvation came with a Conscience—with a capital C—that prodded him to fess up and tell his wife and son what he had done.

The car sat idle as he vacillated. No, he could not do it. The more he thought about it, the more he was convinced that there were some lies that should remain in the past. God had forgiven him and tossed all of his sins in the sea of forgetfulness. He would hold on to that.

Ryan sighed. He was forgiven, but if only he could forget. He leaned back into the leather seat and hit the back of his head several times against the padded headrest before closing his eyes. Determined, he shook his head and groaned, "No no no," but that did not erase the guilt gnawing at him. There was no other option. He had to tell the truth. He knew it.

Patricia "Patti" Oakes opened the front door and poked her head out. Ryan's eyes raked her five-ten slender frame, olive skin, and flowing auburn curls. One look at her sultry smile and pouty mouth and Ryan switched gears. Anxious, he undid the locks and crooked his finger.

She ambled toward him with a seductive sway of her hips. Patricia was a neurosurgeon, which meant she was a heady combination of smart and sexy.

Ryan hid a small smile. He knew what she was thinking, and he liked that idea. He waited for Patricia to open the passenger door and watched as she swung her long legs to hoist herself into the vehicle. As soon as she was settled, he placed his hand on her left leg and inched upward. "I've missed you," he whispered. "As I sat in business meetings all day, I only had one thought. Coming home to see your face."

"I've missed you too." Her skirt hiked higher. "I didn't expect to be in surgery all night, and by the time I came in this morning, you'd already left."

He heard her plaintive voice and knew what she needed. Ryan reached for the seat adjustment and slid his seat backward. In a swift move, he lifted Patricia like a rag doll and positioned her so she straddled his lap. He drew her close to him and sniffed. She smelled like lavender. "I can't wait," he said, while his lips and hands proved his point.

"I figured as much," Patricia groaned.

He was going to have her here and now. Ryan shifted the car in drive and curved his head around her body so that he could see. Then he pressed the garage door opener and pulled into the huge space. He did not care about being discreet, but if Brian, their only son, pulled up and saw them in such a compromising position, he would have their heads.

Ryan and Patricia loved each other almost to the point of obsession. Their consuming passion had made them oblivious to all, including Brian. For most of his formative years, Brian had felt ignored and unloved, which had led to his acting out, truancy, and aberrant behaviors. Ryan and Patricia had not known how Brian felt, and if they had not met Tiffany Knightly before she passed, they would have lost their son.

Tiffany had taken Brian under her wing as a surrogate mother. She fed him and encouraged Brian to quit smoking, get his act together, and improve his grades. Thirsty for love, Brian had clung to her and flourished under her attention.

It was because of Tiffany—and later her daughter, Karlie—their son was now in college and on the right path toward becoming a contributor to society. Brian, Karlie, and her boyfriend, Jamaal, attended New York University.

"I can't wait, honey," Patricia moaned. As soon as the garage door closed, she undressed.

Ryan eyed the tempting display and smiled. He was all too willing to comply. After almost twenty-five years together, Ryan still found her desirable and insatiable, and he loved that about her.

"Me, either, honey," he whispered. He kissed her with passion before tearing his lips away. "Patti, we're behaving like teenagers when we have a king-sized, four-poster bed inside the house."

"I don't need a bed," she pouted. "I just need you."

Patricia made a valid point. Throwing caution to the wind, Ryan made love to his wife. Afterward, when they exited the vehicle, they did not make it past the living room. Ravenous, Ryan and Patricia clawed each other with unbridled passion. He knocked over one of the $300 Murray Feiss lamps from an end table. Both ignored it.

Fortunately for them, Brian had not decided to pay them a visit that day. As they lay on the carpet in each

other's arms, Ryan cradled his wife's head and played
with the tendrils of her hair. Her skin glistened from the
effects of their passion. Again, his conscience pricked
him.

Tell her.

"No, I can't." He uttered the words in a low tone of
voice, but Patricia heard him. She turned her body
toward him and kissed him on the neck. "Can't what?"

I can't tell you the truth. Ryan rubbed his nose in her
hair. *Mmm.* He smelled apricots. "I can't have you again,
though I want to." It wasn't a complete lie. He wanted
Patricia all the time.

"Oh, Ryan, I love you," she sighed. "How did I luck out
with such a good man?" She took his face in her hands
and kissed him gently on the lips. "I hear women at
work gripe about their husbands, boyfriends, and baby
daddies, and I consider myself blessed that I don't have
any worries like that. You're a rare breed of man, Ryan
Oakes, and I love you always."

Ryan gulped, and his conscience gave him a swift kick
in the gut. He closed his eyes because he knew that he did
not deserve that trusting look on her face. Not anymore.
But, he could not bear to see Patricia's trust turn into
disgust. What was he going to do?

Nothing.

"Wake up, sleepyhead." Patricia poked him in the
chest.

"Lord, help me," Ryan prayed. He pried his eyes open.

His wife misunderstood and chuckled. "Yes, He's going
to have to help you because of what I've got planned . . ."

Ryan felt her body shift and knew what she intended to
do. *Tomorrow.* He would tell her tomorrow. Never mind
that he said that yesterday—and the day before that. He
would keep his word this time. Tomorrow would be
the day.

Chapter Two

"What do they mean my sound is too sweet?"

Karlie Knightly swept her shoulder-length curls out of her face. She crisscrossed her long legs on her king-sized bed in the Marlton Hotel.

Karlie had wanted to rent an apartment, but her adopted father, Neil Jameson, convinced her to live in the hotel. That way she would not have to cook or worry about housekeeping with her coursework load. She had stepped into the luxurious building resplendent with rich burgundy undertones and had fallen in love. Though the rooms were small, she loved the crown moldings, brass fixtures, and the private marble bathroom. The onsite restaurant and café added to its appeal.

She clutched a printout from a quack blogger who was gathering clout. Her debut song, "How Great Thou Art," had released to not-so-stellar reviews. According to this twit wannabe reporter, Karlie's voice was nothing like her "dearly departed mother's."

In fact, Brenda Northeimer called her sound "too sweet, saccharine, and filled with fake sentiment to grasp the raw emotion needed for a song like that."

Try losing your mother and see how you would feel.

Karlie grabbed several tissues from her nightstand and blew her nose. She knew she could not sing like her mother did. She was not trying to. She was her own person. Karlie crumpled the paper and tossed it against the wall. It landed on the herringbone wood floor with a thud.

Karlie strolled in her bathroom to throw out the soiled tissues and wash her face. She looked in the mirror at her almond-shaped face, so much like her mother's except Karlie had honey-colored eyes and slightly fuller lips.

Brenda Northheimer did not know what it was like to be left alone because cancer had reared its head and torn her life to pieces. Five years had passed, but that did not stop Karlie from wetting her pillow at night for a mother who she would never see again.

Neil and his wife, Myra had taken her into their home and hearts. Their daughter, Addison, Addie for short, whom she adored, was the sister she never had. But Karlie missed her mother. Tiffany Knightly was irreplaceable.

Karlie's cell phone buzzed. She jumped to retrieve it from her computer desk, hoping that it was her boyfriend, Jamaal Weathers. She had texted him earlier, but he still had classes, and then had step rehearsal after that.

It was not Jamaal. It was Brian.

Let me in.

Ugh, why didn't Brian ever give her advanced notice? He just popped in whenever the mood struck. Karlie wiped her face. Since she lived on the second floor, she knew he would be at her door any minute. She scrambled to make her bed and picked up the crumpled paper. She was about to throw it into the trash can when she heard the knock.

Holding the paper in her left hand behind her back, Karlie opened the door. "Hey, Brian."

"Hey, yourself, Sweet Cheeks." He squeezed her cheeks and entered her small space.

Trying to be discreet, Karlie tossed the paper into the trash can, but Brian zeroed in on her action.

"What's that?" he asked.

"It's nothing," Karlie replied, shooing her hand and moving away from the can.

Brian squinted his eyes. He was not buying her act. He bent his six-foot-five frame and pinned his light brown eyes on her face. "Your eyes are puffy. Have you been crying?"

"No." She shook her head.

Brian studied her before walking over to the trash can. He reached in and picked it up.

Karlie lunged toward him to get the paper out of his hands. "What're you doing? You can't just come in here and rummage through my trash!"

Brian held his arm above her head.

Karlie jumped to get the paper. "Brian, give it to me. You're so juvenile."

He swayed it out of her reach. "Considering it's the only thing in the garbage, I wouldn't say that was rummaging. In fact, I was only searching for a piece of paper to stick my gum in."

"You're such a liar, Brian Oakes," Karlie said. "You don't have any gum in your mouth. You're being nosy as usual, and this is a severe breach of my privacy."

"Whatever." Brian unrolled the paper.

Mortified, Karlie tromped over to her bed and plopped down, not the least bit comforted by the plush Duvet covers.

Brian's head moved from left to right as he read the contents of the article. With a frown, he walked over to sit in the chair by her computer desk.

She saw his brow furrow and his lips curl and knew that he had gotten to that part.

"Who writes this trash and gets away with it?" In a fit of rage, Brian shredded the paper and hurled it back into the trashcan. "I hope you don't believe any of that filth written solely to gather a following of people who have nothing better to do with their time."

Karlie's eyes widened. Brian was so articulate. He had an artful way of manipulating words. He would make a great journalist, or was it attorney? He had changed his major four times already.

He jumped to his feet and in two strides sat next to her on her bed. With a gentle touch, he placed one large hand under her chin. "Karlie, I hope you didn't let that get to you. Fat Brenda is just doing her job. She's stuck doing that because she'll never have your figure, your finesse, and your future."

"Great alliteration," Karlie said with a smile. She shrugged. "She wasn't the only critic though—and she's not fat. Other reviewers said I had no right singing 'How Great Thou Art.' They said I hadn't been through anything. I have a silver spoon in my mouth. Blah . . . blah . . . blah . . ."

"Let them talk," Brian said. "Karlie, they don't know you. They've forgotten your pain of losing your mother. Because they don't know better, they feel your being stinking rich is the solution to all your problems."

Karlie winced. It was true that she didn't have to struggle financially, but it didn't mean that she didn't have struggles. When Winona Franks had approached her about launching her singing career, Karlie had fought tooth and nail. Winona had been her mother's friend and longtime manager. Winona was a business whiz and under her guidance, Tiffany had made more money than she knew how to spend. Winona was ready to take Karlie under her wing.

Karlie agreed to do the well-known song as a trial to get her feet wet. Never had she imagined how much the rejection would hurt. Never had she realized how much she wanted it. She wanted to sing.

"Come on." Brian stood. "Grab a jacket. Let's go get you some ice cream."

"I don't know if I feel up for ice cream. Why don't we just go downstairs to the Espresso Bar or even Margaux?" She especially loved Margaux's alcove. The floral hangings gave the place cozy warmth.

Besides, she had another reason why she wanted to stay close. Karlie didn't want to miss Jamaal if he decided to check in on her.

"Why? Is Jamaal coming over?" He raised his eyebrows.

Brian could be so astute at times it was scary. Karlie gave him a playful slap. "Shut up. It's not what you think. Get your mind out of the gutter, Brian. We're saved. You know that."

He looked heavenward. "Yes, I know. But you guys have been dating since you were fifteen. That's a long, long time for a couple to be abstinent."

"And your point is?" Karlie arched her eyebrow.

She and Jamaal vowed to remain celibate until marriage. It was difficult, but they knew they could do it—with God's help.

"You mean to say Jamaal hasn't tried anything in all these years? And you'd better not lie to me because I'll know."

Karlie squirmed, not wanting to stretch the truth but not wanting to confess either. Instead, she attacked. With her nose in the air, she said, "Not every man behaves like a Neanderthal like *some* people."

"Ouch." Brian grinned and stepped back. He held up his hand. "Take it easy, young one. I meant no harm."

"Don't call me young one. You're only two years older than me. Twenty-three is not old."

"Yes, but I've been through a lot."

That was true. Brian had grown up with two parents who made him feel as if he did not matter. As a result, he had been a juvenile bordering on delinquent until Karlie's mother had rescued him from himself.

Karlie touched his arm and gave him a squeeze. "Yes, Brian, but you've turned your life around."

He looked at her with a penetrating gaze.

For the first time in their six-year friendship, Karlie felt awkward. This strange tension had been happening between them of late, and she could not explain it. Not that she was trying too hard to figure it out.

She drew a deep breath and grabbed her sweater from the back of the chair. Maybe going out would not be such a bad idea. "I've changed my mind. Let's go to Yooglers. I'll text Jamaal and tell him where to meet us."

Yooglers Frozen Yogurt was located on 791 Broadway and was a quick seven-minute walk.

He smiled. "Yooglers sounds good."

Karlie noted Brian's pearly whites and felt a small shift. What was happening here? How come she never noticed that Brian had such a beautiful smile before? In fact, he was fine. *Super* fine.

Confused by her sudden thoughts, Karlie distracted herself by putting on her sweater. They exited her building on Eighth Street and walked toward Broadway and made a left.

She shoved her hands into the pockets of her jean jacket. The March air felt nippy. Spring was taking its time arriving this year. She and Brian made small talk but concentrated on navigating their way through the busy streets of Manhattan. It was a few minutes shy of nine p.m. when they arrived.

Brian held the door open, and Karlie breathed in the smell of cookies, candies, chocolate, and syrups, not to mention yogurt. She rubbed her hands together in anticipation.

"What are you having this time?" Brian asked.

Every time Karlie went to Yooglers she tried a new flavor. So far, she had had seven of their forty-six different flavors, ranging from Cappuccino to Snickerdoodle.

"I think I'm getting the Fudge Brownie Batter this time," she said, wrinkling her nose. Glancing around the orange and green establishment, she was glad there were only a few customers.

Brian headed toward the huge cow on the wall, near the entrance to the play area.

"Don't even think about touching those balls. They were meant for six-year-olds not a six-footer."

He executed a U-turn and grabbed a container. Brian chose the French Toast yogurt before trailing after her to get toppings. He piled his cup high with brownie bites, crushed chocolate mints, cheesecake bites, and marshmallow sauce.

Karlie stuck to just the yogurt. They strolled to the counter to weigh their yogurt and paid for their treat before finding a table.

Brian scooped a large spoonful of his concoction and popped it into his mouth. After he licked the spoon, he said, "As much as I hate to admit it, Karlie, I think Brenda what's-her-name has a point."

Karlie plopped her half-eaten yogurt on the table and glared at him. With careful enunciation, she asked, "What do you mean 'she has a point'?"

"Whoa. Hear me out." Brian held both hands up. "What I mean is that your voice is beautiful, but it lacks an edge—it lacks the haunting tone of someone who has experienced some things."

"You're contradicting yourself," Karlie replied. "What about all that talk back at my place, when you said . . ." She looked around and lowered her voice. "What about when you said that losing my mother is tough and all that."

"Yes, but you're the quintessential poster girl." Brian took another scoop of his treat. He pushed Karlie's yogurt back toward her.

After a couple seconds, she dug in. "What's wrong with being a good girl, Brian?"

"Nothing, but it's boring," he said. "No one cares about the good girl. You're a yawn. You've got to get some edge. Do something crazy—out of this world—you know, let more people notice you. Get to know you. You've got to get out of your mother's shadow. You can't be Tiffany Knightly's daughter. You've got to be you—Karlie. Who is she anyway?"

Karlie's mouth popped open. She did not know how to answer. She was still searching for her identity. "I'm—I'm me."

Brian yawned for effect. His point hit home.

Karlie used her spoon to flick a dollop of frozen yogurt toward his left cheek.

He laughed, swiped at it with his thumb, and tasted it. "You need to do some crazy stuff and post it to YouTube. You know like Miley Cyrus twerking all over the place."

Twerking was the name of the dance move where young ladies jiggled their rear ends in a sensual, suggestive manner.

Karlie splayed her hands. "You can forget about that. I'm not twerking or doing all that crazy nonsense. I'm a church girl, and I like it." She folded her arms in stubborn protest.

"I didn't mean for you to shake your booty and post for the world to see—although, I *would* like to see that." Brian grinned.

Karlie wasn't amused.

He hoped to redeem himself. "Karlie, all I am asking is when are you going to stop being and start living?"

Karlie knew her eyes were wide. "I *am* living." She slid her chair away from the table.

Brian leaned over. "You need to try things—mudding, parasailing, snorkeling—you know, atypical adventures for a black woman."

"That sounds crazy. I'm not trying to kill myself. You should know me better to even suggest that."

"I do know you better, which is why I'm suggesting you step out of your comfort zone. You won't be killing yourself. You'd be living. And stop looking at me as if I have horns on my head."

Karlie propped her elbows on the table and rested her head in her hands. "I'm looking at you that way because your idea is borderline certifiable. How do you propose I do all these adventures? I'm in school, or did you forget *that* pertinent fact?"

Brian finished his yogurt. He reached for hers and ate it. "Like the use of the word *pertinent,* by the way. But, I digress." He tossed the empty containers into the trash receptacle. "I've already thought of that, and I have a quick and easy solution."

Karlie leaned in to hear his option.

"You need to take a semester off."

Her mouth hung open. "You must be out of your mind. My dad would hit the roof if I fixed my mouth to tell them that. He's not like your dad who was cool with you taking a year after high school to backpack through Europe. He has plans—I mean, *I* have plans for my life."

"Aha. Your own words betrayed you. You are operating off everyone else's plans and expectations." He waggled a finger at her. "You, my friend, are a people pleaser."

Karlie wondered what was wrong with doing the right thing. Brian made her sound boring. "I'm not pleasing anyone but myself."

Brian waved his hands dismissively. "You're in denial, Karlie. You're all about making everyone happy. You need to do this and shake things up a little. Neil would be fine with it—eventually. We both know you've got him wrapped around your finger, just as your mother did."

Neil and Tiffany had been best friends. Tiffany trusted him with all her secrets and with her past pain. He had been the last person to see her mother alive.

Karlie could not believe she was even continuing this conversation with Brian. Nonetheless, she asked, "And what about Jamaal? There's no way he's going to take time off from school, and I'm not about to do this by myself. So, noway, nohow."

"Yes, way. And I'll tell you how. I'll take a leave myself. I'll be with you."

Karlie narrowed her eyes. "And what about Charlie, or Nikki?" She hid a smirk.

Brian shrugged. "They know the deal. I have a no-commitment clause with all my women."

Karlie shook her head at Brian's dismissive tone. "I don't understand how you manage to convince two adjunct professors to date you at the same time without pulling each other's hair out."

He patted his stomach. "It's my duty to spread love in the world." Then he got serious. "Say the word, and I'm all yours."

Chapter Three

"What will I do while you're gone?" Charlotte Hollingsworth moaned before kissing Brian's chest. Her light British accent tingled his ears.

He swatted her on the butt. "I'm sure you'll be fine."

"I know I won't," Nikki Thatcher pouted.

Spooned between two voluptuous women, Brian lay on his back on his king-sized bed in his spacious one-bedroom apartment. While other students had to share suites, Brian's parents had hooked him up in style.

One auburn-colored head and another dark-haired head graced each arm. He crossed his legs. *What a place to be.* "I'm sure neither one of you will suffer with your choice of men. Besides, I'm not going anywhere until the end of May."

Nikki's hand grazed his body. She gave him a sly smile. "We'll keep you busy till then."

"How did I get so lucky to have both of you?" Brian mused, bobbing back and forth between the two of them. Honestly, if he could merge the two of them into one being, he would have the perfect woman. Knowing him, however, he would still find something wrong. The problem was they were not a certain someone, who would remain nameless.

"It isn't luck," Charlie said. "It's called skill. This has been one of the most satisfying eight months of my life."

Nikki kissed his cheek. "I agree."

"I need to help Karlie," Brian explained for the third time.

Nikki shifted to rest her head in his arms. "What does she have that we don't?"

Before he could answer, Charlie stood. "I've got to use the bathroom and head back to my dorm. I have papers to grade."

"She's my best friend," Brian said to Nikki, once Charlie closed the door to the bathroom. "Karlie is like a sister to me." He swallowed.

Liar.

Brian ignored the inner voice. He wasn't ready to delve into those emotions.

Nikki snorted. "Please. I don't believe you two never smashed."

Brian turned to face her. "We're friends. It is possible for a male and female to be platonic."

Charlie opened the door and caught the tail end of the conversation. "What are we talking about? Let me guess, Karlie?"

Nikki sat up, unashamed of her nakedness. Eyeing her, Brian knew she had no reason to be. Her body was well toned from hours in the gym. "Yes. He's trying to convince me, or rather himself, that they're just friends."

Charlie wiggled into her jeans and searched under the bed for the rest of her clothes. Though the lights weren't on, the moonlight provided enough light to help in her search. Nikki dressed as well.

"You're leaving too?" Brian asked.

The Puerto Rican beauty faced him. "I have a practicum at five-thirty in the morning and two classes to teach in the afternoon. I need my rest because you wore me out. I can't be next to that soft butterscotch skin and not want more."

It was half-past eleven, and Brian cracked a self-satisfied smile. Another satisfied customer. He looked at Charlie. Or, rather, *two* satisfied customers.

His cell rang. Karlie's face flashed on the screen. Brian sat up and swiped to answer. "Are you okay?"

"Yes," she breathed.

Brian waved off the two women who blew him kisses. His mind was now preoccupied with the other person on the line. He swung his legs to the floor and switched on the small bedside lamp.

"It's almost midnight, so this is not nothing."

"Did I disturb you?" Karlie asked. "I didn't even think that you might have company."

He heard the slight hesitation in her tone and quickly reassured her. "I did, and they're gone. Get on with it. What's on your mind?"

Karlie sighed. "I can't sleep. Winona called me. The record label isn't sure they want to back my next project after such lackluster reviews."

"That's why I told you to start a YouTube channel. Once your stunts go viral, that will all change. Believe me."

Another dramatic sigh resounded through the line. "I guess."

"Where is your faith, Christian woman?" Brian asked. "You're always telling me about God, and how He can do anything. Why can't He do this for you?"

Karlie chuckled. "Not *you* voluntarily bringing God into the conversation. I'm usually the one trying to convince you to trust Him."

Brian smiled. "Well, He must be growing on me." He stood. *Ugh.* His lower back hurt. Uh-oh, he knew what that meant. While Karlie rambled about telling Jamaal and her parents about their plans, Brian ambled over to his closet. It boasted a huge mirror so he could investigate what was on his back. Sure enough, he saw the beginnings of an outbreak. Brian groaned, knowing what was coming next.

"Brian? Are you listening to me?"

Huh. What did she say? His brain couldn't recall. "I got a little distracted for a second. Repeat your last sentence."

"I said that I'm meeting up with Jamaal tomorrow to talk. I told him about my taking a semester off, and he wasn't too thrilled."

"Yeah, I saw him at the gym, and we talked about it. I tried to persuade him to tag along, but he shut me down."

Brian wandered into his bathroom and opened a drawer. Rummaging around, he searched for his topical cream. It had been months since his last outbreak, and he had foolishly believed that he had been cured.

"I . . . Maybe this isn't a good idea . . ."

He could almost visualize her playing with the bridge of her nose. That was her habit whenever she was deep in thought or unsure about something.

Brian put the phone on speaker and unscrewed the cap to his prescription ointment. "Karlie, there's a time when you have to be decisive. The last thing you want is to look back at your life and have regrets. Consider this an adventure before you and Jamaal settle down to the proverbial white picket fence with two-point-one children."

Karlie's laughter echoed in the small space. "Thanks for being a good friend to me." She emitted an unladylike yawn. "I'd better get some sleep. Professor Stewart does not tolerate tardiness. Her words, not mine."

Brian saw The end sign flash across his screen. He twisted his body to get a look at the red blister on his lower back. With deft maneuvering, he applied the ointment. Then he washed his hands and trudged over to his bed. He lay on his stomach not wanting to soil the five hundred-dollar linens Patricia had insisted on purchasing when she decorated his space.

Psoriasis. How he hated the disease. He'd been twenty-one when he had suffered his first outbreak. At first, Brian had thought it was a rash or an insect bite, but then debilitating pain followed. That was when he had called his mom. Patricia referred him to a dermatologist who slapped him with the diagnosis. He had researched for hours to learn more about the incurable immune attack.

To make matters worse, Brian had psoriatic arthritis, which is why he felt such pain. Besides his lower back, his feet flared up sometimes. Lucky for him he could hide it. And he did.

No one except his parents knew about his psoriasis. None of the women Brian had been with knew, and he planned to keep it that way. The condition was not contagious so he was not worried about spreading it to anyone. But he was afraid. Afraid of being scorned and rejected.

Brian touched his lower back. His fingertips told him that this was a small flare-up. Relief seeped through him. That meant he would be able to function. He would know in a few hours if he would make it to his eleven o'clock class. Sometimes, the pain would become so unbearable that he cried like a baby.

Brian curled onto his side. He took deep breaths to relax his body and mind. He knew from experience that he needed to rest. With quiet determination, he closed his eyes.

"Lord, please," he whispered into the night.

No one knew he prayed. It was always just those two words, but Brian prayed. When it came to his condition, he had no other choice.

Chapter Four

"I can't believe you're seriously considering doing something so ridiculous!" Jamaal said, heedless of the throng of passersby in Washington State Park. Birds circled by the monument where he stood, but he did not care.

Dressed in a wool jacket, battling wind-tossed hair, Karlie nodded. "I know Brian's idea seems crazy, but it's growing on me. I have been thinking about it nonstop for weeks."

The spring temperatures were delightful, but the winds were strong for April. Dusk was about to fall, but neither noticed as the streetlights would beam brightly enough to keep the park well illuminated.

"But, what about me, the church—Neil, Myra, and Addie?" he asked. "What are we all supposed to do while you're off on your grand adventures?" Jamaal stood close to her, eye to eye. His breath fanned her bangs.

Karlie's voice cracked. She touched his cheek. "Jamaal, I'm already torn at the thought of taking a semester off, but it's not like I'm going to Timbuktu. I'll still be on U.S. soil most of the time. I'm just living a little. It's time I expand my horizon and broaden my experiences."

Jamaal huffed and moved out of reach. Steam emanated off his body as he continued his tirade. "Are you even listening to yourself right now? You sound just like *him*. Brian and his harebrained schemes! He's in graduate school and still doesn't know what he wants to do. He's cool and fun to hang with, but he's just too—I don't even know the word. Now you're going off with him to try some crazy nonsense like skydiving."

"Well, I *suggested* you come *with* us, but you're being stuffy. As *always*."

He got in her face. "I'm not stuffy, and might I add, up until a month ago, you felt the same way I did. Well, I refuse to let the opportunity Tiffany gave to me go to waste. Your mother gave me money to better myself. If it weren't for her, I'd be hustling on the streets. But here I am studying journalism as I said I would all those years ago. I won't apologize for my ambitions."

Properly chastised, Karlie regretted her choice of words. Jamaal had been abandoned by his mother when he was a newborn. Tossed in the neighborhood garbage bin. Fortunately, his grandmother found him and raised him as her own. He lived in a dilapidated area all through high school before moving into Carlyle Court at New York University.

Karlie shuddered remembering the smell of pee and debris scattered all over. It had been eye-opening for a girl from Los Angeles who was used to the finer things in life. From the revenue of his investments, Jamaal had purchased his grandmother a home in Uniondale. That was the only big purchase he had made besides paying his tuition and room and board.

With a small voice, she apologized. "I didn't mean it like that, Jamaal. I know what my mother did for you. I applaud her generosity, and it warms my heart to see how you excel at everything you do. You're amazing—and ambitious."

Jamaal straightened. His eyes lost their fire, and he softened. "That's why I can't take a semester off, Karlie. I have to keep going. Besides, I'm the lead stepper for most of our routines. I can't leave my frat brothers in the loop, and don't forget basketball."

She nodded. "I know you feel I'm being irresponsible, but I've always done what's expected. And where has it gotten me? Lukewarm results."

"This decision of yours has me floored," Jamaal said. "It's way out of character. I hope this is a fluke, and your common sense will return by summer."

Karlie smiled, but she knew her mind was almost 100 percent made up. Brian made it sound exciting. Secretly, she had envied his decision to take off and go backpacking on his own in Europe. "I want to live."

"You *are* living," he said.

She exhaled. "Ever since my mother died five years ago, I've not been living. I've been existing. I did all the right things, said all the right things, but . . ." She shrugged. "I can't explain it. I feel unfulfilled."

Brian's comment about knowing herself had really hit home. Seeing Jamaal's mouth open and predicting what he was about to say, Karlie added, "I know I have joy in God, but He created a beautiful world that I have yet to see. Right now, I'm all boxed in."

"Then plan a European excursion or go on a cruise," he said. "*Don't* mess with your future."

The wind gushed at her skirt. Distracted, Karlie grabbed at the hem before she experienced a Marilyn Monroe moment. When she straightened, she saw Jamaal's face. He wasn't unaffected by the view of her long legs, and he was ready to ditch their previous conversation.

He reached over to cup her face in his hands. The timbre of his bass voice deepened. "Let's get out of here."

She felt herself respond but sought to steer both their minds elsewhere. "Let's get moving. We're going to miss the entire Bible study." She looked at her watch for emphasis. "We've already missed the first fifteen minutes." She grabbed his hand, then gestured that they needed to start walking.

Jamaal remain rooted to the spot.

She tugged again.

"You know where I want to go," he said. "My roommate is at his girlfriend's tonight. So we can have the place all to ourselves."

Karlie reached over to kiss him full on the lips, and Jamaal's long arms circled her waist. After a few seconds, she ended the kiss. "It's not that I don't want to," she confessed. "It's that God is there. He's everywhere."

Jamaal rubbed his head and exhaled. "Don't you think I know that? But I'm getting tired of feeling left out of the locker room conversations. That's all they ever talk about, and I—"

Karlie stormed off. He followed, as she knew he would. Her boots clicked as she pounded the pavement. "When you met me, I knew you weren't a virgin, but you told me I was worth it. You told me that you could wait until marriage."

He kept up her vigorous pace. "You are worth it, and if I could marry you, you know I would."

Karlie stopped short. "You could. Thanks to my mom, you're not destitute. So I really don't get what the holdout is for."

He grabbed her arm. The wind howled, and his baseball cap flew off his head. Grunting, Jamaal sailed after it.

Karlie tapped her heels and waited. She admired his well-defined physique honed from years of basketball. His forehead glistened when he returned. The two walked to the end of the block.

She plucked the hairs on his beard and joked. "What a way to end a conversation."

"No, no. We're not done talking. You're not going anywhere if I have my say. And, to answer your question, I haven't proposed marriage because I want to purchase your engagement ring with my own money. I wouldn't feel right buying you something so meaningful with someone else's money. The ring I put on your finger must be bought with my own hard-earned funds."

Karlie said, "That's why I love you, Jamaal."

"So don't leave me."

Here we go again. It took some effort, but she resisted the loud groan. This was how all their discussions went lately. When he wasn't trying to boycott her taking time off, Jamaal was talking about their love life—or lack of one. *Lord, help me.* He was driving her crazy, and it wasn't as if she wanted to say no all the time.

She knew she had to.

If it hadn't been for God, Karlie wouldn't have made it these past five years. Neil had introduced her to Christ, and she read her Bible daily. But her flesh was rising up. Parts of her tingled. Her body was so ready.

Karlie debated. *What if Jamaal seeks release in someone else's arms?* Her heart revolted at that thought. Girls flocked the games. The groupies followed him around the gym, not hiding their intent. It was only a matter of time. Maybe she should just give in. What did he say? He had needs.

Karlie's stomach knotted at the thought. She had plenty to pray about.

Just before they went into the study, Jamaal squeezed her hand to reassure her. But Karlie was far from reassured. She was scared.

When she returned home from Bible study that night, she called Brian, but he wasn't answering his phone. Karlie wasn't too concerned, though. Brian sometimes retreated into his own world for a day or two. He'd pop up soon enough. Instead, she focused on her upcoming conversation with Neil and Myra the following night.

As soon as she was done with her classes the next day, Karlie hopped on the train. She would then catch the Long Island Railroad and venture into Hempstead where Neil and Myra lived. Karlie housed her SUV in the Marlton's parking lot, but she preferred taking the train during rush hour.

She hailed a cab from the railroad that would take her to the place she had called home for the past five years. She smiled when she passed the pizza shop where she and Jamaal had hung out together on many occasions.

In fifteen minutes, Karlie was in front of her home. She paid the cabbie and stood outside. She looked down the block. At the end of the cul-de-sac was her mother's childhood home. Tiffany and Myra had been friends before her mother found fame. When Tiffany learned she was dying of cancer, she had packed them up and returned here to Hempstead.

Karlie had not known it at the time, but Tiffany's main purpose was to find Karlie's father. When her stepfather, Clifford Peterson raped her, Tiffany acted out by being promiscuous. During the space of one month, Tiffany slept with four men, one of whom, she married. For most of her life, Karlie had believed Thomas Knightly was her father.

It was not until Tiffany learned of her impending death that her mother had confessed. Tiffany was bedridden in the hospital by the time the paternity results came in. Neil convinced Karlie not to tell her frail mother the truth.

Karlie shook her head. Her mother died not knowing that her stepfather had been the culprit. Karlie took a step, wondering if she should go down there. No one lived there. She paid to keep it maintained, but the house was otherwise unoccupied for now.

She would go another time, she thought. That was what she told herself every time. Neil had asked her on several occasions to sell, but Karlie could not let it go. God would tell her what to do. Until then . . .

Karlie turned and opened the gate leading up to Neil and Myra's house. As she drew closer, she smelled Myra's lasagna. Her mouth watered for the spicy spaghetti sauce and three-cheese combination that melted on her palate.

As soon as she opened the door, Addison Jameson, her five-year-old sister, raced over to her. "Karlie!" Addie vaulted into Karlie's arms.

"Hey, what brings you here?" Myra asked as she wiped her hands on her apron. "You just missed dinner. I made lasagna. It's wrapped in foil on the counter. Your father is in his office."

Karlie nodded and headed to the cabinet to retrieve a plate. She scooped a generous serving and heaped it onto her dish before grabbing a fork. Once she was finished eating, she rinsed her utensils and put them in the dishwasher.

Neil Jameson walked in. "Look who decided to pay us a visit," he said.

Dressed in a short-sleeve shirt and slacks, his body was toned from hours in the gym. Judging by his tight fade, Neil had paid a recent visit to the barber. Looking at his square jaw and broad shoulders, Karlie remembered how she had wished her mother had married him. That had not happened, but Neil had adopted her as a daughter. Thomas had offered to be her guardian and moved her back to L.A. but Karlie had been miserable. She remembered her jubilation when Neil flew out to get her. Thinking of it now made Karlie smile. That was the first time she had called Neil dad.

Every day Karlie thanked God for parents like Neil and Myra. From the moment she had moved in at sixteen, Karlie had felt right at home. They were the best parents a girl could ask for.

Bringing her mind to the present, Karlie told Neil about her plans to take off a semester in the fall. His reaction was as she expected. Neil was cool and charming, but he was every inch Karlie's dad.

"Karlie, you've lost your mind if you think I would give you my blessing for something so preposterous. If Brian were here, I'd wring his neck for even putting such an absurd notion in your head."

Neil looked at her as if she were insane. Karlie resisted the urge to touch the top of her head to check to see if she had sprouted horns. She bristled on the inside but kept a respectful tone. "How do you know it wasn't my idea?"

Neil snorted, "It's a no-brainer. Because frankly, you're too smart for that. You've never even gotten a traffic violation, Karlie. You're not a risk taker by nature."

Karlie hated how he described her. She sounded like a google-eyed librarian and not a vibrant twenty-one-year-old. She squared her shoulders. "My not being a risk taker, as you put it, explains why my song came across as bland and lifeless."

"Who said that?" Neil took a step back.

"Brenda Northeimer."

"You actually read that junk she spews out daily under the pretense of news?"

"Yes, yes, I do read it. My mother was a famous celebrity. I just released a song. It is top entertainment news and subject to open scrutiny and ridicule."

Neil flailed his hands. "Listen to you. Now you even talk like *him*."

"Who?" Karlie shook her head.

"Brian. Since when do you use phrases like 'subject to open scrutiny'?" Neil asked. He folded his arms like the Mr. Clean man.

Karlie could not decide whether to be amused or insulted at his answer. "Dad, I'm educated. Brian's not the only one with a prolific vocabulary."

"There you go again." Neil arched his eyebrow.

Was she *seriously* having this conversation right now? Not for a second would Karlie admit that those were indeed Brian's terminologies. Maybe he was rubbing off on her. If so, would that be such a bad thing?

She shook her head. "Dad, I can't believe you're going along with the stereotype that black people can't speak intelligently."

"Leave her alone, Neil." Myra walked into the kitchen with a bath towel drooped over her shoulder. She had just given Addie her bath. Myra meandered her way between the two of them. Though she was smaller and rounder in stature, Myra wasn't the least bit intimidated by Neil. "I see nothing wrong with Karlie taking time off and seeing the world, so to speak. She's young. Isn't that what young people do?"

"Thanks, Mother." Karlie smiled. She bent over to kiss Myra on the cheek.

Myra gave her a comforting pat on the back.

"So, you're saying that it's okay for our daughter to go jumping out of airplanes and swimming with sharks? How many black people do *you* see doing that?"

"Neil!" Myra covered her mouth. "I can't believe you would say something like that. You sound ignorant. As the young people say nowadays, YOLO."

Karlie stifled a giggle. Myra considered herself hip and trendy and was pleased to be on top of the latest jargon.

Neil gestured for her to interpret.

"You only live once," Myra explained. She gave Karlie a high five.

Neil was not backing down. "I don't know about no YOLO or YONO, but I'm taking a stance. Karlie, you're not gallivanting all over the United States with Brian Oakes. He needs to get his act together."

Karlie wanted to argue with him about that, but a part of her agreed. Brian did need to declare a major and stick with it for good this time. She crooked her head toward the clock in the kitchen. "Dad, if you don't leave now, you'll be late for Bible study."

Neil looked at his watch for confirmation before he sighed with obvious reluctance. "I've got to get going, but we're not done." He tapped the bridge of her nose. "I know you picked this time to drop your bombshell because you knew I'd have to leave. But we're not done."

Karlie blinked. He knew her so well.

"Well?"

She smiled. "Yes, Dad. We'll talk later." *Not if I can help it, though.*

Karlie made her way into her room and closed the door. She scanned the light purple wall lined with pictures she had taped hodge-podge to the walls, then she sank to her bed and took out her phone. Brian had not called yet. That meant he had not yet told his father.

A message popped up. Startled, she exhaled at what she'd just read.

If you go we are through.

Chapter Five

Patricia knew her husband better than he thought she did. Her smarts weren't limited to brain surgery. Nope. She was not fooled by the plastic smile when Ryan caught her studying him. At night, she heard him grinding his teeth—a sure sign in the past that he had something on his mind. Patricia bided her time, though. She knew how to get Ryan talking. She was patient enough to give him space.

Patricia shuddered as she remembered the last time she had felt this way. It was six years ago, but it felt like yesterday.

"Honey, I've got to tell you something . . ."

She had felt her insides swirl and knew that she wasn't going to like it. And she hadn't.

Ryan had confessed to having a one-night stand with Tiffany Knightly before they were married. Almost sixteen years later, he had faced a paternity test and the real possibility that he had another child. Patricia had stood by him. Patti had even befriended the fifteen-year-old Karlie during her mother's last year. Why? Because Patricia loved him. Loved Ryan Oakes from the moment she had rested her golden eyes on him. He was her world—her everything.

Lucky for her, the feeling had been mutual. He loved her with the same intensity. Their passion had blinded them to everyone else—including Brian. Fortunately, that was water under the bridge. She and Ryan now had a healthy relationship with their son. Brian knew he could depend on them to be there for him.

She went into her lab at the Nassau University Medical Center to look at several films. Clasping her hands behind her back, she studied the frame for several minutes. The human brain was magnificent. Its intricacy never ceased to solicit awe and wonder.

She heard the lab door creak open and turned her head. Whoever it was knew better than to invade her turf when the door was closed. She knew it had to be important.

Dr. Timothy Newhouse poked his head through the open space. In a deferential tone, he said, "Dr. Oakes, sorry to interrupt, but you have a phone call."

"Thanks, Tim, and for the millionth time, please call me Patricia, or Patti. Dr. Oakes sounds too formal."

He nodded his assent before closing the door, but she knew the other physician would not take her up on the offer. He hadn't yet. Walking over to her desk, she picked up the phone.

"Mom, I've been calling your cell like crazy," Brian said.

"Oh, I'm sorry. I'm in the lab." She sauntered over to the door where her lab coat hung. She dug into the pocket and located her cell phone and looked at the screen. Sure enough, there were seven missed calls. Concerned, Patti asked, "What's going on?"

"I wanted to let you know I'm going to take a semester off. I'm putting the papers in but wanted to let you and Dad know first."

Brian's carefree words got her attention. Patricia didn't sanction that idea. Not one bit. He needed to get his career going full speed ahead. However, her son was a free spirit with a mind of his own. She knew better than to push or he would rebel.

"What did your father say?" she asked.

He cleared his throat. "Uh—well—I didn't tell him yet. I was sort of hoping you'd tell him, or at least be there with me when I tell him."

Figures. It all made sense now. She was the chosen buffer. Ryan was going to hit the roof when he heard this news. For some reason, Brian had a bad case of wanderlust. He never seemed to settle down but was always on to the next thing. He was like that when it came to women too. Thankfully, he'd only brought one or two home. Otherwise, she'd need to install a revolving door.

Patricia sought to dig into his thought pattern. "Get ready for a fight tonight. Honestly, I'm not thrilled with your plan, either. What brought this on?" Maybe there was some method to his madness.

"Karlie" was his one-word explanation.

"Oh?" Patricia drummed her fingers on the desk.

"Well, her debut song got slammed," Brian said. "I mean, people are bashing her left and right. I think I can help her. Karlie must build a name for herself. You know, build a fan base—one not connected to Tiffany."

Patricia didn't understand how Brian could be of assistance. He was not a music major, and neither was he studying management. "And how do you propose she does that?"

"Well, I've convinced Karlie to get some edge by doing some stunts and posting it to YouTube. She'd be an instant sensation. When she sings, her songs would mean something. I'm telling you, Mom, Justin Bieber was a YouTube sensation and now look at him! Who knows, Karlie might even land a reality show. I don't care for some of them, but they are hot right now, replacing actual TV shows."

Does he know how crazy he sounds? This had to be Brian's most farfetched scheme yet. Wisely, Patricia held her tongue. How could she come across as conciliatory but convince Brian to abandon this foolish plot?

Patricia swallowed. Gathering her thoughts, she said, "Brian, I think I see your thought pattern, but why you? Why do you have to be the one who drops out of a renowned university to do this?"

"Why not me?" he countered.

"Well, what about Jamaal? Is her boyfriend in on this?"

"No, he's not intrigued with our plan."

For the first time she detected what could be a kink in Brian's plan. "I applaud Jamaal for demonstrating good sense," she said. "I can't even see Karlie going along with this. She always seemed so—"

"Straitlaced? Goody Two-shoes?"

In spite of herself, Patricia laughed. Brian's wit was impossible to resist. She looked at her watch. She had surgery at two p.m. and needed to get back to her prep work.

"I have to go, but we need to discuss this further," Patricia said. "Are Neil and Myra on board with this?"

"I don't know yet," Brian said. "Karlie is telling them tonight."

Patricia pictured Neil and Myra in her mind. They fostered a close-knit family. There was no way Neil would condone their children's actions. Maybe after speaking with her father, Karlie might drop the idea and focus on her studies. Patricia hoped so.

"I can only imagine Neil's reaction," she mumbled. She knew she would hear it soon enough.

Chapter Six

"Brian, I didn't expect to see you here." Ryan raised his eyebrows. "What's going on?"

He thought he was coming home to see his wife in all her glory. Instead, she was dressed in a pair of white linen slacks and a chic blue wool sweater. He went over and kissed her on the cheek.

Brian did not wait for a hug. "Dad, I'm taking a semester off."

"Don't you think you have done enough exploring to last a lifetime?" he said. *Don't you think you've wasted enough of my money on frivolity?* he didn't say.

"It's for a good cause," Brian said.

Ryan glared. "Earning a degree is for a good cause. You need to establish a career. Spababies could use you."

Ryan had wanted to spend more time at home and build his relationship with his son so he had sold businesses. But once Brian graduated from high school, Ryan wanted to return to work. Then he had met real estate tycoon, Michael Ward at a caucus, and the two decided to venture into business together.

Spababies was born amidst two platters of steaks and potatoes. Michael had the connections, and they both had the resources. Spababies was a deluxe childcare service for mall shoppers. Parents no longer had to hassle with their children at the mall. They could drop them off at the center and shop to their hearts' content. Michael had designed the center with state-of-the-art security systems, and Ryan was pleased they had a 100 percent positive rating. Hard to get, tough to maintain.

Brian shook his head. "I'm not interested in working for you."

"What's wrong with working with your father?" he asked.

Patti put a hand on his arm. "Let's just hear him out, honey." She gestured to Brian to continue.

"I don't want to hear him out," Ryan said. "Brian is impulsive, reckless, and has a bad case of itchy feet."

"Wow. You're talking about me like I'm not standing here," Brian mumbled.

"Give him a chance," Patti said. "There's no need for things to get ugly."

Ryan clenched his jaw until he simmered down. *Keep calm. Kind words.* "So where are you planning to go this time?" he asked, shedding his jacket and slinging it across the couch.

"We're thinking of starting with L.A."

Ryan arched an eyebrow. "We?"

"It's not just Brian, honey. It's Brian and Karlie," Patricia interrupted.

Ryan's chest caved in after she delivered that bombshell. He staggered like a drunken man and dropped into the couch. This, he had not expected.

"Karlie? Karlie? What do you mean, son?"

"Yes—uh—Karlie's song didn't do so well, so we're going to build her a fan base," Brian said. "Our plan is to embark on atypical adventures for her, and then post them on YouTube."

"Have you lost your mind?" Ryan roared, jumping to his feet. "That is a cockamamie idea. Right now, you don't sound like a college graduate. You sound like a buffoon—a nincompoop."

Patricia's eyes were the size of saucers. "Ryan! How dare you speak to our son like that! Words have life. You will *not* be demeaning!"

Ryan was about to respond when Brian laughed.

"Dad, you're hilarious. I didn't expect such a spewing of outdated words. But, I'm an adult, and I can make a decision like this without your consent."

"Well, how do you plan to fund this scheme? Because I'm not paying for your shenanigans. It's about time you become responsible," Ryan challenged.

Brian met him eye for eye. "We don't need your money, Dad." He shook his head. "Karlie's got plenty of her own. Or have you forgotten? She's been frugal, but as I've told her, she needs to live a little."

Live a little! Ryan was beside himself. He couldn't believe this was happening. Was this all some sick joke? *God, are you there?*

Ryan strove to gather his wits. He threw his son a curveball. "Brian, you're not thinking this all the way through. Karlie is inexperienced and gullible. You don't want her developing feelings for you, do you?"

He shouldn't have asked.

"To be honest, I wouldn't mind," Brian confessed. His confession seemed torn from him as if it were something he had been walking around with for a while.

I would, Ryan thought. *I would mind a lot.* In less than five minutes, Ryan had entered the Twilight Zone. Or, maybe this was a nightmare and he would soon awaken, hopefully.

"Is that what this is about Brian?" Patricia asked. "You like her?"

Brian wrinkled his brow. "I'm not sure, but I'm drawn to her somehow."

This cannot be happening. Ryan did an about-face and walked outside his home, leaving the front door ajar. He stood by his well-manicured lawn and sniffed the air with appreciation. The beautiful flowers were in bloom, and the scents greeted his nostrils, but they did nothing to ease his troubled mind.

Now was the opportune time for him to confess the truth. But he held back. With gripped fists, he took several deep breaths. To tell would mean losing Patricia—and Brian.

Ryan felt sweat beads form around the nape of his neck. Even his upper lip felt moist. In rapid strokes, he undid his tie and slung the noose from around his neck. Then he held his head in his hands. *This cannot be happening*.

Ryan heard footsteps behind him and knew Patricia had come outside to check on him.

She put her arms around his midriff and hugged him.

He cradled her against him and prayed. *Please, God, I'm going to lose everything.*

"What is it, honey?"

Patricia's gentle inquiry was almost his undoing. If only he could tell her. If only it were that simple.

"I'm just afraid for him," Ryan said. "And I can't do anything."

Patricia smirked. "Short of sabotaging him every step of the way, your hands are pretty much tied on this one, love." She patted him on his chest. "Brian has good sense and street smarts. He and Karlie will be okay."

Ryan wasn't listening. His mind had grabbed onto one word. *Sabotage*. It was evil. It was childish . . . It was his saving grace. There was no need to confess if he could put a wrinkle—no, a tidal wave—into their plans. He would ask Brian to give him his itinerary. Ryan perked up and swung his wife in his arms. Bending her over, he gave her a kiss befitting a princess. "Thanks, Patti. You always know exactly what to say."

And thanks to her, he now knew what he had to do.

Chapter Seven

Karlie tried to reach Jamaal several times, but he didn't answer. Finally, she left a voice mail. "Jamaal, please call me. I read your text, and we need to talk." She swiped her phone to end the call. Next, she called Brian. "How did it go?" she asked.

"It wasn't as bad as I expected, although my dad blew a fuse," he said.

"My father wasn't thrilled either. But, I'm in if you are." Karlie quivered with a mixture of fear and anticipation.

"Yes, I'm in," he said. "I'm not backing out of this."

Karlie breathed a sigh of relief, but some straggling doubt reared its head. "Do you think we're doing the right thing?"

"Only one way to find out," he chuckled.

Karlie took exception at the glib reply. She wondered if Brian had thought things through. Their decisions today affected their tomorrow. She was plagued with nights of worry.

"How can you be so nonchalant about this? This is our life we're interrupting, all for a grand scheme that may not work."

"Correction, this is our life we're living. And it *will* work. We must speak it into being. Positivity is half the battle."

His confidence was reassuring. Karlie blew out a huge gulp of air. She knew she was wavering, but a part of her was also curious to see how this would all play out. "I'm tripping out about this, but I'm also looking forward to it. You know what I mean?"

"Sure do."

"I've been praying for God's direction and for Him to lead us. I know God won't steer us wrong."

"Well, make sure you bring Him along," Brian said.

In spite of herself, Karlie laughed at his somewhat irreverent tone. "You know you can only avoid God for so long, don't you?" She'd been trying to get Brian into church ever since her conversion, but he avoided church as if it were the plague.

True to form, he changed topics. "I've got to go," he said. "I need to make some preparations and plan our excursions. My dad wants a detailed list of our where and when."

"Good idea," Karlie said. "E-mail it to me when you're done." She shivered with glee. "Summer can't come soon enough."

Karlie confronted Jamaal as soon as he exited Jerome S. Coles Sports Center. It was a fifteen-minute walk to his studio apartment in Carlyle Court or a three-minute ride on the 6 or R train. It didn't matter to her. Either way, she wasn't leaving his side until they had thrashed things out.

"I called you all night. Why didn't you answer the phone?" Karlie asked.

He wore his basketball garb with a towel slung over his shoulder. Jamaal was funky and dripping wet. Sweat poured down his body, but Karlie couldn't have cared less.

Jamaal dropped his gym bag to the floor. He wiped his forehead, his face, and his neck—and everything else he could to keep from answering her question.

She clenched her teeth to keep from screaming at him, already knowing he would answer her only when he was good and ready. "Are you going to explain that text you sent me last night?"

"You can read," Jamaal said. "You saw what it said." He hefted his gym bag over his shoulder and walked away from her.

Dressed in thigh-high three-inched heeled boots, Karlie had hoped he would've hopped on the train. Ignoring her protesting feet, she rushed after Jamaal and strove to keep up with his longer strides.

After almost tripping on a crack in the sidewalk, Karlie grabbed his arm and applied pressure. They stood by the crosswalk of Eighth Street and Broadway. Jamaal stopped, but he refused to make eye contact. Mutinous, she maintained her stance. They were tackling this conversation, even if it took her all night.

"I'm not letting you go, Jamaal Weathers," she insisted. "I love you. You love me. We're a team."

His nostrils flared. "Oh yeah? If we're a team, how can you be okay with leaving me and going off with Brian on some escapade? What am I supposed to do when you're gone? I thought it was a fluke that would pass, but I see you're serious about this"—he formed quotation marks with his hands—"adventure." He peered down at her with an imperially arched eyebrow.

In all the years she'd known Jamaal, he'd never been so condescending toward her. Karlie shook her head. "What's with you? You're not yourself."

"I'm fine," Jamaal wheezed. "It's just . . ."

Karlie gestured with her hands. "Go on."

A passerby pushed past her, and Karlie hobbled to maintain her balance. Jamaal reached out a hand to steady her.

"Okay, I'll speak plain," he said, pulling her out of the pedestrians' paths. "It bothers me that I can't even spend the night with you or vice versa, but you've got no problem sleeping with Brian in a tent or wherever it is you'll be."

Karlie rocked backed on her heels. Her mouth popped open. Jamaal was jealous. *Of Brian?* "It's not the same, and you know it. Brian and I aren't dating, so there's no need to worry about anything." She shook her head. "The three of us have always been close. We've all hung out numerous times before, so I don't get why this is any different."

He jutted his jaw. "It is different. Brian's mostly your friend. I tolerate him most of the time, but I think he's flaky." He stooped to stare into her eyes. "Have you taken a good look at him? Don't think that just because I'm a guy I don't notice how the girls are crazy about Brian. And if I have to spell it out for you, then you're even more gullible and naïve than I thought."

Stung, Karlie stepped back. Jamaal was being insulting, and she wasn't having it. She liked that he was opinionated and had a mind of his own, but she was nobody's doormat. Karlie stormed off, leaving him standing there.

She strutted back to Mercer Street with the practiced precision of an experienced New Yorker.

"I don't know who he thinks he's talking to, but he's not talking to me like that. Imagine the nerve of him calling me gullible and naïve. There's nobody more gullible than he is. He's the one worried about his friends and what they think because he's not having sex. He's the one without a backbone to stand up for his principles," she mumbled, walking hastily.

Karlie waited at the crosswalk by Waverly Place when she heard a clap of thunder. A huge downpour followed. She pouted. "Perfect. Hours of straightening my hair down the drain in less than five seconds." She wrapped her jersey tight around her waist and stomped toward her hotel suite, which was ten blocks away.

Brian's apartment was on MacDougal Street. Karlie bit her lip and debated. From her current location, his place was the quickest choice. Normally she wouldn't hesitate to seek shelter at his place, but Jamaal's comments had her rattled. Another huge boom echoed in the sky.

Decision made.

She raced toward Bleecker Street and made a sharp right on MacDougal. She felt like a bedraggled rat as she shivered from the cold rain. Racing into his building, Karlie waved at the doorman and jumped on the elevator to his floor.

Karlie pounded on his door. "Please be here."

The door swung open.

With a towel draped around a six-pack and well-defined hips, Brian took a moment to examine her from head to toe.

Then his arm snaked out and pulled her in flush against his chest. He used his other arm to slam the door shut. Karlie exhaled as she came in contact with muscles that flexed upon impact. Awareness hit her being. Who was she kidding? Brian was every inch a man, and one who was definitely pleased to see her.

Chapter Eight

"Thank you, God."

It had to be God who had sent him to his son's apartment. He had driven up into the city to see Brian and had spotted Karlie rushing into Brian's place. His chest concaved, and Ryan had to take several deep breaths. He swerved down several streets hunting for a parking spot. It was divine intervention when he managed to snag one as a Nissan Altima vacated it.

Heedless of the rain, Ryan sprinted. His heart pumped against his chest as he willed his feet to move faster. Rain pelted his Armani suit, but he didn't care. He had to get to them. He had to stop Brian and Karlie.

What's Karlie doing there, anyway?

His pants legs were soaked. His seven-hundred-dollar Church & Co. walnut-colored Chetwynd wingtip shoes were ruined, but Ryan didn't care. He had to put a stop to what may be transpiring behind that door. It was untenable—unthinkable.

Ryan strove to catch his breath and pounded on his son's door.

Brian opened the door. Ryan saw the surprise reflected on Brian's face before a grimace formed. Brian wasn't happy to see him. Well, that was too bad. He was coming in anyway. Ryan pushed his way in and closed the door. He greeted Karlie before facing his son.

Arching his brow, Ryan asked, "Shouldn't you put some clothes on?"

Brian swiveled around to get dressed.

Cupping his mouth, Ryan yelled, "And bring me a towel on your way back."

"I'll get it," Karlie said. She went to retrieve one for him and one for herself.

As Ryan's eyes followed Karlie, he couldn't help but notice how she seemed to know her way around Ryan's apartment.

Taking the towel she offered, Ryan shrugged out of his jacket and tossed it to the ground. He dried himself off as best as he could. A puddle formed on the tile floor, but he ignored it.

Ryan's only focus was on the woman standing before him. Entranced, he only had eyes for Karlie as she busied herself wiping her face and using the towel to dry her hair. Ryan was unaware of his frozen stance.

Karlie gave him an awkward smile and crossed her arms against her chest.

With a start, Ryan realized he was staring, which made her uncomfortable, but he couldn't help it. Just the sight of Karlie transfixed him. He did not afford himself this luxury too often because he was too afraid of what his face might tell—too afraid of the truth he had done so much to keep well hidden.

He saw Karlie bite her lip and look heavenward. He knew she was searching for something to say to fill the void. Ryan held his empty hand out toward her. He willed her to come to him. He would have laughed at her pretense of not seeing his proffered hand if his heart hadn't been crushed at her rejection.

Eyes identical to his own tore into his soul before she admitted, "Mr. Oakes, you're making me uncomfortable."

"Uh," Ryan mumbled. "I—"

What could he say? Karlie had good reason to think he was a sick, perverted old man. But he loved her. She was a part of him. He could deny it no more. At least not to himself.

"Dad, you're looking at Karlie like you've seen a ghost," Brian observed with a chuckle.

Ryan jumped. He hadn't noticed when Brian had reentered the room. Thankfully, Brian had dressed in a light sweater and jeans.

Ryan felt bemused at his son's wisdom. He *was* looking at a ghost—a reflection of himself—

His child.

His daughter.

Ryan adopted a blasé attitude, feigning ignorance. "Was I staring? I didn't realize. My mind was miles away." With a practiced smile, he addressed Karlie. "I didn't expect to see you here, Karlie. I was caught a little off guard. By the way, where's Jamaal?"

On the inside, though, Ryan trembled. Here he was talking to Karlie as if everything was normal—when it was far from it. He had denied her existence. For five years, he had pretended as if Karlie was only a mere acquaintance. Was God paying him back for what he'd done?

No, God didn't do paybacks, but He did allow consequences—being saved didn't spare you from that.

Karlie looked down at her feet. "We sort of got into an argument."

Ryan's ears perked up. *Trouble in paradise. Hmm . . .* "This wouldn't have anything to do with your and Brian's upcoming escapade, would it?"

She squirmed. "Well, yes, among other things."

"Say what?" Brian exclaimed. He shook his head. "But we invited Jamaal to come along. Did you tell him we're not doing this until summer? It's only if you're a hit that we would take off the fall semester. Plus, we can always change our mind. It's simple paperwork to reenroll. I don't see what the big deal is."

"That's a long time for a couple to be apart," Ryan said. He savored the indecision crossing Karlie's face.

Karlie twisted her hands together. "I've been with Jamaal forever. I don't want to lose him over something like this."

"Karlie, if Jamaal really loves you, he'd support you," Brian said. "You want to sing—make a name for yourself . . ." Brian's voice trailed off. He searched to find the words.

"All that's good, Brian, but YouTube isn't the way to do it," Ryan said. "Karlie, you need to be in a studio rehearsing, honing your skills, not traipsing all over the world. It's ludicrous, really."

Karlie placed her forefinger across the bridge of her nose and slid it down to the tip before landing on her upper lip.

If that don't beat all, Ryan told himself. He did the same thing when he was thinking. Genetics was amazing.

Ryan's conscience gripped him. His legs weakened, and his insides whipped him like brutal waves attacking the sea. He closed his eyes from the truth and covered his forehead with his hands.

"Do you need some aspirin, Dad?" Brian asked.

No, he needed to tell the truth and set himself free from this agony. Ryan shook his head. Sometimes he wished Brian was not so observant. With a calm he did not feel, Ryan said, "I'm fine, son. I hope you change your mind. Both of you need to come to your senses."

Brian took Karlie's hand and pulled her next to him for support. "Dad, we're going. At the end of spring semester, once we've handed in the last paper, we'll be leaving for California. First stop—zip-lining."

"Zip-lining!" Karlie's eyes were wide. "But I'm afraid of heights."

Brian nodded. "And I have the perfect remedy—Zip-lining."

***

"Zip-lining!" Ryan raged to Patricia that night. "He wants to go zip-lining! He must have a death wish or something, and there's nothing I can do to stop them. He and Karlie . . ."

Patricia placed both hands on her hips. "Oh, now it's making sense. This is about Karlie."

Ryan reared back. "What?" Had she figured it out? He studied Patricia's face but saw no signs of distress.

"Yes, you're attracted to her," Patricia said.

Oh no, she was way off base. "Whoa! I'm not attracted to Karlie," Ryan said. "What do I look like, a pedophile? Where would you get such a ridiculous idea? She's young enough to be my . . ." He stopped, unable to say the word.

"Yeah, you think?" Patricia flailed her hands. "I had a hard time convincing Brian otherwise."

Ryan couldn't hold back his surprise. "Brian? When did you have time to talk to him? I just left there."

"He called as soon as you left. After you made sure to drive Karlie home."

Ryan pursed his lips at her tone. Now was the time to confess and tell Patricia the truth. He looked into her eyes and saw her pain. "Wait. If you're expecting a confession, you can forget it. Nothing happened with Karlie and me. I'm not interested in her. You're the only woman for me."

He approached Patricia and massaged her shoulders. Leaning over, he kissed her neck. "You're all I've ever wanted," he whispered. "I can barely keep my hands off you. Honey, you must know that." Ryan's lips met hers in a gentle kiss.

"Then why haven't you touched me these past weeks?" Her lips quivered. "I feel like there's a big gulf between us, and I don't know why this is happening."

Yet another opportunity to spill the beans.

He let it pass.

Instead, Ryan chose the lake of denial. "There is no gulf. We're fine."

Chapter Nine

"Come unto me, all ye that labour and are heavy laden, and I will give you rest," Pastor Keith Ward said, quoting Matthew 11:28. "This verse urges us to cast all our cares on Him. And it's true, if you put everything in God's hands, you'll find a peace you never knew existed." Pastor spread both of his arms wide as he beseeched the crowd to come to the altar for prayer.

From his seat in the fifth row, Ryan felt drawn to make his way down the aisle, but he stayed in his seat. He had entered Zion's Hill Church that Saturday, heavy-hearted and weighed down from his lie. He had had to cancel several business trips because his head wasn't in the game. At night, Ryan tossed and turned so much that Patricia had taken to sleeping in the guest room or Brian's room, which bothered him to no end. Since their marriage, they had always shared a bed unless he was out of town. He couldn't sleep without Patricia next to him. So, of course, he had been cranky.

"What's the matter with you?" she had asked one morning with troubled eyes. "You say there's no gulf between us, but I know something's wrong."

"I think my wisdom tooth is bothering me." That had gotten him a trip to the dentist—which he abhorred—followed by a teeth cleaning and a filling.

Ryan looked over at Patricia, who was nodding her head at whatever Pastor Ward was saying. She must have felt his eyes on her, for she turned toward him and smiled.

Seeing her radiant face made him feel like a worm. After a perfunctory smile, Ryan looked away. He watched Patricia stand and walk down to the altar. He sat rooted in the pews while she received anointing and prayer. Ryan experienced a rare bout of spiritual envy. He wanted what she had, but he did not want to pay the price.

It was not until one of the prayer warriors gave her a tissue that Ryan realized Patricia was crying. Why did he have the feeling that he was the reason behind her tears?

Unfortunately, Ryan didn't have time to ask her as one of the ushers approached to tell him that Pastor Ward wanted to see him. Ryan texted Patricia to go home without him while he made his way through the crowd to the side exit leading to the pastor's office.

Dianne Hupert, the pastor's secretary, said, "Hi, Brother Oakes. Pastor Ward should be here shortly." She tilted her head toward the door. "You can wait in his office if you'd like."

Ryan thanked Dianne and sat in one of the chairs across from the pastor's desk.

While Ryan waited, he thought about his path to conversion.

Since its conception, Spababies blew up in ways neither he nor Michael had imagined. It morphed into exclusive childcare services for mall employees as well. Future surveys would show increases in job performance, attendance, and employee satisfaction because mall workers knew their children were safe.

Spababies expanded into malls across the country. Now, England, China, and India wanted in on the franchise. Ryan and Michael had their hands full. Michael and his wife, Verona, had relocated to California to oversee the groundbreaking of Spababies in hundreds of malls. Ryan and Michael employed Verona's law firm, Lattimore & Ward, to oversee every legal aspect of the expansion project. The senior partner, Nigel Lattimore, was the lead consulting attorney for their firm.

He and Michael grew close, and eventually Michael extended an invitation to his brother's, Keith's, church. On his first visit, Ryan had given his heart to God. Yes, one message was all it took for him to see the light. Patricia had not believed him, but within a month, she also converted.

The decision was easy. The walk was not. Life with Christ, he was finding, was 100 percent sacrifice and 0 percent selfishness. Ryan sighed because he was still a work in progress.

Pastor Ward rushed into the room with a burst of energy. He thumped Ryan on the back. "You want some water?"

Suddenly thirsty, Ryan nodded.

Pastor Ward retrieved two bottled waters from a refrigerator and threw one for Ryan to catch.

Ryan guzzled most of the water and placed the half-empty bottle by his feet.

"Brother Oakes, God directed me to speak with you."

Caught off guard, Ryan cracked his knuckles. "What did I do?" On the inside, Ryan pleaded with God, *Please don't tell him about Karlie and me.*

"I didn't say you did anything." Pastor Ward chuckled. "But you're a new convert. God pointed you out to me. He told me He meant for you to lay out at the altar, yet you stayed in the seat."

"I can pray from my seat, Pastor. Isn't God everywhere?"

"If I had a dollar for how many people have said that to me . . ." Pastor Ward laughed. "Yes, God is everywhere, but sometimes He wants us to take the step of faith." He zeroed in on Ryan. "God wanted you to do that today. I don't know what it is, but I do know what He wants you to do."

Ryan nodded. "You're right, Pastor." There was no use denying it. He knew what God wanted him to do too. God had been speaking to him for weeks. Now, God was using Pastor Ward as His voice to prompt Ryan to man up and tell his wife the truth.

Still, he wished he had not sat close enough for Pastor Ward to see him. Maybe he should change his seat. Ryan preferred to be close so he could soak in the Word. Michael had urged him to do so, saying the back rows were the gossipers' and gamers' lounge. He did not know if that was true, but it would keep him out of the pastor's radar.

Ryan sighed. There was nowhere far enough to keep him from God's eyes. Pastor Ward prayed with him and offered words of encouragement.

Ryan thanked him, and Pastor Ward drove him home. He remained quiet for most of the ride because Ryan experienced his first spiritual skepticism. While gospel music blared, Ryan wondered, *How do I know for sure Pastor Ward was speaking on God's behalf?* He peered out the window. Pastor Ward had eyes. He had seen Patricia crying and wanted to find out if Ryan was the culprit.

For all he knew, Patricia could have spoken to Pastor Ward about her concerns. Ryan didn't ask him, though. He wasn't bold enough to call the man of God out like that. He would, however, bring it up with his wife.

Pastor Ward pulled up in front of his house. Ryan thanked him for the ride and waited for Pastor Ward to pull off before going inside. Patricia had dinner laid out, and Ryan washed his hands. He would play it cool.

After dinner, Ryan suggested that he and Patricia go out for ice cream, and she agreed. He had pistachio, and she chose rum-raisin. Once they were enjoying their treat, he posed the question.

"Patti, I saw you bawling your eyes out at the altar—well, everyone did. Sweetheart, what's wrong?"

His wife looked at him from underneath those long lashes of hers. "Nothing's wrong, honey. Just talking to God. The Word touched me—that's all."

Ryan knew she was lying through her peach-tinted lips, but who was he to call her on it when he had been lying to her for days—make that years?

It's time.

Ryan's ears tingled. It was almost as if someone clearly whispered the thought to him.

He didn't get where he was by giving in that easily. He refused to listen. Ryan studied his wife as she licked her spoon. His passion surfaced. Ryan wanted Patti as if she were a cold glass of water on a hot summer day. He took her hand and stroked it.

No, he could not risk their marriage. Patricia could *never* know. Turning his back on his child was the one thing that would separate them.

Many waters cannot quench love . . .

That line from one of his favorite scriptures entered his mind. Again, Ryan didn't take heed.

Yes, but a daughter you denied you had would do it. It would quench their love for an eternity.

Chapter Ten

Patricia twisted and turned on her side of the bed. Not even the Tempur-Pedic mattress would help her sleep tonight because Ryan filled her mind.

She had hoped that his conversation with Pastor Ward would have made him open up. When Ryan had texted her to go home because he had to talk with Pastor Ward, she had uttered a quick praise. But Ryan hadn't enlightened her about his strange behavior.

Tears again flowed. Maybe her hormones were out of whack, and she was overreacting, but Patricia could not help it. Never in their relationship had she felt herself questioning her desirability. But it had been a couple of weeks since her husband had touched her.

Now, for some people, that may be nothing, but not for them. Ever. Something was bothering him. Or, rather, *someone* if Brian were to be believed.

Though Ryan denied it, there could be no other explanation for his sudden withdrawal. Withdrawal was a classic sign of cheating. Patricia thought of Karlie. She was a beautiful, miniature replica of her mother, who had been a pop icon in her day. Was Ryan attracted to the daughter as he had been to the mother? She wondered for the umpteenth time. After all, he had slept with Karlie's mother.

Patricia sighed. She did not know what to think. In one rapid motion, she flung the blanket off and trudged out of bed. She went into Brian's bedroom and slid under his sheets not caring when last he had washed his linens. She gazed up at the ceiling.

Maybe Ryan was experiencing a midlife crisis.

A part of her found it improbable that he would have feelings for Karlie, but stranger things had happened. Articles in the *Huffington Post* or *NewsOne* proved that. But then another part of her felt fear gripping her heart. Why else would her husband react so strongly against Karlie and Brian traveling together?

She pinched her hip. Maybe she wasn't thin enough. Then she snorted. She was smaller than when she had had Brian, and Ryan had never complained about her weight. Patricia knew she was obsessing, but she sniffed anyway.

She really should just ask him, but Ryan might give her an answer she didn't want to hear. She wasn't prepared for that.

Patricia closed her eyes and prayed. Her recent problems had drawn her even closer to God. He was the only one she could talk to about her concern. He was the only one she needed to talk to besides her husband.

She had accepted Christ a month after Ryan had. They had gotten baptized together and often studied the Word in bed. However, when Ryan became buried with Spababies business, Patricia had taken to reading during work breaks and on her own at work. She tried to memorize her Bible scriptures, but she couldn't recall the last time they had prayed as a couple.

Patricia poured her heart out. Pain added to her eloquence. "Lord, I just need your comforting presence to surround me at this moment. I need you to bind my marriage closer than before. Keep us from the plan of the adversary who only wants to steal, kill, and destroy. I pray for my husband, Lord, and ask you to help him face whatever is bothering him and to make the right decision. Amen."

She meditated in silence, allowing God's Spirit to soothe her frayed nerves, and soon she drifted to sleep.

It seemed as if she had barely closed her eyes when her cell vibrated with a text from the hospital. After reading the message, Patricia dressed with speed. Stuffing her feet into her sneakers, she scribbled Ryan a note and sped out of her driveway. Patricia called Timothy as she navigated her way through the empty streets. It was 5:30 a.m. and most people were still in bed.

However, death didn't have a bedtime. It came knocking any hour of the day. She pulled her black Mercedes next to Tim's gold Camry and swiped her fob through the back entrance. Her sneakers made squishy noises in the quiet hallway until she opened the door to Trauma Room 2.

All sorts of beeps and noises greeted her. Patricia took in the bustle of the emergency staff. It was obvious they were in over their heads. She stuffed her hair under the cap, scrubbed her hands, and donned a protective mask and her lab coat before heading into the fray.

"What do we have here?" she asked.

"Four-year-old craniopagus twins, Anna and Alyssa Velasquez. Anna's the one on the left. She had the seizure. Lucky for her, Dr. Newhouse was here."

More like God was here. She studied the charts before walking over to where the twins lay. Her eyes traveled from their skinny little legs and up their small frames. By the time she reached their faces, Patricia's heart tripped. Anna was asleep, but Alyssa observed her with curious eyes.

"Anna's sick," she breathed, her huge brown eyes filled with fright.

"Your sister's okay," Patricia said, patting her on the leg.

When a single tear rolled down Alyssa's face, Patricia had to turn away. She had never had such an emotional reaction to a potential patient. She cleared her throat and addressed Jaclyn Desmoines, the nurse on duty.

"Where are the parents?" she asked.

"They're in the waiting area. Dr. Newhouse went to speak with them." Jaclyn lifted Anna's limp hand. Then she whispered, "Can you separate them?"

"I'd have to look at their charts and order several scans to see what I'm dealing with. To separate craniopagus twins is usually a four-stage operation. It's an extreme high-risk case because of the blood flow between the brains." Patricia was one of the best, but she was not a miracle worker. She would need a strong team to complete the surgery.

Jaclyn continued, "They've traveled a long way—from Venezuela—to see you. Everything was fine until Anna had a seizure."

"I want my mommy," Alyssa yawned.

Promising the youngster to return with her mother, Patricia walked the short distance to the ER waiting area. Timothy stood talking with a couple she knew must be the Velasquezes.

With confident steps, she introduced herself.

"Can you help my babies?" Mrs. Velasquez begged. "Alyssa is stronger, but my Anna is a fighter."

From years of experience, she knew better than to make empty promises. First, she would have to use tissue expanders to stretch the skin over their heads. Then after a month or so, she would do a final separation. The survival rate was rare, and neurological damage was a possibility. Knowing all this, Patricia said, "I'll do the best I can. We'll have to wait for Anna to become stable before even attempting the surgery."

Later that morning, Timothy entered her office with two cups of coffee. "Dr. Oakes—I mean Patricia—I'd like to consult on the Velasquez case."

She rubbed her eyes, accepting the steaming cup. She took a sip. "Just the way I like it."

"Two sugars, no milk." Timothy smiled.

How did he know? Her face must have asked the question.

"I make it my business to know everything about you," he said.

Patricia was not sure how to take that so she opted to go the professional route. "You and I will work closely on this case. We'll admit the twins and run some tests."

"I've looked at the x-rays. I understand why the Velasquezes didn't separate them. One or both could die."

"Or neither." Patricia injected a note of hope. She had not achieved her status as a neurosurgeon without taking risks.

Timothy acquiesced. "You're right, of course. So, how many sleepless nights have you been having?"

Patricia straightened her spine, upset at what she viewed as his invasion into her personal life. "What do you mean by how many sleepless nights I'm having? Where do you get off asking me a question like that?"

Timothy lifted a hand. "Easy now. I didn't mean it the way it sounded. Your eyes look puffy, like you haven't been sleeping well. I'm concerned. That's all."

Hating the compassion in his eyes, she got frosty. "I don't need your concern. I wouldn't be chief of neurosurgery if I couldn't go days without sleep."

Timothy wasn't intimidated by her feisty bravado. He tilted her chin with a finger and said, "Get some rest, Patricia. You need it."

Oh, now he wants to call me Patricia. She rolled her eyes but held her tongue. She was too tired to argue with him.

Tim gathered their coffee cups and deposited them in the trash. Then with a wink, he left the room. When the door closed, Patricia released a huge yawn and bent to touch her toes. She remained in that position until her muscles eased.

Glancing at her watch, she saw that it was fourteen minutes to ten. She picked up her phone and called Ryan. She needed her husband. She needed to hear his voice.

He didn't answer.

She threw the phone across the room. *Calm down,* she told herself, but her mind didn't heed. "I'm losing him. I'm losing my husband." With a heavy heart, Patricia accepted the truth.

Chapter Eleven

Karlie snuggled closer into her jacket and knocked on Jamaal's door. "Jamaal, this has gone on long enough. I don't care if I have to wait out here until midnight. You're going to talk to me."

A couple of apartment doors opened and people peered out, but Karlie didn't care. She knocked even harder and called out, "I know you're in there, and I'm not leaving until you open this door!"

Karlie knew his roommate, Pharell Smith, was out because she had seen him leave. He had been the one to hold open the door for her as she entered the building.

She raised her fists to give the door another hearty knock when Jamaal opened it and moved aside to let her in. Karlie swooshed past him, bumping arms on purpose. Not for one moment would she let on how her elbow protested against meeting his firm muscles.

She refrained from rubbing her arm. "You're not breaking up with me, Jamaal, because I'm not letting you go. You hear me?"

The stubborn blockhead only looked at her. If it were not for the blinking of his eyes, she would think he was a statue. Karlie grabbed onto his shirt and shook him. The mule would not budge. She pummeled him with her fists until he snatched her hands in a viselike grip.

Jamaal's gentle tone belied the strength he displayed. He loosened his hold on her hands and pulled her against him. "I can't do this," he whispered. "I can't be so close to you and not have you. I love you so much it hurts."

"But, Christ's love is enough to constrain us." Karlie tilted her head back to look him in the eyes. "I know it's hard, but we can resist. We're not the only couple who committed to remain celibate until marriage. I'm telling you that we *can* get through this."

Jamaal groaned. He released her and put some distance between them. "Even now . . . your smell . . . your hair . . . Everything entices me. It's intoxicating. Being with you is all I think about." He sniffed the air. "What is that scent you're wearing?"

Karlie blushed. "Almond passion."

He clenched his fists. "See what I mean. That smell is driving me insane. I want to hold you and show you how I'm feeling, but you say hands off. I want you so much I daydream about you in class." He snatched her and crushed his lips onto hers.

Sensations rocked her being as she returned his heated kiss. She was alone with Jamaal. In his bedroom. Not a wise move on her part. He was an uncaged tiger, and she was his chosen prey. She would be mincemeat at his hands. *Help me, Lord. Now.*

Jamaal's hands moved into one of the designated no-no zones.

Her body flared. Karlie sucked in a breath. *What's happening?* Things were getting out of hand. Her flesh weakened.

Jamaal must have felt her acquiescence because he deepened his onslaught.

Karlie basked in the sensations riding her body. She felt like putty. Now she wasn't sure if she wanted to stop. Before she knew it, she was lying on his bed.

Jamaal broke contact. He opened the nightstand and pulled out a condom.

Karlie's haze cleared when she heard the distinct sound of a something being ripped. Suddenly, it all became real. She could not do this.

"Where did you get protection?" she asked, rising up to rest on her hands.

"Uh . . ."

"No, Jamaal, please don't tell me you . . ." She covered her mouth.

Cold water washed over and cooled her emotions. Had Jamaal stepped out on her? She knew there was no ring on her finger, but they were in a relationship.

Jamaal held both her shoulders and made her look at him. "Karlie, I haven't done anything. Pharrell gave this to me that night I invited you over. You remember, don't you?"

Karlie closed her eyes. She nodded but did not know if she believed him. She wasn't naïve enough to eat the bologna he was feeding her. Karlie recalled his expertise from moments ago. She had never been with anyone, but Jamaal seemed to know what he was doing a little too well.

She opened her eyes and jumped off the bed. "If you haven't been with anyone, then how come you seem so . . ." Karlie searched for the appropriate word. She arched her eyebrow with practiced calm. "Knowledgeable?"

Jamaal stood and met her glare for glare. "Are you accusing me? Don't you trust me?"

Karlie pointed at him. "Don't you turn this around on me. I'm not falling for that, so you'd better change tactics fast."

He gulped. "For six years, Karlie you've been my world. We've been together since we were fifteen. I haven't been with anyone else. I'm man enough to own up to what I do."

Karlie's heart eased. Her nagging suspicions rested. She reached up to touch Jamaal's cheek and gestured between them. "Do you really want to end this?"

"No."

"Good."

"Are you still going with Brian?"

"Yes."

Just like that, they were back to square one.

"We're planning a send-off dinner before we start our adventure," Karlie said. "Will you come?"

"Who's the 'we' that's going to be there?" he asked.

"My parents, Brian's parents, and Winona. Oh, and I was thinking about inviting my grandmother, but I'm not sure. She and my father are not the best of friends, as you know. "

Jamaal did not commit to coming but seemed intrigued with her guest list. "You're considering giving Merle an invitation? Are you asking for a brawl between her and Neil? Did you forget how he threw her out of your mother's funeral?"

Karlie shook her head. "No, I haven't forgotten, but Merle has been on my mind. She's reached out to me before, but I ignored her. I thought it might be a nice gesture."

"More like a foolish one."

"Are you going to shoot down everything I try to do? I don't have much family. Like it or not, she's blood. I know she was horrible to my mother when she was alive, but she's been apologizing for five years. I have the letters to prove it. I think it's time to let it go and move on."

Jamaal grabbed her jacket. "That woman is pure evil. I think you need to stay away from her."

Karlie lifted her chin. She was tired of everyone telling her what to do. She was grown and able to make her own decisions. She pierced him with her gaze. "If I want to take time off from school, I will. If I want to start a relationship with Merle, I will. I'm not helpless. I'm not stupid. I'm more than capable of looking out for myself."

"Fair enough," Jamaal shot back. "But don't come running to me when all of this backfires in your face."

Chapter Twelve

"I can't believe I'm doing this!"

Karlie had almost backed out several times, and it drove Brian crazy. Good thing it was summer break or she might have chickened out. Brian persuaded her to come, telling her they would tackle the semester issue come fall. Karlie and Brian had nixed the idea of a dinner as neither of their parents celebrated their taking time off from school.

Brian wiped the sweat from his face. He was sweating bullets. Summer had come in with a bang and some serious heat. California was hotter than he thought it would be even if it was mid-June. Just their luck, they were in the middle of a serious heat wave.

For their first adventure, Brian had booked with Margarita Adventures. They offered five zip-lines in their tour. Though they had purchased the full tour, Karlie had only committed to doing one. Brian had made special arrangements for them to do The Pinot Express where they would travel 1,800 feet at 125 feet in the air. A bus would be waiting to drive them back to the site.

Dressed in jeans, a white long sleeved shirt, safety gear, and her helmet, Brian noticed Karlie quivering. Her teeth chattered, and he knew it was her fear.

"Relax, it's going to be fun." He turned to the cameramen. "Are you guys ready? Because there will be no retakes or do overs. We're only doing this once."

Brothers Yentl and Griffin Moffitt gave him toothy grins and thumbs-up signs. Brian couldn't imagine why someone would name his or her child Yentl or Griffin, but he wasn't about to debate that now, not when the Moffitt brothers were the fifth film and editing duo they had had to hire so far. His past four hires had quit, feeding him excuses like a better gig, a conflicting engagement, or not enough money.

He held Karlie's arm and rapped on the metal on her head. "You ready?"

"No," she said, biting her bottom lip. She crooked her head toward the cameramen. "At least these two didn't quit on us."

"I wised up and made them sign a contract," Brian said. He addressed their guides. "Let's run through the directions one more time before we go." They were going to zip-line at the same time. However, Karlie would be the primal focus of Yentl's camera lens. Then they would be ready to post on YouTube.

He used his arm to wipe the sweat off his brow before bending over to get his water bottle. Brian took several huge swigs before extending it to Karlie.

She declined. "Not trying to pee my pants while I'm being taped."

Brian laughed. "Okay, let's get this going."

Within minutes, they were zipping through the air. He enjoyed the scenery, but Karlie's hollering had him distracted. He couldn't resist laughing as he saw her terror-filled face. She was screaming some notes at the top of her lungs.

"Lord, help me!" she yelled. "Ahhhh!"

Music to my ears, Brian thought. But just before they reached the end, Brian heard a slight snap. *Was it the wire?* His head shot up to look at the line. Nothing was out of place. If it was not the line, then it must be . . .

Brian looked down and saw that his strap was loose. *What the—*He squinted. *Did the harness give way?*

Don't panic, Brian warned himself as his suspicions were confirmed. Taking a deep breath of courage, he tightened his grip and shouted over at Karlie, "My harness broke!"

"What?" she turned her head to look at him with suspicion. "Are you trying to distract me? Because it's working."

"I'm not kidding. Now, I feel like *I* might pee my pants." His joke fell flat and real fear set in.

Karlie screamed, "Help! Help!" at the top of her lungs.

Brian held on though his hands felt clammy. They were about 100 feet from the end of the line. He gritted his teeth. He would make it. He saw Griffin zoom in on them with the camera and tried not to look like a wuss.

Brian's bravery, however, ended with another distinct snap. *"Oh no!"* He used his lower body to propel himself forward. He was not going to die out here. Not today. He kept moving until his feet touched the other side.

There is a God. Brian bent over and kissed the earth with utmost relief. A couple of seconds later, a frightened Karlie landed.

She was at his side in a flash. She spun toward the guides and snarled, "What happened? I thought you double-checked everything. We were hundreds of feet in the air, and he could've fallen."

The men looked confused. They rushed to Brian and assisted him out of the faulty device.

Brian flung off the harness.

While Karlie raged, they hemmed and hawed. "Uh, sorry, man. That never happened before. I . . . don't know . . . I can't imagine . . ."

Before Brian could say anything, Karlie grabbed onto one of them. Her hands twisted the man's shirt as she shook him with rage. "You can't imagine. He could've died, you buffoon!"

The cameras kept rolling, but Karlie was past the point of caring. The lens zeroed in on her face.

Brian saw the worry, the fright, and his heart skipped a beat. His mouth went dry, and he swallowed. She walked over to him and placed her hands over his heart. Brian prayed she did not feel the thunderous vibrations as his heart rate escalated.

Her voice broke, and her chin quivered. Then she looked up at him through tear-spiked lashes. He had to close his eyes for a second to keep from becoming overwhelmed by those honey depths.

"Brian, this is a sign," she sniffed. "I think we should call it quits. You could've died. You could've died."

He jutted out his chin. "But I didn't. I'm not going to back out because of one mishap."

Karlie shook her head. "Mishap? What an understatement!" She chuckled. "How can you be so calm about this? Don't you value your life?"

Brian looked at her and for once let the emotions surface that he felt but could not say. "I value my life. But I believe in you, and you're worth it."

"It wasn't what he said, Karlie, it was *how* he said it," Jamaal yelled through the line. "He was looking at you like a lovesick puppy."

In her bedroom at the Pismo Lighthouse Suites, Karlie squatted on her bed as she fielded Jamaal's questions.

"He almost died," Karlie said, shifting her long legs under her body. "It was an emotional moment. I . . . I think Brian said it to boost ratings. You know he has a way with words."

Jamaal snorted. "Well, his plan worked. You have over half a million hits, and it's only five p.m. our time. 'Your Adventures of Karlie Knightly' video is trending on every social media site. TMZ even called me trying to get a statement. I don't even know how they got my number."

Karlie clutched her chest. "I'm sorry, Jamaal. I didn't mean to get you involved. This wasn't how I imagined our first trip."

His heavy breathing echoed through the line.

Karlie hoped Jamaal was trying to compose himself.

"Come home, Karlie, before Brian kills himself or you over some stupid stunts," Jamaal said. "You two need a heavy dose of common sense."

"We both are college-educated, and Brian's idea isn't stupid," Karlie said. "It's working. I was scared out of my mind, but I'm proud of myself." She heard a snort of derision and gritted her teeth.

"What's next?" Jamaal asked. "Swimming with sharks?"

Jamaal doesn't know how close to the truth he is. "FYI, we're not swimming with sharks. We're going kayaking next in Florida."

"Kayaking? Now, I've heard it all. Aren't there gators in Florida waters? Listen, Karlie, I'd better not get a phone call that you've been eaten by an alligator."

Jamaal's words fell on deaf ears. She heard a light rap on her door and cupped the phone. "Enter," she said. Brian strolled inside. They had chosen to stay in the two-bedroom Family Suite as both rooms featured king-sized beds.

Karlie placed her finger over her lips and pointed to her cell phone.

"I'm hungry," Brian mouthed. He snatched the menus placed near the phone.

Karlie gave him a thumbs-up sign. "Jamaal, I've got to go. My flight to Florida leaves early in the morning, and we're scheduled to go out on the water at about three p.m."

"Have Neil and Myra seen the video, yet?" Jamaal asked.

"Yes. He wants me to come home."

"Well?" Jamaal demanded. "Since my opinion doesn't matter, what about Neil's?"

Karlie's gaze met Brian's. He was openly listening in on the call. "I'm staying with Brian. I'm going to Florida."

Brian's eyebrows shot up close to his hairline. "I'm surprised you told him that," he said once she'd ended the call.

Karlie shrugged. She didn't want to recount her entire conversation with Jamaal. It drained her. "Let's order our meal."

Once they called down for room service, Karlie warmed up her vocal chords. She ran through several notes. Tentatively, she belted out, *"This is my Father's world . . . and to my listening ears . . ."*

Brian cut in. "Can you go five minutes without mentioning God?"

"Can you go five seconds without His breath?" Then she continued with her song. *"All nature sings, and round me rings . . ."*

Brian rolled his eyes and observed her from under hooded lids.

Karlie closed her eyes and visualized the scenery "This Is My Father's World" evoked. *"The music of the spheres. This is my . . ."*

"Now I understand," Brian interrupted.

She stopped singing and glared at him. He was messing up her groove. "Understand what?"

"The reviews. Where's the emotion? Because I'm not feeling it."

She spoke through gritted teeth. "Well, *I* am. I don't care if you're not feeling it. I just want to sing my song without any rude interruptions."

"I have to intervene when you're butchering a perfectly good song. When you sing, it should evoke an emotion not a yawn." He added an exaggerated yawn for effect.

Karlie cupped her mouth. "Stop," she breathed, touching her chest. "You're brutal."

"Truth often is," he said in a gentler tone. Crooking his chin at her, he said, "Close your eyes. Think about today when you realized I could've been killed."

Karlie complied. Her chest constricted. She felt her pulse quicken and shook her head. "I don't want to remember."

"You need to," he said.

Karlie heard his steps and felt the bed sink beneath his weight.

"How did you feel?" he asked.

"I felt . . ." Tears pricked her eyes. She swiped them away. She continued in a shaky breath, "I didn't want to lose you. My best friend."

"Now sing. Not that tired song but a better song. Let your soul sing and reach my soul." He placed her hand against his chest.

She felt the thump of his heartbeat. Karlie opened her mouth, but the words would not come. She released short, raspy breaths. "I can't. It's. Too. Much."

"Why do you keep running away from emotions?" he asked.

"I can't." Karlie gulped. She folded her arms about her, feeling exposed.

Brian jumped off the bed so quickly she opened her eyes and noticed his clenched fists. "Ugh! I know what the real problem is. You need to get laid!"

Her mouth popped open. Had he just said what she thought he said? "Don't get crass with me!" she snapped. "Why must your mind always be in the gutter?" She was surprised to hear him use such everyday words. Surely Brian had more eloquent terminology to use.

Brian moved into her space. He dared her. "At least if you got laid, you'd have something worth singing about! I'd listen to *that* song."

Chapter Thirteen

At the Spababies corporate offices in Garden City, Ryan slammed the phone down.

Yentl and Griffin had increased their price. The morons. Since they had been under contract, he could not buy them out like he had the other cameramen. So, Ryan had told them to tamper with the seat only enough to scare—and they had almost killed his son!

Now, it was a YouTube hit.

Ryan replayed the video and stopped when Karlie touched Brian. Shivers ran up his spine seeing her hand on Brian's arm. Curling his hands into a fist, Ryan did not want to believe what was happening before his eyes, but it was.

His son and his daughter. Together. It was unseemly. No way could he let that happen. He had to come clean.

Fast.

Ryan leaned back in his chair and visualized Patricia's reaction when he broke the news. She would be surprised at his deception. No, surprised is too lenient a word. She would be furious. He shuddered. Ryan had no doubt Patricia was borderline certifiable. She knew her way around a scalpel. How else could someone cut into a skull and enjoy it? Ryan made a mental note to avoid spilling his guts in the kitchen.

Prim Baker entered the room. "Mr. Oakes, there's a Kyle Manchester here to see you from Manchester and Barnes."

"What's going on?" Ryan straightened.

"He wouldn't say but was persistent he needed to see you."

Ryan adjusted his tie and ran his hands through his hair. "Send him in." He kept his eyes peeled on the glass doors. Within seconds, a stocky gentleman came into view. His gait and mannerisms made him seem as if he owned the place.

Kyle Manchester held out his hand. "Mr. Oakes, thanks for your time. I was in the neighborhood getting a haircut and decided to personally deliver my news."

Ryan returned the perfunctory greeting but remained seated. He wanted to show he was not intimidated by the other man's presence. He affected a relaxed pose. "What can I do for you?"

"You're being sued by Jackson Higgins," Manchester said, showing a set of white teeth. "He says that you stole his ideas when you went into business with Michael Ward of MJW Conglomerate. He is asking for 60 percent of the proceeds you've made from the Spababies franchise."

Sixty percent was an obscene amount of money. Ryan slinked further into his chair. An instant headache formed around his temples. *Why is this happening now?*

"Mr. Manchester, I assure you, your client has no grounds. I hired Jackson *two years* ago to complete a task, and I paid him double his fee. I can show you the contracts to prove it."

Ryan moved to press his intercom.

"That won't be necessary," Manchester said. "We'll discuss everything at mediation on August twelfth." He placed the legal documents on Ryan's desk. "I'll see myself out."

Ryan observed the other man's confident swagger and resisted the urge to slam his fists on his desk. He grabbed the envelope and tore it open. He scanned the documents and bit back an expletive. *Forgive me, Lord.*

He stormed into the hall, sailed past the receptionist, and barged into Prim's office. "Please set up a meeting with Nigel Lattimore of Lattimore and Ward. Urgent."

"Will do," Prim said, pulling up her contacts list.

Ryan needed to deal with the man on top. Ryan admired Nigel's expertise and work ethic, and he claimed Nigel as the closest person he had for a friend. Once Ryan had met Patricia, he had dropped his pals and latched onto her.

Ryan yanked his cell phone out of his jacket pocket intending to call Patricia. His call went to voice mail. He hung up without leaving a message and exhaled. Then he sent her a text message: Meet me for lunch? Lunch was code for a hot and heavy lovemaking session at their home ten minutes away. Ryan had not chosen this location by accident.

His intercom signaled. He pressed the button. "Yes?"

"Nigel will be here to meet with you at twelve thirty. I've ordered lunches from The Garden City Bistro."

"Nigel will be pleased." For the first time since Kyle Manchester flounced into his office, Ryan smiled. "Make sure you order something for yourself."

"I did," Prim said.

Ryan's thoughts returned to Patricia. He needed his wife's arms about him and the heat of her body beneath his. He eyed the papers on his desk, and he eyed the clock. It was two minutes past ten a.m. He might be able to get some alone time with Patricia and still make it back to meet Nigel. It had been awhile.

The quicker he handled the case, the quicker he could get back to the Brian and Karlie issue. These situations took preeminence over making love to his wife. He groaned, knowing what he had to do.

Ryan sent Patricia another text: Have to cancel. Another time.

After pressing the Send button, Ryan shook his head. When had his priorities changed? His wife always came first to the point of obsession. His secret was changing him for the worse.

Though he was in shape, Ryan felt every single inch of his forty-five years. Fatigue seeped through his being. Having skipped services since his talk with Pastor Ward, Ryan decided it was time he quit avoiding God.

He sank to his knees. "Lord, I need your direction. Help me make the right decisions. Forgive me for my many mistakes and help me make things right."

You know what to do, the Holy Spirit whispered in his ear.

No, anything but that, Ryan bargained. *I'll pay more tithes and help with the ministries. Help me provide a distraction for Brian and Karlie.*

Ryan stood and brushed off his pants, satisfied with his deal. His cell phone rang. Pastor Ward's face popped up. *God worked fast.* Ryan swiped the answer button and cheerily greeted him.

"Brother Oakes, I haven't seen you for a few weeks. I'd like to meet up with you sometime tomorrow."

"Sure, I'll have my secretary check my schedule and contact you. I'd like to share some of my ideas with you as well."

"Ideas?"

"For ministry," Ryan said. "I want to donate . . ." He saw Nigel holding up some containers. "Ah, Pastor, I have to go, but we'll be in touch."

"See you tomorrow."

Ryan led Nigel into the conference room. The men scarfed down their lunch and caught up on their day. Once they had finished their wraps and salads, Ryan told him about the lawsuit.

Nigel perused the documents before looking up. "There are pretty serious allegations here. Jackson claims Spababies is his brainchild."

Ryan shook his head. "No, it's mine. I hired him to help me flesh out the concept before I presented it to Michael Ward."

Nigel nodded several times and stroked his chin. "It sounds like a case of he said, she said, or in this case, he said, he said. Did you log his hours spent on the project? Did you hire a secretary or did he type the presentation? Who was involved in the official meeting and presentation?"

Ryan's eyes widened. It wasn't easy to do, but Nigel's barrage of questions had rendered him speechless.

"That look on your face says you're clueless," Nigel said. "Ryan, you've owned several businesses, you know the drill."

"I . . . I might have . . . What I mean is, Prim might have chronicled his visits and his billing statements." Ryan knew he was a stuttering fool, but the past two years were hazy in his mind.

"For your sake, I hope she has copious records because Jackson's main argument is he invested more time and effort because you were involved with your other interests." Nigel looked up at the ceiling.

Why? It was not as if the stucco surface had the answers. "I'm drawing a blank."

"Not surprising. I suggest you get a notepad and jot down all you can remember. Open the project files and specify areas in which you were directly responsible. Itemize everything. I mean, *everything*."

A chill crept up Ryan's spine. "I'm on it. I have cameras installed, and I will create a detailed sketch for you. Believe me, if Jackson crapped at twelve twenty-one p.m., I'll know it."

Nigel used his feet to swivel the chair from the desk. "I know a man. Frank Armadillo. I've used him, and Michael has as well. He's . . . I don't even have the right word to describe how good he is."

Ryan arched an eyebrow. "Discreet?"

Nigel gave him a knowing glance. "Very."

Grabbing a stack of Post-its from the center of the table, Ryan flicked one down to Nigel. "Put his name and number here."

Nigel swiped through his phone to find the digits.

Ryan squirmed. His spirit felt ill at ease. Nigel's connotation about this Frank person was not sitting well with him. If Ryan needed evidence, it sounded as if Frank would magically be able to provide it. He did not feel comfortable with all that, but he was less comfortable giving Jackson millions of dollars.

Nigel must have seen Ryan's pensiveness. "Frank is legit—if you need him to be. Keith used him on Michael's case."

Ryan's tension eased. If Pastor Ward employed Frank's services, the man could not be all that bad. Ignoring his inner vibes, Ryan folded the sticky note and slipped it into his shirt pocket.

Why am I even on here?

Patricia scrolled down her social media profile page. She had been on her page for about an hour. She typically lurked, reading updates and statuses but didn't stay on for any length of time. It was 2:30 a.m., and she was still in her office. She had not bothered going home. What was the point?

Patricia blew out a breath and picked up her cell phone.

Ryan had texted her for the tenth time. She rolled her eyes, not wanting to see his face. Not after he had gotten her hopes up with one text and dashed it with another.

Patricia missed her husband.

And it was high time he missed her.

She spun her chair back to the films lining her display board. She had been studying the X-rays for several days. On her table, Patricia had created a simulated life-form of the twins. With tired eyes, she observed the still frames.

A verse from Genesis teased her mind. What was it again? With quick steps, Patricia went to her computer and clicked on her Bible app. Then she clicked the search button and typed in the words. After typing "living soul" in the search bar, her verse popped up.

She gave a sound of exultation. Genesis 2:7 said, "And the Lord God formed man of the dust of the ground, and breathed into his nostrils the breath of life; and man became a living soul."

Walking back over to the dolls, she pondered on the Word. Though man can create humanlike structures, they could not breathe life into them. She smiled. Now, if God would breathe some life into her marriage . . .

Patricia pushed the thought aside. She needed to think on positive things to prepare for what many deemed an impossible surgery. Though she had studied the charts in depth, Patricia opened the folders and snuck a look at the snapshot of Anna and Alyssa. The twins drew her to them, especially Anna.

Patricia knew why.

She used a small key from her keychain and went to her desk to unlock the middle drawer. With a slight tremble to her hands, she withdrew the sole content of the drawer—a 3-D photograph of a baby. Hers.

A tear escaped. *Where had that come from?* Patricia had stashed it away. She dropped the picture back inside and slammed the drawer shut. She whipped around and closed her eyes, wishing she could forget the little face and tiny hand on her daughter's face.

Patricia wandered into the small back room and pulled out the couch bed. She didn't bother to make the bed or change her clothes. Instead, she plopped on top of the hard mattress to catch a couple hours of sleep.

But her mind was on the picture.

Her baby had been four months in utero when she died. Patricia had named her Anna . . .

She raked her hands through her hair. Tomorrow, she and Timothy would begin their first simulated surgery. They would practice together before bringing the other doctors and nurses in. Then there would be several practice runs before she attempted the impossible.

Her Anna hadn't made it past the womb, but this Anna had. Anna Velasquez was her second chance. Patricia clenched her fists. *Lord, help me. Help me save this one.*

Chapter Fourteen

"Do gators sleep?" Brian nudged Karlie with his elbow.

They were waiting in line to rent their kayaks at the Almost Heaven Kayak Adventures in Sarasota.

Brian had chosen the Myakka River route because of the huge number of alligators in the water. He said viewers would tune in for that.

Karlie thrust her chin in the air, ignoring him. She waved her hands in circles to keep the Florida lovebugs from getting in her face. Ugh, they were a pesky nuisance. Somewhat like Brian, who was pulling on her hair.

She pushed his hand away and stuffed her hair further into her straw hat.

"May I use your sunscreen?" he asked.

That request, Karlie wouldn't deny. She dug into her backpack for the lotion and handed it to him. Through her Gucci shades, she watched him squeeze a dollop into his hands and rub it over his body.

"We'll be in the kayak right behind you," Yentl said, holding the camera.

Karlie nodded. "Just be sure to keep a safe distance."

"Don't worry," Griffin said. "We will. We're experienced kayakers. All will be well. Did you attach the microphone?"

Karlie nodded and tapped at the small device on her shirt. She certainly hoped all went well. The broken harness still plagued her mind. She crooked her ears as the guide went over all the safety procedures. Despite the biting heat, she shuddered. Brian put his arms around her. She tensed up, not wanting him to touch her but too afraid to reject his assurance.

"You can't *not* talk to me," Brian said. "I've said I'm sorry so many times, but if it helps, I'll say it again." He cleared his throat. Heedless of the cameramen and other people in the tour, Brian said, "Karlie, I'm sorry I said you needed to get laid!"

Karlie's mouth hung open. She knew her cheeks were bright red. From the corner of her eye, she saw Yentl turn his equipment on. No way did she want this conversation on air. She shook her head to signal Brian to shut up.

When she saw Brian open his mouth, fear prodded her to say, "All right. All right, I forgive you. Just shut up."

Brian exhaled. "Thank you." He sauntered up to the counter to pay for their double kayak and to get their paddles and life vests.

Karlie tapped the guide on the shoulder. "Will the alligators attack?" She could not disguise the tremor in her voice.

The young man gave her a friendly smile. "No, alligators are naturally afraid of humans. Just respect them and they'll respect you."

Karlie did not know how to deal with his scripted response.

Soon enough, Karlie and Brian took off in their kayak. The first part of the tour required energized paddling as they were going upstream. Karlie admired Brian's powerful strokes. Sitting with him made her feel secure.

Then she spotted her first alligator, and her heart jumped with fear. She sat as still as a statue and exhaled short, stucco breaths.

Brian asked, "May I have some water?"

He was a little loud for her taste. "Shh," she pleaded, looking around. "I'm not trying to rile any of these gators." Gosh, she had not realized there would be so many or that they would be so huge.

"Water?" he asked.

"I'm not trying to make any unnecessary movements," she whispered. "You can drink when we get back to land."

"We have to keep hydrated." With an exaggerated sigh, Brian reached past her to get the bottled water. He took a huge swig.

Karlie gulped. Her throat felt parched, and she licked her lips.

Brian bent over to put his bottle between his feet. His movements rocked the kayak.

"Argh!" she gasped, looking around for angry gators.

"Relax," Brian said. "The gators are sunning and minding their business. You can check this off of things to do."

Karlie turned around to see Yentl and Griffin following along in their kayak and training the camera on her sweat-filled face. She cracked a brave smile. Brian gave a wave and wiggled his body to jar the boat.

"Quit it!" Karlie squealed.

At that moment, a gator swam close to where they were.

"Oh, Lord," Karlie breathed. "Though I walk through the valley of the shadow of death I will fear no evil."

"Paddle, not pray."

"If there is ever a time to pray, now would be the time," Karlie said.

Brian stopped paddling. He brushed at his arms. "This hot is hotter than a—"

"Brian!" Karlie interrupted. "Watch your language."

"I was going to say hotter than a mug." He took another gulp of his water and crooked his head toward her. "You need to drink some water. I don't want you getting dehydrated."

"I'm afraid to let go of the paddles," Karlie said.

"For the love of—open your mouth," he commanded, holding the water close to her lips.

Karlie sipped the cool liquid. On a day like today, nothing soothed thirst like water. "Thanks," she sighed, licking her lips with gratitude.

Suddenly, they felt a boom underneath their kayak.

What was that? Karlie knew her eyes were wide from fright. She clutched the paddles. "Is that an alligator?"

Somber now, Brian said, "Could be. They sometimes sun on the bottom of the river. We might have rolled over one."

Karlie sniffed. Her body shook as tears fell. "We're going to get eaten by an alligator."

"No, we're not." Brian used his paddle, but the kayak wouldn't budge. They were stuck.

Yentl and Griffin drifted close.

Karlie's heart was beating so loud and fast she swore the alligators could hear it. She put a fist in her mouth. She was two seconds away from a major panic attack.

Brian rocked the kayak back and forth.

"Be careful," Karlie shrieked. "The boat might topple."

"Do you have another idea of how to get it moving?"

She shook her head. The urge to pee was strong.

"Then relax and let me do this." Brian rocked his body. The kayak tilted dangerously to the right. Karlie moved to the left to add weight on that side.

"Hold on tight," Brian said, before giving the kayak a forceful rock.

Karlie's heart thumped. She screamed at the same time the boat slid off the gator's back.

"Thank you, Jesus!" she shouted.

"You were a brave girl," Brian said and reached over to wipe her face. Then he began to paddle. "We're heading downstream now."

"Never again," Karlie moaned clutching her stomach.

"Hey, look on the bright side, at least nothing—"

"Look!" Karlie pointed. "There's a small speedboat heading straight at us."

Brian looked in the direction of her finger. "Hey!" he shouted. "Slow down!"

If anything, the man inside seemed to increase his speed. Karlie and Brian furiously paddled. The end of the tour was in sight.

"He's not slowing down!" Karlie cried.

"Jerk face!" Brian yelled. "Slow down!"

Karlie and Brian's skill levels were no match for the would-be attacker. Just as they neared the bank, the speedboat swerved away, its wake slamming into the side of the kayak and rolling it over. If they had not been securely strapped in, they would have flown out into the water.

"Jump out!" Brian shouted, undoing his seatbelt. "We can swim the rest of the way!"

"I'm not jumping in a river full of gators! You've lost your mind! Why is this happening? This is not an adventure, it's a *mis*adventure! I never should've listened to you! I'm going to die here! I want to go home!"

Brian jumped into the water and found it was only about two feet deep. While Karlie kicked and screamed, he undid her seat belt, covered her mouth with one hand, and sprinted to the shore.

The guide and others were there to help them to safety.

"You're brave!" someone said.

"You're a hero!"

"Did you see that man in the speedboat?"

Karlie's body shook. She clutched Brian even when her feet hit the dirt. Never had she been so terrified. Then, everything went foggy. She fainted away, not knowing the camera captured every minute of the harrowing ordeal, including Brian's tender kiss to her forehead.

Chapter Fifteen

"I've had a lot on my mind," Ryan explained when Pastor Ward asked about his absence from services. How Pastor noticed his absence when Zion's Hill boasted three thousand or more members was beyond him. As promised, Dianne had called to set up this mid-day Monday meeting with Pastor Ward. Ryan loosened his Burberry tie and draped it on the back of the chair.

Seated in his chair behind the desk, Pastor Ward stared at him.

Ryan's excuse withered underneath that stare. The charade of pretending all was well was getting old. He needed to talk. "I've done something terrible, and I don't know what to do."

"I'm here if you need a sounding board."

Ryan shifted in his seat. "I . . . I've been praying, but God hasn't done what I've been asking Him to do."

Pastor laughed. "It's been my experience that He does what He wants. His will is not our will. His ways are not our ways."

"I know that for sure," Ryan said. "I mean, I keep telling God I'll give more tithes and offerings and I'll get involved in ministries, but does He listen to me? No!" He laughed, hoping Pastor Ward would join in. However, Pastor Ward was no longer amused.

Slowly Ryan's smile faded. He must have crossed some spiritual line or something.

"We cannot bargain or tempt God, Ryan. When we become saved, we submit to His will, knowing God knows what's best for us better than we do."

Properly chastised, Ryan squirmed and closed his mouth. Both men were quiet until Ryan exhaled. "I need to tell someone."

"You've got my attention." Pastor Ward gestured with his hand.

Ryan gathered his courage. Telling Pastor would be practice for telling his wife. *Just say it.* "I think my son is in love with his sister." After he uttered the words, relief seeped through his spine. He practically sprawled in the chair. He faced the ceiling and rejoiced. "Thank God. I've said it aloud. I've been thinking and thinking, but to say it aloud is like a boulder lifting off my chest. Whew! Who knew?"

Ryan knew he rambled, and so he stopped. He straightened and waited for Pastor Ward's reaction.

Pastor Ward furrowed his brow. "I think you need to start from the beginning."

"Now this is all before I gave my life to God," Ryan said, adding the disclaimer. "I wasn't saved then."

"I know that," Pastor Ward said. "I was there when you got saved."

Ryan had a small view of what Pastor Ward was like when he was in the courtroom. Pastor Ward used to be a criminal attorney, and his cases were usually big news.

Thinking of his own criminal actions, Ryan asked, "You're not obligated to report me when you hear what I've done, are you?" He chuckled nervously.

"I won't know unless you tell me. So tell me what's on your mind." Pastor Ward relaxed against his chair. He seemed prepared to wait all night for Ryan to share.

Ryan inhaled and squared his shoulders. "Six years ago, Tiffany Knightly—the pop singer who died of cancer—approached me. Well, let me back up. Before she was rich and famous, we had a one-night stand. Brian couldn't have been more than two years old, and Patti was in medical school. I wanted Patti to quit and stay home to raise our son, but she's an ambitious woman. We argued and I left the house. I met Tiffany at a bar, and we had sex." In those few short sentences, Ryan summed up the beginning of drama in his otherwise perfect marriage.

"I don't know why I did it when Patti was my world. I've never wanted another woman besides her. Well, I ignored my guilt, and Patti and I went on with our lives."

Pastor Ward rose and retrieved two bottled waters from his mini-fridge. He handed one to Ryan and sat by the edge of his desk. Ryan untwisted the cap and drank, appreciating the cool contents.

"Then Tiffany tracked me down and tells me she's dying of lung cancer and has about a year to live. She informed me I needed to take a paternity test. Tiffany had been with four men and didn't know which of us was the father of her teenaged daughter." He shook his head. "I tell you I felt like a contestant on Maury Povich's paternity show. Tiffany shook up my home with that news, but Patti was my rock. She even reached out to Karlie—that's Tiffany's daughter—and they became friends. Tiffany befriended Brian, who'd been messing up in school, and he straightened out." Ryan tossed his empty water bottle into the basket by the door. "I do have that to thank her for. Tiffany put me in my place and commanded I make Brian a priority."

Restless, Ryan couldn't stay in the chair. He stood and glanced Pastor Ward's way, but Pastor Ward signaled for him to keep talking. The pastor's impassive face didn't give a clue as to what he was thinking. Ryan found it disconcerting to spill his guts and be unsure of his listener's reaction. Nevertheless, he continued because he needed to talk this out.

Ryan paced the room. "The time finally came for me to take the paternity test. Tiffany organized it, but what she didn't know is that I paid off the tech. I paid him an obscene amount of money to give me the results first. I don't know why I did it. I think I felt that if I knew ahead of time, I'd be able to prepare myself." He stroked his chin. "Maybe deep down I knew Karlie was mine. I don't know."

He stopped pacing and found he had Pastor Ward's undivided attention. "The results were 99.9 percent conclusive that I was Karlie's father."

Ryan pulled out a handkerchief to wipe his face. "I was stunned. Stunned to know that a fling with someone I didn't care about had made me a father again. I panicked. I was a horrible father to Brian. Besides my work, Patti consumed me. I had no room for more children in my life. So I bribed the tech to change the results."

Pastor arched an eyebrow. "Bribery is never a good idea." He rubbed his chin. "So, Karlie and Brian have remained friends?"

"Yes, best friends." Ryan wiped his hands on his pants. "I must have the worst luck in the world! I couldn't believe it, but I wasn't concerned. Karlie was—and still is—dating Jamaal Weathers. They've been together all this time. I thought my secret was safe, especially when Neil and Myra Jameson adopted Karlie. They were trusted friends of Tiffany's, and I knew she would be in good hands."

Ryan closed his eyes. Guilt ate at him. He was a weasel who had wormed his way out of his God-given responsibility. Since he could not look Pastor Ward in the face, Ryan wandered over to the bookshelf and scanned the plethora of Bible commentaries. He pulled a random book out and scanned the pages.

Then he trudged on with his disgraceful tale.

"As our children were good friends, it was inevitable that my family and Karlie's would hang out occasionally."

He stroked his chin. "I think we were at dinner when Neil told me about Merle. Merle was Karlie's grandmother who had rejected Tiffany and Karlie." Ryan returned the commentary. "Pastor, are you with me? Because this is a big information dump."

Pastor nodded. "Yes, telling your past helps me understand your decisions of the future. Continue."

"Neil doesn't want Merle involved in Karlie's life, but my daughter has a forgiving heart. Neil told me how Merle was tormented that Karlie had Clifford's eyes. I laughed at that ridiculous notion. I see myself in Karlie all the time. It's downright creepy. She has a lot of my mannerisms." He shook his head. "Genetics is amazing, you know? Anyhow, I was content to let things stay the way they were, and then I got saved. My conscience is killing me. And now that Brian concocted this crazy scheme to take Karlie on all these adventures and . . ."

"You're worried about them developing feelings for each other from being in close proximity," Pastor Ward said.

Yes. Pastor Ward understood his angst.

Ryan exhaled. He sat in the chair. "To make things worse, both Patricia and Brian believe I have a thing for Karlie. Patti and I haven't made love in weeks. I still want her, but this guilt is eating away at me. God has been speaking to me to tell the truth. Every day I tell myself I will own up to my wrongs but . . ." He glanced at his watch, shocked that he'd only been speaking for just over ten minutes. It felt like hours.

"Ryan, the thing about secrets is that they do come out eventually," Pastor Ward said. "Look at me. You've heard me talk enough about my past to know nothing remains hidden. I was in love with my brother's wife and had children with her. I kept my secret until the whole thing played out on national television. I'm sure you've seen the clips so I won't elaborate. What I will say is you're right about God telling you to confess." Pastor Ward leaned forward. "You need to tell Brian and Karlie the truth immediately. How do you know something hasn't already happened?"

Ryan shook his head. "No, Karlie isn't that kind of a girl. She's a Christian, and she's with Jamaal."

"She's also a woman with feelings. Temptation is a strong force even for the most stable believers. How does Brian feel about her?"

Ryan chewed his bottom lip. "See, that's what has me up at night. I can't sleep. Brian likes her. He told me so himself."

Pastor shifted further into his chair. "That was your opening to tell him the truth. How could you let your son and his raging hormones go on the road with your daughter?"

Ryan clutched his stomach. "It's repulsive. I tried sabotaging them so they'd give up and come home. But they're thickheaded. Like me, I guess."

Pastor Ward stood and came over to him. "Ryan, I urge you not to let another day go by keeping this to yourself. Tell Patricia, Brian, and Karlie tonight. I'm going to pray with you, and, yes, God will forgive you, but you still have to face the consequences. You were man enough to do it, so be man enough to own up to it. I want us to meet again soon. Bring Patricia in with you next time. I'll ask Dianne to check my schedule and arrange a day and time."

Ryan put his face in his hands. "Patti won't forgive me for this so easy. And, Brian," he sobbed. "Brian will hate me. He won't want to have anything to do with me." He shook his head. "Then there's Karlie. I can't even imagine how she'll react." He looked up at Pastor Ward. "I don't think I can do it. I can't lose my family."

Pastor Ward helped him to his feet. "Think about this. You made Karlie because of one careless night. What if

Brian and Karlie do get together by chance? Your son and your daughter might give you your first grandchild. You're worried about your future, but what about theirs? Would they be able to live with themselves after that?"

Overcome, Ryan shook his head. "I've made a mess of things."

"I do have a question, though," Pastor Ward said. "Why was it easier to tell your wife about your indiscretion with Tiffany Knightly, but not easy to tell her that you had a child with her?"

Oh, Lord, Pastor is good. Nothing gets by him. Ryan voiced his deepest pain. "Brian wasn't our only child," he whispered. "Around the time of all this madness, Patti hinted she might be pregnant. She was elated. Just before the paternity results, Patti had lost our baby, who, as it turns out, died in utero. She was actually four months along." Ryan lowered his head. "Our Anna, that's what we named her, died." His smile was filled with sadness. "A little girl. We've never conceived since though we tried, and we never spoke about Anna to anyone. I know Patti still grieves for her."

Ryan shook himself to the present. "I knew I didn't want to bring a daughter into the mix. It would've been a slap in Patti's face."

"Karlie could've been a comfort," Pastor Ward said. "Why didn't you consider that?"

Chapter Sixteen

"You need to keep your hands off my girlfriend!" were Jamaal's first words, five p.m. that Monday evening, before pushing his way into Brian's suite at Sarasota's Ritz-Carlton Hotel.

Brian stepped back. "Whoa! Dude, I haven't touched Karlie."

"You think I don't know you want her? I've seen the YouTube videos. It's written all over your face."

Jamaal's squared shoulders said he was here for a fight. Brian wrinkled his lips. He was no punk and was ready for whatever Jamaal was bringing.

Brian pounced into Jamaal's space. "You were the one who didn't want to come. Whatever happens is on you."

Jamaal shoved him so hard, Brian lost his balance and fell to the floor. He scrambled to his feet, raised his fist, and clocked Jamaal on his lower chin, snapping back Jamaal's head.

Jamaal's responding fist just missed Brian's face.

Karlie must have heard the commotion. She raced through the connecting door and grabbed Jamaal. "Jamaal! Stop this nonsense this instant! You two are behaving like children, and I'm not having it."

Jamaal rounded on her. "Why you jumping on me?" He swung his head to where Brian stood, huffing. "He's the one who's all up in your Kool-Aid, and you're too stupid to see it."

Karlie's harsh intake of breath propelled Brian into motion. "You're not going to talk to her like that."

Jamaal set his face like a boxing champion in the ring. Brian could see he meant business, but so did he.

"I'll talk to *my* woman any way I please," Jamaal spat.

"Not while I'm standing here," Brian snapped back. His body shook as he struggled to rein in his temper.

"Brian, I don't need you jumping to my defense like you're Superman," Karlie said. "I'm capable of handling my own business." She turned to face Jamaal. "I don't know what's gotten into you, but I'm not some ghetto girl off the streets. You're not going to be demeaning toward me because I'm not having it."

"I know you're not," Jamaal said. He placed his hands on his knees and took several breaths to calm himself. "I'm sorry, Karlie. I shouldn't have come at you like that."

Her neck rocked back and forth. "Don't get it twisted. You'll be picking yourself up off the floor if you try a dumb move like that again."

Jamaal held up his hands. He wandered over to the chair by the hotel desk and slumped into it.

"Brian, can you give us a minute?" Karlie asked.

Brian wasn't going anywhere. No way was he leaving Karlie with this hothead. Brian folded his arms. "I'll stay."

Karlie tugged on Jamaal's shirt for him to stand.

Jamaal meekly complied.

"Let's go into my room and talk this through," Karlie said. She cut her eyes at Brian before shutting the connecting door with a click.

Brian relaxed. He could kick himself for getting riled. Jamaal had every right to be upset. If Karlie was his girlfriend, he would be beyond mad.

Brian grabbed his MacBook off the bed and pulled up the most recent "Adventures of Karlie Knightly" YouTube video. As he watched the clip, he relived every moment and every scene. He admitted that the forehead kiss was intimate. Putting himself in Jamaal's shoes, Brian could see how Jamaal could mistake the kiss for something more than it was. However, a kiss on the forehead didn't mean love.

Brian doubted he had ever been in love.

The closest he had come to feeling such strong emotions had been when he was with Tanya McAdams, Karlie's best friend through high school. But once she had moved away, he had returned to his old ways. He loved women, and there was enough of him to go around, so why settle for one?

Brian moseyed into the bathroom. Looking at himself in the mirror, he acknowledged that Dr. Kirkpatrick had been right. At fourteen, when he was acting up and getting kicked out of every school, his parents had taken him to see a psychologist. Dr. Kirkpatrick had made him recognize his anger at his parents for being so consumed with each other that they had excluded him. She had pointed out that he kept himself emotionally detached because he was afraid of getting hurt.

That all changed because of Tiffany and Karlie. They touched his heart. He had loved Tiffany as a mother, and now he admitted that Karlie warmed his heart. She inspired protectiveness, a rare tenderness that he welcomed.

Was he in love?

No. Brian would not go that far, but Karlie made him feel something. She loved him, and she saw the good in him. If he were ever to take a chance on love, it would be with someone like Karlie. She was beautiful, intelligent, and almost as smart as he was. Qualities he found hard to resist.

Brian smiled, remembering how he had tutored her in math in high school. Karlie had been a capable student and the two-year difference had seemed more like twenty. Then as the years went on, she became his best friend, and he realized every day she was very much grown and a woman. Brian and Karlie had never crossed the line of friendship, but he toyed with the idea. The more he was around her, the more appealing it became.

"Why was the connecting door open?" Jamaal asked.

Karlie creased her forehead. Was he insinuating something? "Why should I close it? Brian's my friend. He's not a pervert or a rapist who's going to attack me in the middle of the night. Take a good look at him. He could have any woman he wants! Why would he want me?"

"Why *wouldn't* he?" Jamaal asked in a much-calmer tone. His eyes softened. "You're beautiful. You're sassy. You don't even know your own appeal." He walked closer to her with every word. "I can't be within feet of you and not want to do this."

Jamaal crushed his lips to hers and kissed her until Karlie forgot how mad she was at him.

It wasn't until Jamaal squeezed her bottom that Karlie withdrew from his arms. "Jamaal, we can't do this."

"I know," he said, taking a step back. "But now you see what I mean?" He stuffed both hands into his jeans.

Karlie was surprised he had not argued with her. "I see what you mean."

"You're mine. I've waited all these years to claim you as my bride."

Karlie scrunched her nose. Jamaal sounded a bit too possessive for her tastes. He was marking his territory. Typical alpha male. She was not going to let it slide. "I'm my own person. The only person who has a claim on me is God. He earned it when He died for me."

Jamaal backed down. "All right. I can't compete with that." He looked at his watch. "My flight leaves tomorrow morning at seven. I can't miss my classes. Coach is going to rip into me real good for missing practice tonight."

"That's why you should have taken the summer off," Karlie wanted to say. She hated seeing Jamaal go but knew voicing her thoughts would start another argument. "Well, let's enjoy tonight. I don't want us fighting. I think you owe Brian an apology. He saved my life out there."

"He wouldn't have to save your life if you weren't on these crazy adventures," Jamaal mumbled.

Karlie shook her head. "I'm going to tell you like I told my parents. I'm not going home. I'm seeing this through. With Brian."

Jamaal twisted his mouth but said nothing.

She heard pounding through the connecting door. "Not now, Brian!" she yelled.

"Karlie, open up! You're not going to believe this!"

She eyed Jamaal. He nodded to signify he was cool. *Good.* She could not handle any more fighting between them.

"You landed a TV show!" Brian screamed. "This is so cool. I told you the YouTube videos were a good idea. They want to call the show *The Misadventures of Karlie and Brian* and are looking to start taping sometime in January. I gave them Winona's contact information so she can handle our contract negotiations. They've even offered Yentl and Griffin contracts as well. This is a win-win for all of us." He stepped closer to her with bright eyes.

Karlie had never seen Brian so excited. She giggled at his boyish delight. Brian was always too cool for words. He was jumping up and down like a kid.

"What about college?" Jamaal asked. "And how is this supposed to help your singing career?"

Jamaal asked some great questions. Karlie wrung her hands.

Brian's eagerness deflated. "Reality shows are not twenty-four hours, so she could continue going to school.

She wouldn't need to take a semester off. I'm sure Winona can work that out with the network." He waved his hands dismissively. "And as far as a singing career, are you forgetting Tamar Braxton? Do you think Tamar would have made it if it wasn't for the Braxton reality show?"

Karlie swayed to Brian's side of the argument. He had given this much thought. "They could do snippets of me recording and singing while we go on our next adventure," she said.

"The adventures would be carefully thought out and planned," Brian said.

"I'm not feeling this," Jamaal stated. "Karlie, you hated seeing your mother's face plastered on tabloids. Remember that time we were leaving the movie theater and you saw some crazy headline?"

Karlie nodded. Boy, did she remember. It was after her mother's funeral. Some idiot posted a picture of a gaunt Tiffany with the caption, "TIFFANY'S SECRET BULIMIA BATTLE." The tabloid cover had messed her up that night.

By this time, both men stood by her sides. Jamaal was on her right, and Brian was on the left. *Great.* She did not miss the devil and the angel analogy.

Brian took her hand briefly. Karlie didn't miss Jamaal's reaction. He folded his arms with displeasure but didn't say anything.

"This is your chance," Brian said. "You have to take it. You have to grab onto your dream. What if this was what you were meant to do?"

Karlie went to look out the hotel window. She saw the bright stars and pictured herself up there shining with them. Karlie closed her eyes and visualized thousands of people lifting their hands in worship, calling out the name of Jesus and singing right along with her. In a selfish moment of clarity, Karlie accepted a simple fact.

She wanted to sing.

Her eyes begged Jamaal to understand. When he turned from her, she knew he realized her decision. Then Karlie rested her eyes on Brian. His beaming eyes were like an arrow to her heart. She touched her chest in reaction and a small smile formed that widened as surety set in.

Then she said the words that would seal her fate.

"I'm in."

Chapter Seventeen

Patricia dragged her hands through her curls at a little past eight p.m. She stood with such force that the rolling chair spun across the floor. The twin's first surgery was scheduled for mid-October. Her eyes burned from drills and run-throughs, but she wasn't taking any chances.

Prayers and practice were her game plans for two-out-of-two. Patricia wanted both twins to survive. She would not be satisfied with simply one surviving. As part of the protocol, the team was prepared to save whichever twin proved stronger during the surgery, but she didn't plan to ever have to choose.

Bending over to touch her toes, Patricia released the kinks in her lower back. She needed to go home.

But her home did not feel like home without Ryan by her side. Patricia knew she was throwing a private pity party but could not snap out of her funk. She missed the warmth of his body pressed to hers.

She lifted her hair with her hands and nearly jumped out of her skin when she felt a pair of masculine hands on her shoulders. She would have screamed had she not heard Timothy's voice.

"Shh," he said. "Relax. Let me ease your tension."

Since when did he get so bold?

She shrugged him off. "What do you think you're doing?" She moved away from him toward the exit.

Timothy dropped his voice suggestively. "You've been here for days. I just wanted to see if you could use a *friend*."

Friend? Patricia studied Tim for several seconds. She understood what he was offering. Maybe she had given out a distress signal that she wasn't feeling so desirable, and the hound dog had come barking. Timothy had abs and biceps to spare. Many of the nurses swooned in his presence, yet he had never spared them a single glance. Now, she knew why. He was interested in her. But instead of feeling flattered, she felt exasperated.

Patricia smiled. "Tim, thanks for the offer, but I don't need a friend. My husband has been my best friend for years, so that job's taken."

He blinked. "I um . . . I just thought . . ."

She arched an eyebrow. "Thought that because you've seen me here a few nights that there must be trouble at home?"

He gave a little nod.

She lifted her chin. "I assure you all is well. Anna and Alyssa need the best team, and since that includes you, I'm hoping we can put this behind us as a misunderstanding and move on."

He shook his head. "But I thought . . ."

"No, Tim . . ."

"But the way you've been acting—"

"No," Patricia interrupted. "Are we good?"

"Yes," Timothy said, and he departed.

Her shoulders sagged with relief. Timothy was an excellent surgeon and she would have hated to replace him on her team, yet part of her couldn't respect how he had given up so easily. *If you're going to proposition a man's wife, you should at least display a little gumption.*

Patricia cracked up. She sashayed over to her mirror. "You still got it, girl." Tim was ten years younger, and it was extremely flattering. She raked her hands over her body. "You want a piece of *this,* Tim?" She puckered her lips at her reflection and said in her best Marilyn Monroe impression, "Sorry, it's already been claimed."

Too bad Ryan hadn't been claiming it lately.

She slapped her thighs with sudden decisiveness because that was about to change. God had used that small incident with Tim to show her someone still desired her.

Her fragile confidence restored, Patricia made up her mind. She was going home. No more sleeping in the guest room. Tonight, she was going to remind Ryan of what he was missing.

Patricia gathered her courage and her coral suit jacket. On her way home, she plotted her moves. *First, I'll put on that new French maid outfit I bought online.* Patricia had bought it months ago but had yet to wear the hot little number. She pictured Ryan ripping it off her body. *Oh yeah! Oooh. I'll search for the "One in a Million" song to play at the right time.* They both loved Aaliyah's compilation with Timbaland.

Red light! Patricia hit the brake. She drummed her nails on the steering wheel while she waited for the light to change. *Ooh, I'll light some candles. Maybe draw us a bubble bath. Put the wine on to chill. What to do for food? Takeout.* She did not have time to cook.

The light changed. Patricia smiled. She could not wait to get her seduction started. But when she entered the house, she froze. Her eyes widened.

Lit candles of Cranberry Mandarin Splash—her favorite scent—lined the hallway into the living area.

"What's this?" Patricia's mouth hung open as she scanned her foyer. She saw a Post-it on the huge mirror she had bought on impulse from Pier One:

Take off your clothes.

She sniffed the air and took in the soothing scent. She heard the Midnight Sax instrumental music playing and smiled. Nice to know she and Ryan were in sync. Felt like old times.

From the corner of her eye, she saw Ryan hiding behind the curtains in the living area. She smirked. He had no clue she had spotted his shoes sticking out. Might as well give him a show.

She dropped her jacket to the floor. Her skirt and undershirt followed. Clad in her undies and pantyhose, she made a show of turning her back in Ryan's direction before wiggling out of her pantyhose. Hearing Ryan's heavy panting, she bit back a knowing smile.

Patricia swayed her hips to the music. She pretended to reach for her underwear but decided to stretch the teasing. Making her way toward the living room, she saw another Post-it:

Take a sip of wine.

There was a decanter chilling in ice. Her husband had thought of everything. She poured the red liquid in the Olivia Pope-sized glass. Licking her lips, she sipped, making sure to "accidentally" spill some on her chest staining her Very Sexy Unlimited ivory bra from Victoria's Secret.

Pretending to fuss over the lacy material, she snapped it open.

Ryan groaned. Loudly.

Patricia threw back her head and laughed.

He's back, she thought. Slight tears grazed her eyes. *Thank you, Lord, for answered prayers.*

She executed a dance move seductive enough to make a stripper blush. Boy, was she glad for the belly dancing classes at the YMCA. That did it.

Ryan came out of hiding. He held a third sticky note on his lips:

Tonight, I'll make you scream.

Patricia released a quick breath at the bold sentiment. Ryan's note heightened her senses, and his eyes held promise. She knew from experience that he always kept his promises. Patricia plucked the note off his lips.

Ryan pounced into action, kissing her like a man who had starved for days. With a sigh of bliss, she obliged him, anticipating that she would need a day off tomorrow.

Ryan loved his wife, holding nothing back. He had to. When he confessed the truth, it might be the last time he held Patricia.

For a long time.

His fear made him passionate and desperate. He made love to her three times before his body gave out. "You're going to be the end of me, woman," he said, giving her a love pat. While he spoke, his hands roamed her body, committing every nuance and curve of her perfect-for-him body to his memory.

Don't tell her. How can you give this up?

The familiar fear rose within him. Ryan tensed.

She'll hate you. There must be another way.

Ryan rolled onto his side and pulled Patricia until she faced him. He gulped, ignoring the fearful thoughts. Instead, he grabbed onto Joshua 1:9 for courage, "Be strong and of a good courage; be not afraid, neither be thou dismayed: for the LORD thy God is with thee whithersoever thou goest."

"Patti, I have something to tell you."

She touched his cheek. "Are you finally going to tell me what's bothering you?"

"Yes, I am."

Her sigh was mixed with contentment. "It's about time. Your teeth grinding drove me from our bed."

Her attempt at humor made him hesitate. No, he wasn't backing down.

He held her hand and uttered his secret of the past five years. "Five years ago, I paid the lab tech to tell me Karlie's paternity results before anyone." He took a deep breath. "Karlie is my daughter."

Ryan prepared his body for the slap he was sure was coming. Patricia lifted her hand. He squinted as her hand came close to his face. To his surprise, she caressed him.

Caught off guard, he had to ask, "Did you hear me?" Her odd reaction was scaring him. It took every bit of willpower he possessed to reject the urge to jump out of bed and put some distance between them.

Patricia nodded before uttering the last words he expected her to say. "Baby, sweetheart, is that what this is about? I already know."

Chapter Eighteen

How could a person drop that revelation, and then prance about pretending not to know she had sucker punched him?

Thirty minutes had passed since Patricia's revelation eclipsed his own. They had cleared the candles, and Ryan suggested they move their discussion to their bedroom. She sent him ahead while she washed the wineglasses. Patricia returned with two glasses of water and placed one on his nightstand before going to her side of the bed. For once, his mind wasn't on admiring her attributes. Ryan watched her progress trying to temper his patience.

"What do you mean you already know?" he asked, turning on the ceiling fan.

The woman had the nerve to make him wait. He gritted his teeth. Now she needed to tinkle. Ryan slinked into the chair while he waited until Patricia returned.

She gulped her water before easing under the covers.

"How about you start first?" she suggested. "We'll piece the whole story together."

All right. He would start first. "When Tiffany scheduled the paternity test, a panic set in. I don't know why I felt the need to know before anyone else. But I hated not knowing. Once I submitted my sample, I flirted with the front desk clerk to get the name of the tech responsible for the results. Tiffany ensured complete privacy, but everyone has a price. I paid him twenty thousand dollars to provide me with the results before anyone else."

"Why?"

Ryan shook his head. "Maybe it's my control issue. Who knows why I did it."

"I followed you," Patricia said.

His eyes were wide with shock. "What do you mean you followed me?"

"You think I would let my husband take the most important test of his life without being there? I came, but it must've been too late." She touched her chin. "I was about to pull out of the parking lot when a call came in. I parked my car to answer the phone. It was about a patient. When I finished the call and started to pull out of the lot, I saw your car. You rushed back into the building although you didn't stay for more than five or ten minutes."

"And you didn't call to me?" Ryan asked.

"No, I was more interested in finding out why you returned so quickly." Patricia shivered. She reached for a robe.

"Finish your story," he commanded, rubbing his arms. Never would he let on how he hated her mistrust. Not when she was right to do so. He pushed himself to his feet and joined her on the bed.

"I asked to visit the tech—Geoffrey Turner—the front desk clerk provided his name."

"That's right," Ryan said. "I had forgotten."

Patricia placed a finger over his lips. "No more inter- ruptions. This has been a long time coming."

Ryan nodded.

"Unlike you, I didn't flirt to get information. I played the doctor card." She chuckled. "I made him tell me why you were there. Geoffrey spilled it and told me you paid him for the results. I paid him thirty thousand to tell you Karlie was your daughter."

Ryan's mouth dropped open. He reared back and pinned his eyes on her. "What? Why would you do that?"

Who was this woman he had married? She looked like the woman he knew, but she didn't sound like her. The woman in front of him was deceitful. His Patti wouldn't have played such a cruel joke on him.

Would she?

"Two years passed before I understood my motives. We'd lost Anna. I was grieving. Having Karlie for a daughter would've soothed my aching heart. I was already spending time with her, and I'd come to care for her as if she were my own."

"You wanted Karlie as your substitute?" Ryan asked.

"When you put it like that, it sounds . . . contrived." Patricia bit her lip. For the first time she sounded less sure.

"Thanks to your interference, Geoffrey made another thirty thousand from me to declare Clifford as Karlie's father." He rubbed his temples.

"I thought you would come to me with the news. We would've had a daughter and a son."

Through gritted teeth, Ryan said, "Karlie's not Anna. There is no replacing our child."

Patricia nodded rapidly. "I know that. Now. It was a mistake, honey. I was overcome and I . . . I . . ."

"You what? You wanted to make me pay, is that it?" He swallowed before ripping the pain of the past open. "It was payback, wasn't it? Payback, because you blamed me. Admit it. You blame me."

He lowered his head. Ryan registered the slight rustle of the covers being pulled back before Patricia touched his arm. He hated the tears rolling down her face and shrugged off her arm.

"I don't blame you," she said. "I wasn't thinking."

How could he believe any word out of her lying mouth?

"You've got to believe me," Patricia pleaded.

However, Ryan was past the point of listening to her. "All this time I carried the guilt of hiding my daughter from you when you knew. You knew. You did it because you blamed me for Anna's death." He remembered the night she had miscarried. "We had just made love because, as usual, I couldn't keep my hands off you."

Her lower lip trembled. "I, I don't blame you," she wept. "The cramping wasn't because of anything we'd done. She just wasn't meant to be. We cannot control God's will."

Ryan didn't want to hear that. Her explanation wouldn't soothe the guilt stewing within him. Instead, he found himself becoming angry at Patricia's thoughtless actions. His anger transformed his voice into steel. "Tell me something, *wife*. Why did you accuse me of wanting Karlie if you knew the truth all along?"

"I wasn't sure of the truth anymore." She ignored her runny nose. "I thought Geoffrey betrayed me when you told me Clifford Peterson was the father. I figured he'd pocketed the money and told the truth. I couldn't very well expose him without exposing myself, so I took a loss. What's thirty thousand, I told myself. I put the whole thing behind me as a bad experience and moved on."

"A bad experience? *That's* how you see it?"

Patricia's robe fell open. Her half-naked body taunted him, reminding him of how his passion had killed their baby. No matter what Patricia offered as a clinical explanation, he knew the truth.

Ryan inhaled. "Put some clothes on."

"Ryan, we need to get on our knees and throw all this pain to Christ. Only He can help us. When we got baptized, God washed away all our sins, including these."

No, that's too easy. Ryan was not in the mood to pray or accept salvation as justification for treachery. In a tone laced with scorn, he said, "How convenient. You want to bring God into this conversation now. Where was God when you paid someone to lie to me?"

"Whoa. Don't put this all on me. You paid him as well."

He clenched his fists. "I know that. I've been carrying that burden for *five* years. But I thought Karlie was my daughter. I thought I was doing the right thing. I was a horrible parent to Brian. I was always busy. I didn't think I would've been a good father to her."

She curled her lips and pointed at him. "Your excuses might have helped you sleep at night, but they won't wash when Karlie finds out. She's going to see you as the weasel who betrayed her."

The truth punched him in the guts. Patti was right. He had no justifiable excuse for not being in his daughter's life. "*Is* she my daughter?"

"What do you mean?" Patricia asked.

"You paid Geoffrey to tell me a lie. How do I know what the truth is? I've seen Karlie's mannerisms, and I see myself. But what if I'm seeing the similarities based upon what I think to be true?" He groaned. This was complicated enough without this added uncertainty. Ryan could not tell Karlie his wrongdoing and shred her life apart, again, unless he knew.

"There's only one thing left to do and you must be urgent about it. Brian and Karlie are thrown together. What if they fall . . .?"

Ryan knew what she was going to say. That thought had given him many nights filled with tossing and turning.

"I can't even utter the unimaginable," Patricia said. "You must confront Karlie and have her take an unsullied paternity test. That's the only way you'll know for sure."

Ryan shrugged into his clothes and grabbed his keys. "I'll be back."

She creased her forehead. "Where are you going? It's almost midnight."

His rage broiled and bubbled over. "To get some air. I need to put some distance between us or I'm going to say something I can't take back. I can't stand to look at your face." He cut his eyes at her before turning away. He missed the raw pain slashed across her face at his harsh words.

"We need to talk. Make plans." She came over to him and grasped his arm. "Let's go down to Sarasota and tell them together. We can't waste any time on the off chance something happens between them that cannot be undone."

"I'll book our flights when I get back," he said. Right now, Ryan needed to get out of there.

"You did wrong too," Patricia whispered.

He glared. "I'm not going to stay here if this conversation is going to become a tit-for-tat." Ryan tromped over to the closet and threw some clothes in an overnight bag.

"Where are you going?"

"Where do you think?" He was not about to add he had not thought that far ahead. "I'll be at my office."

"Don't leave," she pleaded.

"I'll call you with travel arrangements."

And with that, Ryan snatched his bag and stormed out the door.

Chapter Nineteen

Lovemaking had loosened her tongue.

"Why did I tell him? I should've kept my big mouth shut."

Disquieted and alone in her bedroom, she banged her head on the back of the headboard.

Ryan had been so fearful to tell her his news. She had seen how he had worked up the nerve to tell her. He must have thought he would lose her with his revelation. Patricia had blabbed to put his mind at ease.

But, no, he was furious with her. Men and their double standards. Why was it when they did their wrongdoings, it was forgivable? But if a woman did the same, they threw a fit.

She had recovered from his cheating, yet he was bent out of shape because she had kept a little secret. What was a secret compared to cheating? Patricia squirmed. Well, to be fair, it depended on the secret, and Ryan and Tiffany hadn't been an emotional affair. It was easier to get past a meaningless one-night stand.

Patti tossed and turned but couldn't sleep. It was now 4:28 early Tuesday morning. Sunrise loomed in a couple hours. She might as well head into work. Patricia entered her marble-tiled bathroom. She eyed the large bathtub and wrinkled her nose. She was not in the mood for a bath. Instead, she opened the glass door to her walk-in shower and turned the water on. Within minutes she was showered and dressed. On cue, her phone rang.

"Dr. Oakes, it's Anna and Alyssa. They're both spiking a fever of over 104 degrees."

Adrenaline shot through her system. Her heart pounded. Fevers. Fevers meant infection or seizures, or . . .

She was a physician. She knew better than to suppose this or that. She had to run tests, get the facts. "Keep them stable. I'll be right there."

"Dr. Newhouse is with them."

She breathed a sigh of relief. Tim would watch her babies until she arrived.

Patricia chided herself. Anna and Alyssa weren't *her* babies. They were her patients. She shouldn't be so attached.

Yet her hands shook. Patricia prayed, "Lord, please watch out for the twins. I'm not there, and I need you to keep them."

When she opened the door, Patricia was surprised to see the light sprinkle. She tore through the slick streets and pulled into the physician's lot. She scurried up to the twins' room and pulled their charts.

Patricia noticed Tim had prescribed Dexamol to lower their temperatures. He also ordered blood and urine analysis. If their fevers remained, Patricia worried she might have to do spinal taps. Hopefully, the fevers would subside within a day or so. She prayed it was a virus just running its course.

Anna's feverish eyes followed her every movement. Alyssa was asleep.

"We want to stay together," Anna said.

Patricia went to her side of the bed. "You are together, honey," she said, touching Anna's cheek.

"Yes, but we don't want surgery. We like being together." Anna coughed.

How eloquent for a four-year-old. For the first time Patricia considered that no one had asked them how they felt. Then she dismissed it. Anna and Alyssa were four years old. Babies, still. What did they know? She could give them quality of life. If all went well, they would be running and playing like normal children.

Patricia nodded. "I know it's scary, but you will be okay."

Anna trembled. "I don't want to. I want to go home."

Patricia's heart melted. She patted Anna's head. "I'll do my best to make that happen."

"We want to go to Disney and meet the princesses. Mommy said she'd buy us princess dresses." Anna's body shook with tears.

Patricia's heart broke at Anna's words. She could picture the little girl in her costume waving a wand in her hand. "Hush," she cooed. "Close your eyes and go to sleep. When you wake up, you'll feel better."

"I don't want to sleep," Anna pouted, then yawned. She reached over to take Alyssa's hand before falling asleep.

Patricia monitored them herself. Within a few hours, their fever broke. "Hallelujah," Patricia whispered. *Now stay better.*

Anna's dream of going to Disney World solidified Patricia's efforts. She practiced another simulation drill. Patricia had a limited time frame once they were separated. Doctors would be on standby to begin the reconstruction while she focused on their brains. She was looking at a huge team of doctors and about a hundred hours of surgery. Every detail of the surgery had to be planned and coordinated precisely or lives could be lost.

Patricia sighed. She had better call it a night. Her brain was on overload. She exited the lab and went into her office to hang up her lab coat and retrieve her purse. On her desk were a huge bouquet and a box of chocolates.

She smiled. *Ryan's apology.* Energy surged through her body, and she rushed to read the card attached to the flowers:

While you're caring for the twins, don't forget to pamper yourself. Tim.

"What the heck is the matter with this man? Doesn't he know that I'm married?" *Geez.* If Tim didn't stop with his not-so-subtle overtures, she might have to file a harassment suit.

Patricia sighed. She was not about to report him, though. She needed him on her surgical team, and could not show cause. It was not harassment to give someone chocolates and flowers. Had she somehow encouraged this? Was she flirting with him and didn't know it? Tim *was* charming and handsome. Patricia did not think she had been flirting, but she would make sure she gave him a tongue-lashing and put him in his place.

She played with her hair while she eyed the flowers. They were a beautiful arrangement. It would be a sin to throw them out. She read the card again.

She picked up the chocolates, intending to toss them into the garbage can. She wasn't much of a chocolate person. Patricia rubbed her chin as an idea formed. With an impish smile, she knew just what she had to do. She reached for a Post-it on her desk and wrote:

Thinking of you. Patti.

Ryan loved chocolates. She would leave them for him in his office. He'd appreciate the gesture. Patricia giggled at her regifting plan.

Carrying the flowers and the chocolates with her, Patricia piled them into the back of her car and drove home. She pulled into the driveway and pressed the garage door opener. She groaned. Ryan's spot was empty.

Her cell beeped, indicating she had a text. Coincidentally, it was from Ryan giving her their flight information to Sarasota. They would leave Wednesday morning. She texted:

Are you coming home? We need to talk.

Patricia felt like the whiny housewife and hated it. In all her forty-four years, she never had to beg a man to be in her presence. She trudged into her house.

Her phone beeped again. She read the incoming text message.

Be there in five.

Patricia brightened at the four words. Ordering take-out, she hopped in the shower and dabbed her ears, legs, and other places with Obsession. Ryan loved that scent. Hopefully, they would do some talking, and then some loving.

The alarm tripped, alerting Patricia that Ryan was home. She shimmied into her lace nightgown. The cream color against her auburn hair would make him drool. She heard the doorbell.

Good, the takeout had arrived.

She rushed down the stairs and watched Ryan lay out the meal on the dining table.

"I didn't know what you felt up for, so I ordered a little bit of everything," she breathed out. *Why do I sound nervous?* Patricia chided herself. This was her husband, not a stranger.

Tell that to her heart which was pounding hard in her chest.

Ryan gave her the once-over and looked at the food. "I'm not hungry . . ."

Her shoulders drooped. She blinked to keep the tears threatening to spill at bay. Forcing herself to appear nonchalant, she blithely replied, "More for me, then." She held her head high and strolled toward the table.

She uncovered one of the foil containers. Her stomach felt like lead, but she was going to eat. The aromatic smells were lost on her. Patricia ate the noodles and garlic chicken with fake gusto. She felt as if she was eating rubber, but she finally finished her meal.

Stone-faced, Ryan sat across from her. "We have an early flight. What did you want to talk about?"

She held her fork midair. Dropping her act, an apology tore from her lips. "I'm sorry. Ryan, I can't have things being like this between us. You're cold and mean . . . and . . ." She hung her head. "How did we get here?"

"I don't like being played for a fool," he said. His face was scrunched like an angry pit bull.

Patricia shuddered. "I wasn't trying to play you." She stood and raked shaky fingers through her hair. "I made a mistake. I see that now. But I'm not the only one who lied. You're acting as if you did nothing wrong."

"I know what I did was wrong, and the truth is, I'm angrier with myself for lying—for everything." He rubbed his head. "Is there anything else you're keeping from me?"

Patricia toyed with the lace on her gown. She knew this was a pivotal moment where she needed to fess up to anything else. She shook her head. "No . . . No . . . Well, there is something . . ."

He arched a brow while she sought the words. Patricia wanted to keep him talking.

"I, I . . ." She said the first thing that came to mind. "I'm really nervous about a set of four-year-old twins who need brain separation surgery. Their names are Anna and Alyssa." She emphasized the Anna.

Ryan gritted his teeth. "She's not our Anna."

Patricia's heart lurched. "Yes, but if I can save her, it would be like saving Anna."

Ryan looked at her as if she were crazy. "Are you listening to yourself? Our daughter is gone. There is no bringing her back. There is *no* substitution."

Of course, she knew there was no bringing her daughter back. But saving this Anna would heal the rift in her heart.

Ryan grabbed his keys. "I'll be at the office. See you in the morning."

A cool wind rushed over her body. Patricia fell to her knees. Ryan was so cold and unfeeling. She lifted her head toward the flowers in the foyer. He had not even noticed the bouquet and card.

Wiping her face, Patricia stood. She meandered her way to read the card. She had left it there to make Ryan jealous. Flipping it over, she saw his address penned on the back. *Someone was a little sure of himself.* But at least Tim cared. Tim understood how significant Anna was to her. Holding the card in her hand, Patricia navigated upstairs to her bedroom. She reached for her cell and dialed Tim's number.

"I was wondering if you saw my gift."

"I did," Patricia said. "It was a thoughtful gesture."

"I'd like to see you sometime."

Patricia thought of Ryan's rejection. Tim wanted to see her.

What are you doing, Patricia? You can't lead someone on because you and Ryan are at odds.

Patricia gulped. She couldn't bring Tim into her mess of a marriage. It wouldn't be fair. "Tim, I'm flattered by your gestures, but let's keep things between us professional. If you don't . . ."

"As you wish," he said, and he ended the call.

Patricia understood his curt response. She had done the right thing, she told herself.

Then how come she did not feel right?

Chapter Twenty

Miles away that same Tuesday morning, Karlie pleaded with Jamaal. "Please don't be upset with me."

"I'm not upset," Jamaal said. "It's your life if you want to throw it away. I can't help but feel you chose Brian over me."

"I didn't choose Brian. I chose myself."

The couple stood at the checkpoint inside the Sarasota Bradenton International Airport. They had thirty minutes to spare for his seven a.m. flight. The airport was quiet. Only a handful of travelers were present.

Karlie insisted on accompanying Jamaal to the airport against his wishes. She detested the way things were between them and hoped they would use the wait time to talk. Jamaal had other plans. He moved toward the entrance to the gate.

"You don't have to rush," Karlie said, pointing toward the empty space. "There's no line at this hour."

"I want to go," he said. He chucked his chin in the universal sign of good-bye before walking off.

"No kiss good-bye?" she quietly asked. Karlie had never had to beg for kisses before.

Jamaal paused midstride. Her sad tone must have touched him, and he returned to stand before her. His strong arms crushed her to him. Jamaal gave Karlie a proper send-off, and Karlie savored the sweet taste of his lips. Something about it tugged at her heartstrings and a tear slid down her face.

Is he saying good-bye, she wondered.

Panicked, Karlie broke the kiss. She held his cheeks in her hands. "This is *not* the end for us. I need you to understand that."

Jamaal shoved his hands into his pockets. He pretended as if her words hadn't affected him. Then with a sarcastic edge to his voice, he declared, "This is not the time nor the place. When *you* find the time, we need to talk."

She wasn't going to let Jamaal guilt-trip her for pursuing her dream. "Listen, we're important to me, but I've got to do this. Music is in my blood. It's my passion and a part of my DNA. I can't come home. I have to make my dreams a reality."

"Dreams Brian put into your head." Jamaal glared. "He's only in this for himself. I hope you know he doesn't care about you. I do."

"He does care," Karlie said. "That's why he's doing this. *For me.*" She resisted the urge to stomp her foot. She was too old to throw a tantrum. She looked down and made circles on the floor with her feet. "I've always supported you in everything. When you wanted to do stepping, I'm at almost all your events. You're on the basketball team, and I'm cheering you on. Why can't you do the same for me? Say what you will about Brian, but *he's* in my corner." Karlie raised her head to look at him. "Jamaal, we could've spent time together and gone out and done something fun last night, but you spent the whole time ranting about Brian and me. It's getting old."

With a furious whisper, Jamaal addressed her through gritted teeth. "It has *everything* to do with Brian. You're crushing on him and he's a *player*. He's messed about with two women for months and you turn a blind eye. You shouldn't even be friends with him knowing his lifestyle. You should be preaching God to him, but instead, you laugh in his face."

Karlie clutched her chest. "I've got news for you. Jesus was a friend to the lowest of the low. Being friends with Brian doesn't mean I condone his behavior. I've known him for years, and I do talk about God with him. Brian's not saved. He's—"

Jamaal cut her off. "There you go defending him again. If it were anyone else . . ." He drew a breath, "But it's Brian. Newsflash. I'm not stupid. I can see the chemistry between the two of you. Heck, the entire world has seen it at this point. You two are all over each other like leeches, and I'm sick of it." Jamaal stalked toward the passengers' only sign.

Watching the stubborn set of his stride, Karlie's heart constricted. These were days where anything could happen. She did not want the last words spoken between them to be, "I'm sick of it."

Karlie shouted, "I love you!"

Jamaal kept walking.

Dejected, Karlie stormed outside to hail a cab. She knew he'd heard her. Jamaal could have at least said he loved her too, instead of leaving her high and dry. How she wished he would drop the whole I-think-you're-in-love-with-Brian episode so they could move on. However, she knew from experience once Jamaal had an idea in his head, it was difficult to persuade him otherwise.

A cabbie pulled in front of her, and she got inside. Her cell buzzed.

I love you.

Instantly her anger evaporated like ice in the Florida sun. She had a smile the size of a Cheshire cat on her face after receiving Jamaal's text. Before she could respond, he sent another:

I'm trying.

Hope rose. He was communicating, even if it was through text. Karlie's fingers flew across the keyboard as she texted him back:

I know. I need you in my corner.

Within seconds, a reply popped up on her screen:

I need you too. I wish you had let me show you last night.

Ugh! This was the real reason he had reached out. To air his other grievance. This man was going to make her yank her hair out. He had a one-track mind.

In time. Be patient.

Don't give him what's mine.

Karlie's mouth fell open. Forget the truce. She was ready to go off, but the cab slowed in front of the hotel. She paid the fare and exited the cab.
As soon as she could, she sent:

That was uncalled for. Stop that!

Karlie swept through the doors and nodded at the hotel clerk. Another buzz came through:

Gotta go. Time to board. Watch the video.

Why? Karlie meandered toward the elevator. Why was it so important to Jamaal that she review the clip? Curious, Karlie pulled up the YouTube video. She relived her and Brian's debacle in the water while trying to remain objective. She wanted to see it from an outsider's point of view. *What did Jamaal see?*

To her chagrin, Yentl captured the terror on her face, but then the camera zoomed in on Brian's expression. Karlie saw the grit and determination on Brian's face. She registered how he swooped her into his powerful arms. Glued to the screen, Karlie held her chest as Brian pounded through the alligator-infested waters with her grabbing on tight.

After the rescue, she fainted. That was one moment she wished was not on display. Brian's forehead kiss made her heart constrict. Brian had done that plenty of times. It was the tender, unguarded moment. Maybe that was what Jamaal saw.

She read several comments. Apparently, people thought something was up between them and rooted for their "relationship." Karlie clicked off. She needed to set the record straight. This wasn't a Chad Murray-Sophia Bush connection like *One Tree Hill*.

Karlie opened the door to her suite. Eager to speak with Brian, she walked toward the connecting door. Pressing her ear against the door, she heard distinct groans. She tried to open the door quietly and discovered it was locked. *Maybe he has someone in his room.* She could not go barging inside.

She looked at her watch. It was only half-past-seven. She would give him until after nine. Twiddling her thumbs, Karlie grabbed her Bible and returned to her bed. Not once would she admit that she felt as if she were on the wrong side of the door.

Hours later, Karlie pounded on the connecting door. "Brian, you've been holed up in there all morning. Let me in."

"I'll come see you in a little bit," he yelled through the door.

"Do you have someone in there?" she asked, hoping she didn't come off sounding jealous.

"What? No."

Karlie rested her head against the door. "Yentl told me you canceled our mudding expedition for a couple days."

"Something came up. I need to . . . think."

As she trudged from the door toward her bedroom, she could have sworn she heard a groan, but Karlie let it go. She moped for a minute before opening her MacBook. She might as well Skype home. Her father answered.

"It feels so good seeing your face," Neil said.

Karlie smiled. "Where's Addie?"

"She's spending the night with her new best friend."

Karlie laughed. Addie changed best friends like socks. "What does this make now? Best friend number six?"

Neil nodded. "How are things going with Brian?"

Karlie thought for a moment. If she hadn't just seen the video, her response would've been less guarded. As it was, she provided a bland update. "Pretty good. We were offered a television show."

"You don't sound too excited about it."

"I'm thrilled," Karlie said. She should have known her father would see through her farce. She weighed her words before speaking. "It's just I'm worried about doing a show with Brian when he can be a little . . . unreliable."

Neil's eyebrows arched. "Unreliable? Why do you say that?"

Karlie touched the bridge of her nose. "Maybe unreliable isn't the word I'm looking for. Brian gets into these moods where he closes off from everyone and me. He usually bounces back after a day or two, but I don't know how that will pan out if we have a television show with deadlines."

Neil nodded. "You know my preference would be for you to finish your degree. I really wish you'd avoid the entire Hollywood scene, but you have to follow your heart. I've been praying for you both nonstop, and I just have to trust God."

Karlie bit her lip. She hated feeling as if she had disappointed Neil, but she had to listen to her inner voice. "I feel this is where God is leading me. I was meant to do this, Dad. Please understand."

Neil softened. "Okay, honey. I'm here for you always. However, you need to have a fierce conversation with Brian. The last thing I want is a phone call telling me that you're being sued or something because you guys failed to live up to your commitment."

He is so right.

"I'll talk with Brian," Karlie promised. "You gave me a lot to think about. The show will have both our names on it. I need to know he's ready. We're shooting our last video before we enter talks about the show and contracts. Winona's handling everything."

"Smart move using Winona. Tiffany trusted her with her estate. She's good people."

Karlie heard Neil's wistful tone when he mentioned Tiffany. She knew how much he had loved her mother. They had been the best of friends.

Karlie too missed her mother. Her dream would have been to sing with Tiffany on stage. She knew that could never happen here on earth, but she was saving some songs for heaven. She was sure Tiffany was leading God's choir up there and ripping out some good tunes.

"What crazy adventure do you have planned?" Neil asked.

"Mudding."

Neil's eyes widened. "Did I hear right? You're going to dirty your hair?"

Karlie cracked up. Her long hair was a chore to wash and set. It took hours to do it herself, which is why she had her hairstylist, Shanna, on speed dial.

"Actually, I'm going to be dirty all over. Mudding is a dirty sport. I'm dreading the dirt caked into my hair, but I keep telling myself it'll wash out. Maybe I should have Shanna on standby."

Neil raised his hands to the ceiling. "Girl, you're going to keep me on my knees, but have fun."

"I'm counting on it."

Just before she logged off Skype, Karlie saw a friend request. Her eyes bulged when she saw who it was.

Merle Peterson.

Her grandmother.

Chapter Twenty-one

Brian curled in a fetal position. He didn't know how much more of this pain he could take. He knew he needed to apply more of the ointment, but he needed help. This flare-up was the worst he had ever had.

He knew it was stress related.

This time he would need help. His help was mere footsteps away in the other room. All he had to do was ask, but Brian didn't want Karlie seeing him like this.

"Lord. Please."

Brian prayed his usual prayer as he shifted his legs inch by inch. He needed to use the bathroom. His body trembled as he tried to keep from crying out in pain.

"Lord, please. Please. Please." This time a sob escaped. Every single movement he made was excruciating. He placed a fist in his mouth before swinging his legs to the floor. Next came the task of lifting his upper body.

This required a new prayer. *"Lord, help me."* Gritting his teeth, Brian hoisted his body in a single determined lunge. Fire laced his back. *"Argh!"* He fell back onto the bed.

Brian's outcry was loud enough for fresh banging on his door. "Brian! Let me in!"

He moved his head toward the sound. If she only knew, he would if he could. Pain and the urgent need to relieve himself quickly conquered his pride.

"I can't," he huffed. "Help!" His voice sounded like a small croak.

"Will my key card work in your door?"

"Try," he said. Even that one word took effort. He wiped his face with his hand.

A few seconds later, Karlie rushed inside waving the key card in triumph.

Brian watched her freeze when she realized he wasn't wearing a shirt. He didn't have time to explain. He had to go.

Real bad.

He lifted his arm like a baby would when asking to be picked up.

Karlie raced to his side. "You can't stand?" she asked.

Brian huffed and shook his head.

She crooked both her hands under his arms and assisted him to his feet. They shuffled over to the bathroom. Brian entered the small space. He heard Karlie's huge intake of breath. She had seen his back.

Hanging his head, all Brian could do was close the door and unzip his pants. "Ah," he breathed. Nothing felt as good as that release. He washed his hands, grabbed the ointment, and opened the door to a waiting Karlie. "Thank you."

With a brisk nod, she helped him back to the bed.

He sat on the edge.

Karlie slipped beside him and rested her head on his shoulder.

He knew she was waiting for him to speak. "I have psoriatic arthritis."

She scrunched her nose. "What's that?"

"It's a kind of psoriasis that comes with crippling pain. When I get a flare-up, the area is tender and painful. Fortunately, my back and sometimes my feet are the only places which act up. Once I apply the ointment and medicine, it usually helps ease the pain."

"I know Kim Kardashian has psoriasis, but I had no idea it could be painful," she said.

"Normally it isn't. I just happen to have the form of it that is."

Karlie touched his arm. "Why didn't you ever tell me?"

"I was ashamed. I didn't want you scorning me or feeling repulsed by it. It's not contagious."

She slapped him lightly on the arm. "I could never scorn you. Silly man. I thought you had a genius IQ. And I know it's not contagious."

"You sure? You might wake up tomorrow with spots all over your lips."

They shared a laugh.

"Can you rub some of this on my back?" Brian asked, holding out the ointment. With a nod, Karlie took the small tube. He angled his upper body to give her access. Brian sighed with relief once the medicine had been rubbed in.

"Thank you," he said, facing her.

Karlie nodded. She rubbed the bridge of her nose. "Wait. Is this the reason why you sometimes would disappear for a day or two?"

He nodded.

"And, here I was thinking you were holed up with some girl or something."

Brian chuckled. "Well . . . that's been true too. But I always make time for you. Always. Unless I'm sick or bedridden." He watched her eyes warm at his words.

"Let me see it in the light."

Brian tensed because he wasn't comfortable with the idea. "Karlie, you're the first person, besides my parents, I'm telling about this."

She touched her chest. "I'm glad you trust me enough to tell me. Now turn around and let me see."

It took every ounce of courage he possessed to allow
her a closer inspection. His heart hammered in his chest.
Would she avoid him from now on? Would she eat with
him? Would she be the same toward him?

Brian jumped out of his skin when he felt Karlie's lips
on his back.

"What are you doing?" he whispered. Not for a million
dollars would he admit how her gesture touched him. A
tear threatened to spill. He blinked it away.

"I'm sorry for your pain," she said.

Hearing the sorrow in her voice, Brian faced her. Her
eyes glistened.

Was she crying for him?

His heart cracked open at her compassion and every
ounce of self-consciousness departed. Brian knew there
was nothing he couldn't share with Karlie from now on.
He pulled her into his arms and hugged her tightly. "I
don't deserve a friend like you," he whispered from atop
her head.

Her shoulders shook. "I'm sorry you've been going
through this all by yourself. I wish you'd told me."

"If I had known that was all I had to do to get a kiss, I
would've a long time ago," he joked.

Karlie pushed out of his embrace. "I'd like to pray for
you."

His feet felt weightless. "You want to pray for me?"

"God is a healer. There isn't anything He can't do."

"I've been praying for two years and so far . . ." Brian
shifted and cupped her face with his hands. "I'm sure you
have a direct line to God, though."

She tilted her head. "You've been praying?"

He nodded. "Yes. It's two words. Lord, please. Tonight,
I added a few more pleases to my prayer." He lowered his
head with slight embarrassment.

"Brian Oakes, are you blushing?" Karlie asked.

He lowered his head. "No. I'm too mature to blush."

"You are!" she exclaimed. "You don't have to be embarrassed about praying. I'm glad to hear it. Maybe that's why God sent me to your door. He knew you needed help. That's answered prayer. I'm going to pray and add my prayers to yours. If the two of us touch and agree on something in faith believing, we can move mountains."

Brian stared into her face. She meant every word she said. How he wished he had her certainty! "I don't know if I have enough faith."

"You don't need a lot. The Bible says even a speck of faith, the size of a mustard seed, is enough to do the job."

He pictured the miniscule seed in his mind. "That's not possible."

"Yes, it is," she assured him. "Faith multiplies exponentially when we put it into action."

Brian nodded. He was impressed. "I'd like to see that verse."

She nodded with excitement. "I'll look it up for you." Karlie rushed to the nightstand and opened the drawer to locate the Bible kept there. She scanned the pages of the New Testament until she located Luke 17:5–6.

"Here it is," she said. "And the apostles said unto the Lord, Increase our faith. And the Lord said, If ye had faith as a grain of mustard seed, ye might say unto this sycamine tree, Be thou plucked up by the root, and be thou planted in the sea; and it should obey you."

Brian rubbed his chin. "All it takes is faith?"

"Yes. Faith is your ticket to heaven—and healing. Let's bow our heads in prayer." Karlie clasped her hands. He followed suit and closed his eyes.

"Dear Heavenly Father, you're a divine healer. There is nothing impossible with you. Whatever you command must be done. Whatever you bind in heaven is bound on earth. I come before you putting Brian at your feet.

He is ailing and in pain. Lord, we thank you for sickness and pain because how else would we know how much we need you? I ask you to heal him if it is in your will. But if it is not in your plan for him, then give Brian the strength to endure. Help him to trust that you know what is best for him. Give him relief, Lord. Help him, please. I hate to see him suffer, but I thank you for this window to prayer. Draw him closer to you. I thank you in advance, Lord, and I pray this prayer in Jesus' name. Amen."

Brian did not understand a lot of the jargon she used, but hearing Karlie pray for a heathen like him touched his heart. All he could say was, "I believe."

Listening to Karlie's earnest supplication on his behalf for a divine healing, Brian knew two things. Karlie was serious about her relationship with God, and he wasn't worthy of her.

She helped him back into bed. He rested on his stomach knowing he would be able to sleep well, thank God.

She stretched out beside him.

"Karlie, what are you doing?" Brian asked.

"I'm staying here with you. What if you have to use the bathroom or something? I have to be here."

"I can't have you sleeping next to me," he said. "Just leave the connecting door open. I'll yell if I need you."

"I can't believe I'm the one saying this, but, Brian, you need to lighten up. This is a king-sized bed. If it makes you feel better, I only intend to stay here until you're sound asleep." She yawned. "So quit worrying and go to sleep."

"There's a couch," he said.

"Go to sleep," she said. "I'll be gone soon enough."

Brian quit fighting. He was too tired and sick to continue the debate. He vowed to remain on his side of the bed. He wasn't going to have God strike him dead with lightning or something worse. With a wide yawn, he closed his eyes.

***

Karlie heard her phone alert through the connecting door. She rushed into her suite leaving the door ajar. It was 2:15 a.m. She hoped it was Jamaal reaching out to her. She looked at the screen and sighed. She had gained another social media follower. Whoop-de-doo!

She wandered back into Brian's suite. He hadn't stirred. She smiled at his sleeping form. He looked so . . . innocent. On impulse, she decided to snap a picture. She held back a giggle as she slipped back into the bed and spooned him. Then she hit the capture button.

Karlie composed a cheeky text: Now you can say we slept together.

Then she hit send, laughed, and went to sleep.

Chapter Twenty-two

"Brian isn't answering his phone!" Ryan exclaimed as they exited the elevator of the hotel. They had caught a first-class flight to Sarasota, Florida.

"I couldn't reach Karlie either," Patricia said. "Maybe they went out last night and they're still asleep."

He knew she was miffed at his less-than-enthusiastic response to her efforts the night before, but Ryan was not concerned about that. Brian and Karlie tortured his mind.

"I keep having nightmares of them wrapped up in each other's arms." He shuddered. "Should I have just texted them last night and told them the truth?"

"No, that would've been a bad idea. We needed to be here. Tell them in person." Patricia walked in step beside him.

"This is it," Ryan said. Holding Patricia's hand, he knocked on the door.

Yentl answered the door and stepped aside. "Good morning, Mr. Oakes. Mrs. Oakes."

"I'm so glad you're up. The front desk wouldn't provide me with Brian and Karlie's suite number."

"Griffin!" Yentl yelled. "I'll be right back." He ushered them out. "I'll take you up there."

Ryan held back his response. He knew what he was getting when he hired them.

"I appreciate your going out of your way like this," Patricia said.

They entered the staircase.

"No worries, ma'am," Yentl replied. "It's only one flight up. I need the exercise."

Ryan eyed Yentl's tight physique and looked heavenward. Yentl was flirting with his wife. He saw her hide her smile. Patricia knew it too. She was ahead of him on the stairs, and Ryan admired her trim form. He couldn't blame Yentl for trying, but he wasn't concerned. Patricia was his. They would jump over their hurdle in time.

Soon they were outside Brian's door. Ryan knocked.

He barely waited a second before knocking again. The door next to them opened, and Karlie peered through. She waved them inside. Yentl waved and headed back to his room.

"Brian's sleeping," Karlie said. "He had a rough night last night."

Ryan's legs wobbled with relief. In his mind, he envisioned Karlie answering *Brian's* door. "We'll have to wake him. Patricia and I wouldn't be here if it weren't urgent."

"I'll go get him. Is everything okay?" Karlie made a move toward the connecting door.

Ryan didn't like the ease at which she approached Brian's room. He gulped. Lucky for him, Patricia stepped up.

"I'll go," Patricia said, tapping Karlie on the shoulder. "I want to surprise him."

Patricia hurried into Brian's room, leaving Ryan alone with Karlie. Though he ached to hug her, his hands dangled by his side and he stayed where he was, unable to think of a single thing to say.

"So did you hear about our TV show?" Karlie asked.

"Yes, I did. Do you think that's a good idea? What about college? I mean, you're young now, but you don't want to have any regrets."

Karlie wrung her hands, looking slightly uneasy.

"Lay off, Dad," Brian said, entering the room. "Karlie already has a father breathing down her neck. She doesn't need you adding to the mix."

Ryan froze. His eyes met Patricia's. She gestured with her eyes for him to tell them. How should he begin? He cleared his throat. Nervousness deepened his voice. "Brian, Karlie, I need to speak with both of you."

They swung their glances his way. Still Ryan hesitated. His throat closed up, and he wiped his face.

"I'll order breakfast," Patricia said. She frowned at him and gave him a look which said, *Get to it.*

"How about we all sit down?" Brian suggested with a furtive glance. "You two are behaving out-of-character and it's kind of unsettling. Please don't tell me you're getting a divorce."

His son's tone was doubtful yet hopeful. Ryan shook his head. "No divorce." From the corner of his eye, Ryan saw Patricia slump with relief. "What I have to say involves Karlie as well."

"Why do I feel as if I'm not going to like this?" Karlie mumbled.

Ryan noticed how they both gravitated to the couch. This wasn't going to be a stroll in the sunshine. *Lord, give me wisdom.* "Let's begin with a word of prayer."

"This is going to be bad," Karlie said. She slapped her knees. "Whenever my dad says let's begin with prayer, I know I'm not going to like what he's about to say."

Nevertheless, Ryan prayed. He needed God's back. He felt Patricia take his hand and give him a small squeeze.

"Lord, we invite your presence among us at this time. We ask for you to lead and guide this discussion." Ryan's voice broke. "I ask that you give me strength and courage to face my wrongs. I ask that you help me make it right. I ask that your peace will fill our hearts as we move forward from today. I ask this in the name of Jesus. Amen."

As soon as he said, "Amen," Ryan focused on Karlie. "Karlie, when your mother ordered the paternity test, I did something horrible."

Her face turned sheet white. She shook her head. "No, please don't say it. Don't say you're my father. That had better not be what you're about to say."

"Dad, what did you *do?*" Brian asked.

Ryan's body tightened. "I paid the lab tech to tamper with the results."

Brian vaulted to his feet. "What does that mean?" he yelled.

Ryan saw Karlie bend over. Patricia rushed to her side and hugged her.

"I think I might be Karlie's father," Ryan said.

Brian's face was beet red. His chest heaved, and he got in Ryan's face. "I don't believe you! You stood there and listened to me yammer on about how I might have feelings for her and you said nothing!"

Karlie's sharp intake of breath was the only sound in the room after Brian's proclamation. She shrugged out of Patricia's grasp and covered her face in her hands.

Ryan stepped in her direction, but Brian wasn't letting him through. His son turned to snarl at Patricia. "Did you know this?"

"No, I learned last night," Patricia said with a slight quiver. She looked away, hating the necessary lie.

Ryan and Patricia had both agreed on partial disclosure during the flight. Brian and Karlie didn't need to know about Patricia's paying the technician to say Karlie was his daughter. He knew if they told them everything, Brian would feel as if this was like old times when they had been too obsessed with each other to pay him any attention. They reasoned that after hearing the news, Brian would need his mother's comfort.

Karlie found her voice and stood. "I can't believe this is happening." She pointed an accusatory finger Ryan's way. "You're a selfish, wicked man. What about Neil and Myra? They've been my parents for years."

Ryan started to speak.

"Why are you telling me now?" Karlie interrupted. "Don't tell me you need a kidney or something because I'm not . . ." Her voice broke. "I don't believe this is happening."

"What do you mean *you think?*" Brian asked. He now stood near the front door. He looked ready to bolt. Ryan suspected if it weren't for Karlie, Brian would have been long gone.

Ryan had prepared the answer. "I paid the technician to say Clifford was Karlie's father."

Brian's eyebrows furrowed. "You're a *vile* excuse for a human being." He addressed his mother. "Why you love him is beyond me."

Ryan's heart hurt. He was going to lose his son. He pinned Patricia with a look of sheer panic. His worst fear was happening.

"I love him despite his mistakes," Patricia said.

Karlie clenched her fists. "You paid someone to tell me the man who raped my mother fathered me."

Fear hit his chest. With staccato breaths, Ryan said, "I'm sorry. I panicked. I didn't think you deserved me as a father. I mean, look at how Brian had been acting at the time . . ."

Brian pounced from the door and grabbed Ryan by the shirt. "You're trying to blame *me* for your deception? You're demented if you think that I'm going to accept that sorry excuse."

Patricia grabbed Brian's arm. "Let your father go."

Karlie jumped in. "Brian, please don't."

Brian complied and snaked her into his arms. "Karlie, I'm so sorry this is happening. We have to get this all figured out."

Karlie cried, "What if I'm your sister? The whole world is going to say I'm sick and twisted. They have us in love and all that. You kissed me on YouTube."

Brian shushed her. "It was on the forehead. You don't know for sure that we're related."

"Karlie, I know you're angry, but I need you to agree to a paternity test. That's the only way to know for sure," Ryan said. He dabbed at the sweat on his forehead with his hands.

Karlie ignored him.

"Ryan, I think it's time we leave," Patricia said, picking up her purse. "We have to catch our flight home."

"But I bought tickets for them to come back with us," Ryan protested. "We need to do the paternity test . . ."

Ryan trailed off. Brian swung his gaze Ryan's way.

Brian's eyes were like a sword cutting into the flesh of Ryan's soul. His heart skipped a beat from certain fear.

As Ryan and Patricia headed back to the airport, Brian's face stayed with him. Deep down, Ryan knew that even if he had gained a daughter, he had most definitely lost his son.

Chapter Twenty-three

Karlie cried until her eyes hurt. Crumpled tissues filled her jeans pockets. Holding Brian's hand, they walked the trail along the path of the hotel. The landscaping and ducks floating in the scenic path escaped her. Her life was about to spin out of control.

"I think we should withdraw from the show," Karlie said. "I've already called Winona and left a message for her to call back."

Brian grasped her shoulders. "No. We're not quitting."

They wandered over to the bench a few feet from the pond and sat close together.

"How am I going to tell Neil?" Karlie asked.

"I'll come with you," Brian said. "I don't think there's an easy way to tell Neil that my father was a selfish . . . Ugh . . . I hate him!" Brian gritted his teeth.

Karlie touched his arm. "Don't say that. Hate is a strong word."

"It's the right word, and you should hate him too," he said. "I'm glad they went home. I don't get why you're not agreeing with me. What my father did was foul. And please don't say it's the God in you or spout some religious jargon like that."

"Believe me, if I was a cursing woman, I'd have peppered his ears," Karlie said. She gazed toward the pond. "Losing a parent changes you. My mother isn't here for me to hate or get mad at."

Tears rolled down her face. Karlie struggled to speak her true pain. "I'm furious with your dad—"

"Call him Ryan," Brian said. "That's what I'm calling him from now on."

Karlie sighed. "I'm furious with your *dad,* but I'm mad my mother isn't here for the truth. I lied to her when it turns out that I didn't have to." She faced Brian. "Do you know what that was like? Lying to a dying woman? I couldn't tell her Clifford was my father. I told her it was Thomas. I lied because I thought it was the best thing to do."

Brian lifted a hand. "Don't even compare the two. You were protecting your mother. Ryan was only protecting himself."

Karlie agreed with Brian's logic. She wanted to hate Ryan, but what was the point? She needed to conserve her energy for her real battle—telling Neil and Myra, and then convincing Neil not to kill Ryan. Saved or not, Neil had a vicious protective streak. She didn't need him ending up in jail.

"I don't think I even want to know if Ryan is my father," Karlie decided. "Why bother finding out?"

Brian's eyebrows shot to the top of his head. "Are you crazy? Of course you need to know. I need to know if you're my sister."

She recalled Brian's declaration earlier in the room. Lowering her eyes to her hands, Karlie asked, "Is it because you think you have feelings for me?"

He cupped her chin and pierced her with his eyes. "Don't go daft on me now. You know there's something between us."

Karlie shook her head. "I . . . I don't know what you mean."

"You spent the night in my bed," Brian said.

"You were sick," she replied.

Brian brought his face an inch away from hers. "Your mouth denies it, but I see your chest heaving up and down. I see your eyes flaring as you wonder if your supposed brother is about to kiss you. I see you're appalled but curious at the thought. You're revolted that even knowing what you know, you're still attracted to me."

Karlie exhaled.

He moved away from her, folded his arms, and faced the water. "Don't pretend otherwise. You slept next to me because you wanted to."

Karlie nervously licked her lips. "I'm a child of God. I wasn't going to have sex with you."

Brian chuckled. "I know that, but you're a woman. You slept with me for intimacy, and that's more dangerous than sex."

She couldn't deny his perceptiveness. "I'm drawn to you," she admitted. "But maybe genetics is the reason." Any other reason was unthinkable. She was in love with Jamaal.

He glanced at her and snorted. "If it makes this easier, then go ahead and tell yourself that."

Karlie pulled out her cell. It had been buzzing with alarming fury. She swiped to check her missed calls and messages. She noted Patricia's and Winona's missed calls, but it was Jamaal's text that made her drop the phone.

"What is it?" Brian bent down and retrieved her phone from the dewy grass. He swiped the screen.

"Jamaal's on his way back here." She grasped her forehead. "Can this day get any worse?"

Karlie watched Brian's mouth hang open as wide as an alligator's as he stared at the screen. "You sent Jamaal a text of us sleeping together?"

"I thought it was you," Karlie said, chewing her bottom lip. "I sent it to you as a prank. I must've messed up and sent the text to Jamaal."

"Yes, well, apparently Jamaal wants to jack me up, and he's on his way here to make good on his threat." Brian looked at his watch.

Jacked up was not the word Jamaal had used in his text. Karlie had been struck dumb at his profanity-laced text message. That was at 5:30 a.m. She half-expected Jamaal to come tearing across the lawn any moment. She did not relish the scuffle between the two men.

"Why did I take that picture?" she moaned.

"Let me see the photo again," Brian asked.

She flipped through her camera shots and held up the photo for him to see.

Brian studied it for several seconds before handing her phone back to her. "No wonder they say a picture is worth a thousand words."

"What do you mean?"

"Look for yourself," he said. "Look at your face, and then tell me you feel nothing."

Karlie forced herself to look at the picture. She was sort of spooning Brian. Her hair hung loose down her shoulders, but her face struck her. Even in the dim lighting she noted her relaxed face and her eyes sparkled with a hint of—seduction? Promise?

"We look . . ." she trailed off. *Like a couple.*

"Peaceful?" Brian said. He took the phone to take another look. "We look like people who have been . . ." he used his hands to form quotation marks, "'sleeping' together for years."

Karlie shook her head. "No, we don't."

"Yes, we do." Brian tucked his hand under her head to rest it on his shoulder. "Even now, sitting here together, our chemistry is undeniable."

Listening to the ripples in the water and observing the beautiful scenery, Karlie gave a tender smile. She captured a brief glimpse of heaven and took a snapshot in her mind.

"You feel it too, don't you?" he asked.

Karlie lifted her head to meet his gaze. Their gazes locked. Brian ran his hands through her hair, then he touched her cheek. An electric shock jolted her.

She jumped to her feet. "Let's go back."

Brian nodded and stood to join her. They strolled up the path.

As they rounded the corner to reenter the hotel, Karlie saw Jamaal bounding their way. She grabbed Brian's arm. "He's here! Oh my goodness!"

Brian assumed a linebacker position. He was ready for the impact.

"Jamaal!" Karlie cried. "Let me explain!" She ran in his direction.

Jamaal cut his eyes at her but kept moving.

"It's not what you think!" she cried.

Both men ignored her. Profanity-laced insults rolled off their tongues like old worn sailors. Karlie's mouth hung open. "Stop it!" she begged.

She rushed to Jamaal and shook his shirt so hard she stretched it to twice its original size.

Jamaal swatted away her hand like it was a pesky fly and addressed Brian. "I'm tired of you eyeing my woman! You can have any girl on campus! Why you want this one?"

Brian's chest heaved. "And you have her but want every other girl on campus."

Jamaal backed up.

Karlie's heart slammed into her chest. Had she heard right? She hoped not. "Brian, what do you mean by that?"

Brian shook his head but didn't answer.

Karlie pierced Jamaal with a steady gaze. Through gritted teeth, she asked, "Care to explain?"

Jamaal looked away.

"Drop it, Karlie," Brian said. He wiped his sweaty face. "I don't know what I meant. Just talking trash."

Karlie wasn't buying it. "I don't believe you." She stomped into Jamaal's space and jabbed a French-tipped nail into his chest. "Is this because I didn't sleep with you? What about the promise we made to God and to each other?" She sobbed. "Jamaal, who is she?"

"Turn the camera off," she heard Brian say.

Karlie hadn't even noticed Griffin and Yentl's arrival, and that they had been taping the whole debacle. "No cameras!"

"We signed with the network so we work for them now, and this is news," Yentl stated.

Griffin kept it rolling.

Never in her life did Karlie think her life would become Internet fodder, but she didn't care. Right now, she needed her boyfriend to man up and admit his wrongdoings so she could wring his neck.

"I'll tell you if you tell me what you meant by *this*." Jamaal dug for his phone and shoved the picture into her face. "You slept with Brian?"

She clenched her fists. She wasn't going to be distracted from his treachery. "Nice try, but I won't be sidetracked."

Jamaal wheeled away and marched in the direction of the hotel. No matter how she yelled and threatened, he kept moving.

Karlie realized he had no intention of slowing down. "Jamaal!" she screamed, springing into motion. Everything was falling apart in her life. Her identity and all she knew was under question. She could not let her one constant go. She raced up the path and made it to the entrance in time to see Jamaal walking toward the cabstand. "Jamaal! Wait! How could you do this to me?" she screamed.

Jamaal stopped.

"Where do you think you're going? You're not going anywhere without telling me the truth. I can't believe you were just going to leave like that." Her chest heaved when she reached his side. "I need an explanation."

He glared. "Brian had no right to bring that up. He's such a troublemaker."

"This is not about Brian. It's about you and me. Answer me," she said through clenched teeth. "I deserve the truth. You owe me that much."

Jamaal looked around. "Can we not do this here?"

"Right here. Right now," she said, pointing to the ground.

"Once. Okay!" Jamaal tore out. "It happened once."

Karlie's stomach lurched. She curled over. "Oh, I can't believe this . . ."

He rested a hand on her shoulder. The fire from her eyes was hot enough to melt steel.

With a rage that would do Carrie proud from the movie bearing her name, Karlie gritted out, "Don't touch me, you . . . you . . . *Grimy sorry excuse for a thug!* You're not who I thought you were, Jamaal. For six years I've been by your side. *Six years!* I haven't been with anyone because I was waiting to marry you. For you to be my first. And you played me. You made me look like a fool before everyone."

"No, Karlie. I promise you it wasn't like that. It just happened. I'm sorry. You've got to believe me."

"Get outta my face. I don't believe a word coming out of your mouth." Karlie clenched her lips. "We're through."

Jamaal's eyes widened. "No. I made a mistake. I love you. I want to be with—"

"Don't even talk about love to me," she yelled. "I wish I never met you. I'm done. Done with you."

Jamaal shook his head. "Please. I'm sorry . . . We can't end like this."

Karlie folded her arms. "We can. I'm done." He must have realized there was no getting through to her.

"For what it's worth, I love you. I always will," he said before hailing a cab.

Karlie stood rooted until the cab disappeared from sight, taking the love of her life with it. She hugged her arms feeling chilled despite the humidity. "I've lost him," she whispered as tears fell. "I have no one."

Brian hugged her from behind. He rubbed his cheek against hers. "Nonsense. You have me. You always have me."

She swung to face him. Karlie had not even heard him approach.

"I was talking with Yentl and Griffin so you and Jamaal could talk without them in your face."

She crooked her head. "Why didn't you tell me about Jamaal? I thought you were my friend."

"I—I wasn't sure if it was true, and it wasn't my place. Besides, I'm a friend to both of you, and there is a brother code. If I had told you, I don't think you would have believed me, but now I see I should have said something. I'm sorry, Karlie," he said. "The last thing I would want to do is hurt you in any way. Please know that."

"You and I are best friends. Forget the brother code. You should have told me. I feel like a fool." Her body shook, and she cried in earnest then. "I feel so alone right now."

Brian hugged her tight. "You're not alone. You have me. I'm here."

Karlie shoved out of his arms. "No, I don't. I don't have you. I can't have you. I don't have anyone."

"Yes, you do have someone." Brian pointed toward the heavens. "You have God."

Chapter Twenty-four

"Man to man, that was a foul move you made, Brian," Jamaal said. "We're boys, and you were supposed to have my back."

Brian had called him three times before Jamaal picked up his cell. He knew Jamaal only answered to press him for information on how Karlie was doing.

Karlie had retreated to her room filled with despondency. Brian's suggestion that she pray fell on deaf ears.

Brian adjusted his earpiece. "I told Karlie the truth because you had no right to attack me when you're doing some creepy things. You say you're all about God, but you're only for Him on Sabbaths. I heard all about you and Camesha Jones."

Jamaal's harsh intake of breath rippled in Brian's ear. "How do you know her name?"

Brian heard the shock in Jamaal's voice. "Nikki and Camesha are friends. She wanted to tell Karlie, but I stopped her."

"I didn't know Camesha and Nikki knew each other. It happened once. One time when I was dumb enough to attend a frat party. But I've wised up since then. I love Karlie. I've loved her since high school, and she's the one for me."

"The fact that you stepped out on Karlie and smashed Camesha proves she's not the one."

"No, it only shows I'm human. I made a mistake. I've gone to God about it, but I had no intention of telling Karlie. I didn't want to hurt her."

"Keeping the truth from her is just as hurtful. With all these diseases prevalent today, it's also harmful."

Jamaal sighed. "You're right. I didn't have an excuse. I just wanted—"

"To get laid?" Brian chuckled. "I do understand, but you knew what you were getting into when you dated Karlie."

"She's worth it," Jamaal said.

Brian pictured Karlie in his mind. Her hair, her smile, her beautiful aura. "I agree. Karlie is a special girl."

"But I'm furious with you for taking advantage of her, Brian," Jamaal said. "When I saw that picture, I nearly lost my mind. How could you do that to me?"

Brian wandered over to the chaise lounge in his room. "I didn't sleep with her. We shared a bed because I was sick, and she was worried about me. Karlie meant to send that to *me* as a joke. That's all it was. A prank gone wrong. Nothing more."

Jamaal snorted. "You must think I was born last night. You're tripping over her. If Karlie let you, you'd hit that without hesitation."

"Yes, I would," Brian said. "Well, before today, I would've."

"What happened today?"

Brian heard the curiosity in Jamaal's voice. He hesitated for a beat, but Brian knew Jamaal needed to know the sordid truth. "My father told us he might be Karlie's father."

Following that announcement, there was a small crash, noise, and bumbling before Jamaal came back on the line. "I was so shocked, I dropped my phone," he said. "Did you say you and Karlie might be brother and sister?"

Brian's heart skipped a beat. "Yes." After that single word, his spirit plummeted. How he wished it was not true. He did not want Karlie as a sister.

"Wow. Here I am thinking you and Karlie had something going on, and . . . I had no idea . . ."

"That makes two of us. So, as of now, the line has been drawn."

Emotionally, though, Brian was confused. He shoved any inappropriate feelings in the inner recesses of his heart. They were filed under the "to be tackled" box of his mind at a later date.

"Now I feel stupid." Jamaal groaned. "I've got to call Karlie. I owe her a big apology for violating her trust."

Brian rubbed it in. "She cried for hours after you left. She was inconsolable. I think she's sleeping now, but you should give her a call."

"I know she'll forgive me," Jamaal said, "but I don't know if she'll give me another chance."

"I don't think you deserve one."

"That's not your call, and you'd better not poison Karlie against me," Jamaal threatened.

Brian wasn't intimidated. "I think you're doing a bang-up job of ruining your relationship without any interference from me."

"I'll be praying. God can help me."

"You do that."

Brian disconnected the call and tossed his phone on the bed. Brothers like Jamaal infuriated him. Jamaal seemed only to know God when it was convenient. He had been messing with Camesha for months, not once as he had claimed. Jamaal preached the Bible and quoted verses in one breath, and then talked trash to the girls with another.

Brian shook his head. He wasn't like Jamaal. He revered God too much to make a commitment he couldn't keep. However, when he expressed that sentiment to Karlie, she dismissed him as making excuses.

"No one is able to keep that commitment," she had said. "Only God can help us."

After Jamaal's actions, Brian believed she was right. He was fast realizing, if and when he needed salvation, he had better rely on God. Karlie had taught him that.

Brian rapped on the connecting door before entering. He meandered through tossed articles of clothing and approached the bed. Burrowed under her blanket, Karlie's body shook and he could hear her sobs.

Without hesitation, he slipped next to her, remaining above the blanket, and cuddled her close.

Karlie convulsed into fresh tears. Brian's heart melted at her pain. He'd only seen her cry like this the months after her mother died.

"Hush, it will get better," he whispered.

"I don't know who I am," she stammered. "I don't know what I'm feeling. I just . . ."

"Did you pray?"

Karlie shook her head.

"We can't have that now, can we?" Brian rolled off the bed to snag some tissues. Gently he made her face him and blotted her tears. Her red, pudgy face tore at his heart. "Pray with me." He took her hand. "I have all kinds of questions for God, and I need your help. Please."

She lifted her shoulders and took a deep breath. With a nod, Karlie sank to her knees. Her strong grip on his hand made Brian bend his knees and join her by the side of the bed.

She closed her eyes and Brian observed her from under his lashes. His admiration for her grew as she gathered her strength. Even in her pain, she was willing to pray with him. Karlie was a true woman of God.

"Lord, I know you're not the author of confusion," Karlie prayed. "Right now, Brian and I are hurting. We're uneasy and so . . ."

". . . discombobulated," he said.

She squeezed his hand. "We need your peace. We need your strength. Brian and I cast everything on you because you are able to take us through anything. We can face anything with you guiding us."

"What she said," Brian whispered.

"Lead us, Lord. Comfort us. Lord, let us see your will even through this turmoil. I pray this prayer in Jesus' name. Amen." Karlie attempted to stand.

Brian tugged her back to the floor. "I have something to say."

She tilted her chin but quickly recovered from her surprise. "Go ahead."

"Lord, help Karlie keep her faith in you. I need her to keep telling me about you because it's working. Also, if by some miracle you can change genetics, I would sincerely appreciate it. Amen."

Brian released Karlie's hand and stood.

Karlie chuckled. "God doesn't change genetics. It's like gravity. It's set already from the foundation."

"That's my prayer," he said. "Didn't you tell me I needed to pour out what I feel?"

"Yes, but . . ."

"But, nothing," he said. "That's how I feel."

Karlie didn't argue the point. Instead, she touched his arm. "I'm glad God brought you into my life. Thanks for always keeping it real."

"That's me. That's what I do."

Chapter Twenty-five

"Thanks for meeting with us on such short notice," Ryan said as he and Patricia entered Neil and Myra's three-bedroom half-dormered cape-style home replete with fireplace and a huge backyard.

He hated to disrupt their lives, but Ryan couldn't have Karlie break the news to them. He had to confront Neil himself. He had prayed plenty on the way to Neil's house because he needed all the support he could get.

Ryan was counting on Neil being a minister because ministers preached about forgiveness and all that. He hoped Neil would live what he preached.

"I made dinner. I figured you might be hungry after your flight. Addison is at a sleepover tonight so it's just the four of us," Myra said, walking toward the kitchen.

"How thoughtful," Patricia said. "I'll come help you."

Ryan inhaled. Whatever Myra had prepared had his mouth watering. His stomach grumbled.

He followed Neil to the living area. Ryan eyed the baby grand resting on a rug in the corner. He wondered if Karlie played as her mother had done.

"So, how are my daughter and Brian doing?" Neil asked, interrupting his thoughts. "Are they ready to come home yet?"

Ryan willed himself to remain casual. "They were adamant about staying."

Neil laughed. "I wish they would give up this crazy scheme and get back into their books. But Karlie wants to sing." He shrugged. "For the life of me, I can't understand what singing has to do with posting stunts on YouTube. What happened to good old-fashioned singing and showcasing your talent?"

Ryan nodded. "I agree. These days it isn't about raw talent. It's about image and followers. You can use technology to enhance everything else."

"The sad thing is Karlie doesn't need anything else," Neil said. "She has the voice. She doesn't need the gimmicks. All Karlie needs to do is sing from her soul. Let everything pour out and bless the world."

"You and I may know that," Ryan said, "but our words mean nothing. Karlie has to see it for herself."

"Still ranting about Karlie and Brian, I see," Myra said, entering the room. "Let's get to the dinner table."

Ryan and Neil complied. Neil said grace for everyone and soon everyone savored the meat loaf, mashed potatoes, and coleslaw. Ryan sopped up his biscuits into the juiciest gravy he had ever eaten.

He wiped his mouth and patted his stomach. "Myra, that was delicious. You outdid yourself. The meat loaf was tasty, and your gravy needs to be patented."

Myra blushed.

"No one cooks like Myra," Neil bragged.

Plunking a huge slice of chocolate cake on his plate, Neil asked, "So, I know you didn't just come here to get fat off Myra's cooking. What's going on?"

Ryan saw Patricia wipe her mouth with her napkin and lower it in slow motion. His chest tightened. The moment had arrived. *Lord, give me the strength to do this.*

"Please don't tell me Karlie is pregnant," Myra said with a hand cupped to her mouth.

"Karlie isn't pregnant," Ryan said. He watched two sets of shoulders relax with relief. "She is devastated, however, and it's all my fault."

Neil dropped his fork and pinned Ryan with a steel glance.

Ryan pushed back his chair and stood, feeling it would give him an edge. "I told Karlie I might be her father."

Myra's breath caught, and Neil jumped to his feet.

Ryan rushed on. "I paid the lab tech to give me the results first. When he told me I was the father, I paid him to say it was Clifford."

Neil gripped the table. "Then why did you say 'might be'? It sounds like you *are* her father. You're the punk who deserted her when she needed you most." He closed the distance between them filled with fury. "Karlie and I lied to Tiffany and told her Thomas was Karlie's father. We lied because *you* didn't have the guts to claim her!"

"How could you?" Myra asked. "Why would you do that to her?"

"I was a horrible parent to Brian," Ryan said. "I know now that's no excuse."

Ryan watched Neil grapple with the words before he lifted his hands. "Why? Why tell it now? And, after all this time!"

"I just gave my life to God and my conscience . . . I had to tell her the truth."

Myra rounded the table to confront him. "No, it wasn't your conscience. You told us because of the YouTube videos. You saw the chemistry between her and Brian. That's the only reason why you're confessing."

Patricia followed the smaller woman. "I'm sorry," she said.

Myra allowed Patricia to enfold her in her arms.

"Well, yes," Ryan said, "but God has been speaking to me. I told my pastor, and he said I needed to right this wrong by confessing."

Ryan watched Neil's muscles flex under his dress shirt as if Neil wanted to hit him. Ryan couldn't blame him.

"I've got to call Karlie," Myra said. She departed from the room with Patricia in tow.

Ryan heard Myra's loud sob echo throughout the house and his insides withered. He felt like the worst human being on the planet.

"You're a selfish . . ." Neil shook his head. "I thought Merle was vicious, but she's a lollipop compared to you. You're a jawbreaker."

Ryan squinted at the analogy. The Holy Spirit was obviously tempering Neil's vocabulary.

"I didn't think," Ryan said. "Once you adopted her, I felt at peace with my decision. Until I gave my life to God."

"I know you keep bringing Him up because you know I'm a child of God," Neil said, "but this is some tough news."

Ryan gulped. "We've become friends. I hope you'll be able to forgive me."

"Don't talk to me about forgiveness! You didn't hurt me. You hurt my child. Karlie has been through so much. I don't understand why you would do this to her. She *needed* a father."

"She had you," Ryan said.

He saw a hand flash near him and curled his body on instinct. *If Neil hits me . . .*

The ladies returned to the room. Both had reddened eyes. Myra hadn't been able to reach Karlie.

"I need to take a paternity test."

"Why?" Neil folded his arms. Probably to keep from hitting him.

Ryan explained Patricia's involvement. She squirmed under their derision but let Ryan do all the talking. He held Patricia close. He wasn't about to let anyone come near her.

"Not cool," Myra said. "You two are playing games with people's lives." She hiccupped as she attempted to control the tears threatening to fall.

"I'm sorry," Patricia said. "I am truly sorry, Myra."

"I need to speak to my daughter," Neil said. "Please get out of my house. You can show yourselves out."

Ryan and Patricia hobbled out of the Jamesons' home.

"We've lost our friends," Patricia sobbed.

"They'll come around," Ryan said. "This is a lot for them to process. They need time."

"I hope you're right."

He nodded with confidence. Neil and Myra were upset, but God would speak to their hearts. His son, however, was another matter. Ryan didn't have enough "I'm sorrys" to cure what ailed Brian.

As Patricia pulled out of the driveway, Ryan hunched into his seat. *How could I let things go this far?*

My son is in love with his sister.

"I wonder how Brian and Karlie are doing," Patricia said. They were almost home. "Neither one would answer my call."

"Mine, either."

Patricia yawned. "I'll try again before they leave on their next excursion. I think they're going mudding, if I remember right."

"Yes, Yentl and Griffin confirmed their plans."

She slanted a glance his way. "You spoke to Yentl and Griffin?"

He gave her a curt nod before turning to look out the window.

Her senses went on alert. Ryan wasn't telling her something. Patricia pulled into the driveway and pressed the garage door opener.

Once inside, Ryan reached for the door handle, but she gripped his arm. "Ryan, why are you speaking to Yentl and Griffin?"

"Um . . . I made contact with them to check up on Brian and Karlie," he said.

Ryan jumped out of the car and went into the house. Patricia watched his jerky movements and wrinkled her nose. *There's something he's not telling me.*

She opened the door and got out, activating the alarm before following Ryan upstairs. He was loosening his tie and doing everything but making eye contact.

"Why are you in contact with Yentl and Griffin?" she asked again.

Ryan shrugged. "I told you. Why the third degree?"

"What *aren't* you telling me?" she insisted.

He met her gaze. "If you must know, I paid Yentl and Griffin to sabotage Brian and Karlie's trips."

She craned her neck forward. "You did *what?*"

"I couldn't pay them off like I did the others, so I had Yentl and Griffin create some minor mishaps to make Brian and Karlie abandon their stupid plans."

Patricia's eyes widened. "*Mishaps?* Is that what you're calling getting our son and Karlie almost killed?" she screamed.

"They . . . I . . . I didn't want them hurt," Ryan stammered.

Her eyes blazed. "Brian was hanging on for dear life hundreds of feet in the air. Then he and Karlie ended up in water full of alligators, and you say you didn't want them hurt?"

He backed away. "That wasn't supposed to happen," he said, "And I stopped after the alligator incident. I told Yentl and Griffin no more."

"So that automatically makes it all right."

"No," Ryan said. He mopped his brow with the back of his hand.

"I don't believe you," she raged. "What kind of man are you becoming? You put your children in danger because you're selfish and wicked. You only think about yourself."

He got into her face. "I don't think about myself. I was thinking of you, Patti. I didn't want—"

"Spare me," she scoffed. She jutted her chin in the air. "Look at you. You've changed, Ryan. You're all about power and money. It wasn't me or Brian you were trying to protect. It was your money. Your business. That's your true love."

Ryan shook his head. "No. I love you, and I love my son."

"And what about Karlie?" she challenged.

"I—I was protecting her too," he said.

"Hah!" Patricia folded her arms. "I have no more words for you. Words that a Christian could say, anyway." She shook her head. "It's a shame because I'm realizing I don't know you. How can I love someone I don't know?"

Patricia roamed the house. She kept replaying the conversation with Neil and Myra. Their faces tormented her sleep.

She couldn't believe Ryan had been desperate and stupid enough to put his children's lives in danger. After twenty-odd years together, Patricia had thought she knew Ryan, but she was fast discovering she didn't know him at all. She didn't even know herself. She felt they were sorry excuses for Christians.

Wandering into the kitchen, she eyed the microwave clock. It was almost midnight. Patricia needed to rest but her cell phone beeped.

Seeing the hospital number on her screen, she swiped the answer button.

"We have an accident victim, Colton Seaver. Severe brain trauma."

"I'm on my way."

Though she didn't feel worthy, Patricia lowered her head to pray. A clear head was a must for surgery, and she was going to need God's help to take her through tonight. She couldn't allow her personal situation to affect her professional life. Lives were at stake.

After several heartfelt words of prayer, Patricia departed. She swatted at a mosquito buzzing in her ear and entered her vehicle. She drove on automatic pilot and snagged the last physician's spot in the hospital parking lot. Patricia sped through the beehive, otherwise known as the emergency room, and asked about her patient.

"He's been taken to the OR," the head nurse said. "Dr. Newhouse is scrubbing in and waiting for you."

Patricia gave the nurse a thumbs-up and made her way to the elevator. She reviewed the chart until she had arrived at her designated floor. This would be the first time since she had rejected Timothy's advances that they'd be in surgery together.

She prayed things wouldn't be awkward between them.

"Dr. Oakes, we're prepped and ready to go," Timothy said as Patricia entered the operating room.

She arched an eyebrow at his professional tone. *If that's how he's going to play it, it's fine by me.* "Thank you, Dr. Newhouse. Let's save this man's life." With a curt nod, she addressed the OR nurse. "Scalpel?"

Eight grueling hours later, she exited the operating room. Pulling the cap off her head, she threw her gloves in the special designated can and washed her hands.

"That was some awesome work in there, Dr. Oakes," Timothy complimented.

She rubbed her eyes. "Will you stop with the Dr. Oakes already?"

Timothy stared. "I thought that was what you wanted. To keep things professional."

"I don't know what I want," Patricia said. She laughed at herself. "My life is all mixed up."

"Patricia, what's wrong?" Timothy shed his professional cloak and placed a hand under her chin for her to look at him.

"I should be talking to God," she said. "Or my pastor."

Timothy made a show of scanning the room. "Well, they're not here. I am."

Patricia crooked her head for them to leave the small area. She didn't need anyone overhearing. She led him to her office. On the way there, the Holy Spirit advised her against letting Timothy into the mess that was her marriage.

Patricia obeyed. She'd share something else.

She strode to her desk and unlocked the drawer. Pulling Anna's picture out, Patricia handed it to him. She told him about losing her baby. "That's why having both Anna and Alyssa survive their surgery is so personal to me."

"I understand," Timothy said. He stared into her eyes. "I don't think this was what you wanted to talk about, but I'll let the matter rest."

Patricia lowered her eyes.

Timothy lifted one of her hands and gently kissed the back of it. "Go home, Patricia. Rest up. Deal with whatever is on your mind. Mr. Seaver doesn't require the concentration the twins will."

Patricia pondered Timothy's words long after he was gone. The twins *would* require serious concentration. For the first time, she wondered, *Am I the right person for the job?*

Chapter Twenty-six

Karlie eyed the Skype invite. Merle's smiling face taunted her. She drummed her hands on the keyboard and debated whether to press the accept button. Neil and Jamaal's warnings against Merle swirled in her head. Merle might be the devil's daughter, but Karlie knew she was blood. There was no test needed to prove that.

She pressed the accept button, and then initiated the Skype call.

It was just a little after nine a.m. Her heart pounded in her chest. She hadn't seen her grandmother since Tiffany's funeral, and then it had only been for a moment, because Neil tossed Merle out of the service.

Karlie bit her lip, second-guessing herself. Just as she was about to press the end button, Merle clicked on. Her image filled the screen. Karlie pressed the video button so that her grandmother would also be able to see her.

"Hi, Karlie, thanks for accepting my request. I was praying and hoping you would."

Karlie didn't know what she was expecting, but Merle's voice didn't sound evil. She sounded young and pleasant. Her face was another matter. Merle had been burned badly in a fire the same night of the funeral. The left side of her face was scarred, but plastic surgery helped. Karlie had footed the expenses, but Neil had banned her from visiting Merle in the hospital.

"I . . . I don't know why I did to be honest," she replied. She shifted in her chair. "Why did you reach out to me?"

"I wanted to get to know my only living relative. It's been years, and as you get older you wise up. I made a lot of mistakes with your mother, and I just need a chance to set things right."

Karlie's nose flared, and she drew a deep breath. Her body overheated. She wasn't as ambivalent toward Merle as she had first thought. Anger bubbled underneath the surface. It surprised her but liberated her tongue. "How can you set things right? My mother is in the grave. She died without you there to hold and comfort her."

"Yes, Tiffany died, and I'm living with that guilt every day. Sometimes I wonder why I didn't die in the fire."

Maybe God knew you would need her.

Karlie's flesh revolted at that sentiment, even though in her spirit she knew it was true.

"Dad thinks I should stay away from you," Karlie said, curious to know how Merle would respond. She wasn't about to mince words or avoid any sensitive topics. If they were going to move forward, or whatever, they had to tackle the issues of the past.

"The way I was five years ago, I would have to agree. I was bitter. It's not that easy to live with yourself when you put a man before your only child." Merle lowered her head.

Karlie's heart moved, but she pressed on. "Clifford violated my mother. She lost her innocence because of him. Why would you think she would lie about something like that?"

Merle shook her head. "No reason I tell you will be good enough. I have been in a lot of therapy following the fire, and all I can tell you is that I see where I've failed Tiffany. I'm trying to fix that by being there for you."

"I don't need you," Karlie said through gritted teeth. In her heart, however, she felt the opposite.

"We're *blood*," Merle said. "Like it or not, *my* blood runs through *your* veins. I'm *family*. You're grown, but you *do* need me."

Karlie straightened at Merle's sassy tone. It was as if she was hearing her mother's voice. She couldn't hold the small smile.

"Come see me in person," Merle pleaded. "I hate this whole Internet thing. I like talking face-to-face. I only learned this thing because I wanted to contact you. Neil won't let me within five feet of you. But I figure, you're grown and old enough to make your own decisions now."

Karlie's eyes filled with tears. She was touched at the gesture but wasn't sure how ready she was for a relationship. "I'll think about it," she whispered. "I've got to go."

"I love you, baby girl," Merle said. "You can hate me for the rest of your life or you can choose to forgive me. It's your choice. I'll still love you, and I'll still be praying for you. I'm a churchwoman now. When I was on my face, it was church folk who reached out to me, and I've been studying with them. God is the only person who would have me. I'm hoping to add you to the list."

Overcome, Karlie nodded and ended the call.

She picked up her cell phone. It was flooded with voice mails and text messages. Neil, Myra, Winona, and even Jamaal. Resting her phone on the desk, Karlie pushed her chair back. She massaged her lower back. She didn't feel like talking to anyone. The only person she had spoken to was Brian, and that was because he was right next door. She couldn't avoid him, and it wasn't for lack of trying.

Yentl and Griffin had posted an edited version of Brian and Jamaal's fight on YouTube. Now the whole world thought she had slept with Brian. What would people say when they learned Brian was her brother?

A month or two ago, she was walking in sunshine. Now she was in the eye of a hurricane in the middle of a dark and lonely forest.

You are not alone. I am your shepherd.

Karlie picked up her Bible. She scanned the pages and read Psalm 23 though she knew it by heart. She closed the Good Book, knowing that she needed a talk with God, but she wasn't in the mood for conversation.

She donned an all-white swimsuit hoping that a swim would clear her mind. Karlie grabbed a huge towel, pushed her feet into some flip-flops, and slipped outside into the lobby. She had just entered the elevator when a hand shot out to hold the door. She rolled her eyes when a shirtless Brian sauntered inside. He had on swimming trunks.

"Are you spying on me?" she asked. She avoided contact with his muscled chest.

"I'm just going for a swim," he replied innocently. "Mere coincidence."

She scrunched her lips, knowing he was lying through his teeth. "I just need some space. Leave me alone." She slapped the towel against her thighs.

"Not going to do that. Until I know you're okay, I'm your shadow."

The small space added to her claustrophobia. Karlie clamped her jaws, squelching down a scream. As soon as the steel door swooshed open, she stomped toward the pool.

Heedless of the cool temperature of the water, Karlie dived in and began her laps. She heard another splash. She turned her head to see Brian keeping pace with her. She was a superb swimmer, but Karlie was no match for his longer, leaner strides.

They continued their brutal pace for fifteen minutes before Karlie trudged out of the water.

Brian completed two more laps before resting in the chair next to her. "That was exhilarating," he smiled and briskly rubbed his hair dry.

Karlie grunted, determined to ignore him. The heat seared her skin. She bit back a groan when she realized she'd forgotten her sunscreen. No sooner had the thought escaped than Brian's hands were on her back. He was lathering some sunscreen on her exposed shoulders.

"Can't have your beautiful skin blotching in the sun," he said.

Karlie stiffened. She hated the feel of his hands on her. Rather, she hated that she *liked* the feel of his hands on her. *He's your brother,* she reminded herself.

Allegedly.

In a fit of temper, Karlie shrugged off Brian's hands. Fixing him with a glare, she held her hands out for him to squeeze the lotion in her palms. "I'll do it myself."

"I didn't do anything wrong," he said.

"It feels wrong," Karlie replied.

Brian emitted a huge sigh. "Let's change the subject then. Have you spoken to Jamaal?"

"No, and I *don't* want to talk about *him* either."

Brian gave a slight shrug. "Fair enough. My mother called. She and Ryan told Neil and Myra and things didn't go so well. Neil kicked them out of his house."

Karlie leaned forward. "Dad kicked them out?"

"Yes," Brian cackled. He shook his legs with delight. "Mom said he told them to show themselves out. I wish I had been there to see that."

"Wow. This is too much." Karlie shifted her body to face him. "I spoke to Merle this morning."

"Your grandmother?"

"Yes. She wants me to come see her."

He toyed with the string on his trunks. "What are you going to do?"

"I'm thinking about it," Karlie said, biting her lower lip.

"Did you pray on it?"

Karlie dipped her chin. "For someone who isn't saved, you sure do speak like one who is."

"You're rubbing off on me." Brian playfully swatted her arm.

Karlie eyed him. She wished . . . No, she couldn't go there. "Are we still going mudding?" Mudding was a popular sport in Florida. She didn't relish the idea of gunk in her hair, but she wasn't going to back down.

Brian shook his head. "The network scrapped that plan. They want us to head back to New York. They think we should start our adventure with learning trapeze arts. That would be the focus of the season. Then for the finale, several staged mishaps will occur. We won't know about them, of course."

Karlie shuddered. "I hate heights. I don't know about being a circus act." She looked around. "Where's Yentl and Griffin?" The two men always managed to pop up wherever they were.

"You'll be glad to know they left an hour ago. We'll see them in a couple months when we start taping."

Karlie's shoulders drooped with relief. "I'm so glad they're gone. They were getting under my skin."

Brian gave her a pointed stare. "You can change your mind about the show. We don't have to do this."

Karlie nodded, but she was hesitant. It was kind of late, but she wondered what her mother would think. She did not have to think long. Tiffany would not approve of the intrusion into their lives. But these were different times.

"I want to do the show." She sat up. "I can't tolerate any more of this scorching sun. My skin is frying in this stifling Florida heat." She swiped at her perspiring brow. "When are we going home?"

"We leave tomorrow," Brian said, coming to stand by her side.

As soon as she uttered the word "home" Karlie gulped. Where was home for her? Once again, her life was being turned upside down. Brian took her hand. "Home is where love is, Karlie. You have plenty of people who love you, including me. So, fix your droopy face."

Suddenly the dam holding her emotions at bay exploded. Karlie pushed out of his grasp heedless of the tears streaming down her face. "Stop saying that. Stop telling me you love me. It's confusing me even more than I need to be. I have all these crazy, unexplained feelings and it's creeping me out. A week or so ago, it was all about Jamaal. I haven't even dealt with his betrayal yet." Karlie tilted her chin toward the heavens. "Lord, what are you trying to show me here? Because I'm not seeing it."

Brian's eyebrows furrowed. He moved into her space. "You think this is easy on me? You think it's nice hearing that Ryan messed with our lives like we're a yo-yo?"

"I don't want to hear any more," Karlie raged. She trotted toward the elevator. Her feelings were unbalanced. If she were a drinking woman, she'd be hitting the club. But since she was a child of God, prayer was her drug of choice.

Unfortunately, she was all prayed out.

Brian raced after her and grabbed her arm. "My life was less complicated without you invading my thoughts . . . and heart."

"Leave me alone, Brian. You're trying me." She jabbed the button, willing the elevator to appear.

Ugh! None of the three elevators were available. Karlie's impatience propelled her toward the stairs. Of course, Brian was fast on her tail.

She whirled around. "Don't you understand what it means to leave me alone? I need air." She sprinted up the first floor.

Brian followed her.

With all the strength she possessed, Karlie ran. Her feet pounded on the steps, but she could hear him a beat behind her.

"I'm not letting you run from me," he said, two steps behind her. He tugged her elbow and forced her to stop midstride.

Giving up, Karlie slammed her body to the ground. Brian almost fell on top of her but caught himself. He settled beside her on the steps.

"I've never been in love before," Brian whispered, his breath close to her ear.

"Don't think it, don't speak it," Karlie warned. "I mean, did you forget about Jamaal?"

He shook his head before running his fingers through her curls. Brian exhaled and buried his head in her hair. "I love you."

His warm breath fanned her senses. She shook her head, denying any feelings. "I can't allow this."

"Then don't do anything," Brian said. "Just let me this once. I've got to know."

Karlie didn't resist. She closed her eyes and imagined the serpent tempting Eve. How appealing the offer was to her senses. Brian's lips teased her neck.

Stop him!

Her body tingled. *I will, in a second.*

His lips were on her cheek.

You already want it in your heart, so you might as well let Brian kiss you. You're already guilty.

No! Finding her strength, Karlie shoved him away.

"I wasn't going to," Brian said, crushing her to him.

A minute passed before he released her. Karlie saw his eyes shimmered with a glassy hue. She could not think of a time she had seen Brian so emotional.

"I'm sorry," she said.

"I'm not." He squared his shoulders. "What this means is that we'll be in each other's lives forever. It'll take me a minute to adjust my thinking, but I'm going to love having you for a sister."

Mere seconds ago, he had been about to kiss her, and just like that he was ready to move on? Under the circumstances, she didn't see a choice but to follow his lead.

The two shook hands on it. Together they returned to their suite. Karlie smiled wide and bright. However, her smile collapsed once the door closed. She plopped onto her bed and beat it with her fists. The last thing she wanted was Brian for a brother. In her secret heart of hearts she could admit that.

With a little laugh, she remembered her prayers for a sibling. What a time for God to answer prayer!

Chapter Twenty-seven

Is there ever a right time to get saved?

Puttering around in his apartment back in New York, Brian knew the answer to that was a big, fat, emphatic, "No." He could never be right enough for God. Karlie told him all the time that God wanted him just the way he was, blemishes and all. But he couldn't help but wonder, *Does God want someone who might be in love with his sister?*

Brian scoffed at that thought. No way would the Lord condone that perversion.

His cell vibrated. It was Neil. "Is Karlie with you?"

"No. Once our flight landed, she hopped into a cab and told me she was headed home."

"She hasn't been here. Neither Myra nor I have heard from her. Do you have any idea where she might be?"

Brian's stomach clenched at the worry in Neil's voice. "No, I'll try to reach her as soon as . . ." The line went dead. "We end the call," Brian said to thin air. Wow, Neil had not even said good-bye, which was evidence of his worry level.

With a quick swipe, Brian pulled up Karlie's number and pressed call. It went straight to voice mail. "Karlie, call me. Your dad's looking for you. Neil, that is." He ended the call.

It was sad he had to specify whom he was talking about. A few minutes later, he received a group text.

Hi, everyone, I'm fine. I need some time to think. I'll be in touch. Don't worry. I'm in good hands.

Thirty minutes later, Brian heard a pounding on his door. Hoping it was Karlie, he rushed to answer before the person broke the door off its hinges. It was Jamaal.

"Where is she? I must speak to her! Karlie!" Jamaal pushed past him. His head swung left to right as if he expected Karlie to materialize out of thin air.

"If by *she* you mean Karlie, she's not here."

Jamaal ignored him as he searched the apartment for himself. Brian folded his arms and waited.

"She's not here," Jamaal said, stating the obvious, slightly out of breath.

"That's what *I* said." Brian's eyes followed Jamaal, who now paced the length of the living area floor.

"I thought . . ."

"Thought what?" Brian raised an eyebrow. "That she would be here with me? Well, I've got news for you and everyone else. Karlie and I aren't joined at the hip. She doesn't want to be bothered, and we must respect her wishes. When she's ready, she'll talk to us . . . although I don't know what she could possibly have to say to you."

Jamaal pierced him with an icy glare.

Brian eyed Jamaal's Retro Air Jordans with matching skinny jeans and T-shirt. He supposed women would admire Jamaal's long, lean build. The brother had serious skills on the basketball court and the brains to match. Tiffany had also left him with a sizable bank account to live a comfortable life.

"Listen, I made a mistake," Jamaal said. "We're boys, man. Don't let this thing with Karlie come between us."

"You hurt her. Of course it would come between us."

"Yes, but she texted me to say we'll talk. That must mean something." Covering his face with his hands, Jamaal moaned, "I can't lose her. She's the best love I've ever had in my life."

Brian wanted to feel sorry for him, but jealousy prevailed. Jamaal had the luxury of being able to date Karlie—something he couldn't do. Brian clenched his fists. He had to temper these inappropriate feelings.

"What about God?" he asked.

Jamaal lifted his head and furrowed his eyebrows. "Huh?"

"Isn't God supposed to be the best love of your life?" Brian tilted his head, curious to see how Jamaal would respond.

"He is. God changed me in ways I can't even begin to explain. The day I accepted Christ as my Savior, my grandmother jumped with joy for days." Jamaal smiled. "Next to God comes Karlie."

Brian shook his head. "See, that's what I don't get. How you could espouse such love for God and Karlie yet betray them so easily?"

"Everyone gets tempted," Jamaal explained with a slight edge in his voice. "Everyone. Even Jesus Himself faced temptation though He didn't yield to it. I allowed my temptation to override my good sense. I failed, but that doesn't change God's love for me. Karlie, on the other hand . . ."

Jamaal's acknowledgment of his humanity touched Brian, and he finally understood. God didn't give His love based on man's actions. It just *was*. Wow. He needed a love like that.

His father came to mind. Ryan had made a mistake. Maybe . . .

No, Brian was not that generous.

He and Jamaal went out to get a bite at Patsy's Pizzeria on University Place. After enduring the other man's constant admission of regret, Brian asked, "What did you do with the picture?"

Jamaal had been about to bite into his third slice. "Nothing. It's in my phone."

"Why haven't you deleted it? Keeping it on your phone leaves room for that picture to end up in the hands of the press." Brian held his hand out, gesturing for Jamaal to hand him his cell phone.

Jamaal pointed to his slice. "I didn't think anything of it. I'll delete it. I promise. I don't want to get my hands dirty while I'm eating."

Brian nodded. He wanted to press the issue, but a young woman approached with her iPod in hand.

"Brian? I'm Myesha, and I've been following your show. Is it okay if I ask you a couple of questions for my video blog?"

Brian gave a wary nod. She hit the record button.

"The last YouTube upload showed you and Jamaal duking it out. Yet, here you are sharing pizza like old friends. Is the show staged?"

Brian shook his head. "No, what you saw wasn't scripted. However, Jamaal and I go back a long way. We've called a truce as everything that went down was a big misunderstanding."

"So, you've squashed everything?" Myesha asked, looking at Jamaal for confirmation.

Jamaal nodded. "Yes, we have."

"Will you be on the show?"

Jamaal wiped his mouth. "No, I plan to get on with my studies."

Myesha curved her body into a suggestive pose. "Jamaal, please give me the scoop. Are you and Karlie over? If so . . ."

Brian narrowed his eyes. Was she hitting on Jamaal? He noticed Jamaal's eyes were taking in Myesha's lovely assets.

"Uh. We're . . . No, we're not finished. Karlie and I love each other, and we'll be all right."

Good for you, Jamaal. Brian was impressed at how he had finally pulled his eyes from Myesha's cleavage and made contact with the camera.

Brian laid on the charm. "We'd like to get back to our pizza now. Thanks for stopping by."

Realizing she had gotten all she could out of them, Myesha stopped filming. She pulled a card out of her snug jeans. Brian wondered how she managed to fit anything into that tight space. She scribbled her number on the back of the card before placing it into Jamaal's palm.

"Call me if things between you and Karlie don't work out."

With a flash of her shoulder-length dreads, she was gone.

"Wow, she's bold," Brian said. He watched as Jamaal flipped the card to read the number.

"I know, right," Jamaal laughed, but Brian watched him pocket the card.

Brian didn't understand what was going on with Jamaal. He believed Jamaal loved Karlie, but the lure of sexual gratification seemed a tough battle to win. He could relate, but unlike Jamaal, Brian hadn't made a commitment to God.

Brian and Jamaal parted ways. Brian walked the few blocks to Washington Square Park. Passing by a street performer playing a wicked tune on makeshift drums, Brian thought of Nikki and Charlie, who had both left him messages to give them a call. He had yet to reply. Brian knew his body wouldn't mind the fun, but there was more to life than meaningless encounters.

He tipped the drummer before finding an empty bench while he people-watched.

Brian attributed his change of heart to Karlie. Her prayers must have rubbed off on him. He chuckled. A man could resist such fervor but only for so long. Or maybe the few Bible verses he had dared to read on his Bible app had comforted him. Ryan's betrayal was not a slice of cherry pie. It was like drinking castor oil. He could only stomach small sips at a time.

Inevitably, his thoughts returned to Karlie. His best friend. Like him, she needed time. Brian knew why she had put distance between them. He needed to adjust his thinking, not just verbally but also mentally. If they were going to do a show together, they had to come clean with their relationship. The world had to know they were brother and sister and not lovers as many now suspected.

Brian had called Winona, who had advised him to do and say nothing. "Wait until people have moved on from the video," she had said. "Then before the show, we'll release the statement. That will generate a nice buzz, and viewers will tune in. You'll be like Bobby Kristina and that 'stepbrother' of hers."

That comparison didn't sit well with him, but Brian understood her thinking. The logical part of him even applauded Winona's cunning, but this was his real life. Karlie also hadn't agreed to the paternity test yet. *Ugh.* His head hurt from all this thinking.

A father walked over to the bench with a crying boy in tow. Brian focused on the boy's chubby hand clinging to his father. The boy had scuffed his knee, and his wail could summon the ghost of Washington himself.

"Hold, still, Elijah," the man said. Brian saw the father use his bottled water to wash the welted knee. He whispered something to the boy, because within seconds his bottom lip quivered but no sound came out.

Once he had finished cleaning up the wound, the father hugged his son. "You're so brave and strong. Daddy is so proud of you."

Little Elijah nodded, and Brian watched him give his father a look of such trust that he had to look away.

Brian stood and gave the father a thumbs-up sign before heading home.

All the way, Elijah's trusting face tore at him. How he wished for that! How he wished he had a father he could look up to with such trust.

You have me.

The whisper of a thought made ice-cold goose bumps rise on his arm. Brian stopped in the middle of the street he had been crossing and looked around. People shoved by him.

A cabbie yelled, "Hey! Moron! Get out of the street!"

Returning to his senses, Brian realized the light had changed. Cars charged in his direction at alarming speeds. Putting his feet in motion, Brian raced the rest of the way to the other side of the street. He panted to catch his breath, and his adrenaline gradually slowed. He looked at the cars crowding the spot where he had just stood. He hadn't imagined it. He knew he had heard something.

Maybe God was calling him. What a sobering thought.

Brian commanded his feet to move. *No no no,* he told himself with each footstep. He was sure there was a scientific explanation for his experience. There had to be. God wasn't calling him.

He knew exactly how to counteract this ridiculous notion flowing through his mind. Brian pulled out his cell. He'd give Nikki a call. *And* Charlie.

Brian could feel and touch them. They were real. Not his feelings for Karlie. Not the voice of a God who had given him a messed up father like Ryan Oakes.

Chapter Twenty-eight

"I need you there by my side, Patricia," Ryan said.

It had been two weeks since the debacle at Neil and Myra's, and he and Patricia were still on the outs. Nevertheless, Ryan asked for her support. His mediation could cost him millions. Having Patricia sitting with him would keep him grounded.

"I have this major surgery in a few weeks," Patricia said. "I must prepare. Anna and Alyssa are a tough case."

In their kitchen, Ryan slammed his hands on the counter of the island. "This isn't about your case. You're mad because I told you about sabotaging Brian and Karlie's adventures."

She whirled on him. "Either one of them could have died. How would you live with yourself if one of them had?"

"I didn't think they'd put them in real harm," Ryan pleaded. "It was meant to break them apart."

"Instead, you succeeded in bringing them closer together," she retorted. "Now Karlie has disappeared, and Brian isn't talking to you. He's barely talking to me, either. He won't answer my calls. I'm lucky he's answered my text messages."

Ryan hunched over. "I know I've messed things up royally, but we need to stay united. The devil wants us divided. He loves seeing us at odds with each other."

Patricia rolled her eyes. "I don't want to hear it. You should've thought about that before you tried to get over.

None of this would be happening if you had just accepted Karlie as your daughter."

Ryan stepped back. "Go ahead! Dump everything on me! What else do you want to blame on me? The Ebola virus? The war in Iran? Go ahead!"

"I don't have time for your dramatics. As it is, I can barely stand the sight of you." Patricia stalked out of the room.

Ryan's chest heaved. Her words cut him in ways he wouldn't be able to verbalize. What was happening to his life? He pumped his fists in the air and railed at God. "This is all your fault! You wouldn't stop needling me until I had to confess, and now my marriage is in shambles." He bent his head. Ryan took everything on himself instead of handing it over to God. "My son hates me. My daughter . . . Oh, I don't even know if she is my daughter."

Ryan took several deep breaths.

He had a case tomorrow. He couldn't afford to wallow in this abyss of guilt. Ryan left the kitchen and climbed the stairs to the master bedroom on leaden feet. He saw the light underneath the guest room.

Oh no. He wasn't having that. Patricia was sleeping next to him in their bed. Ryan stormed over and turned the knob. To his surprise, the door was locked. Fury rocked his being, and he rattled the door.

"Patricia, open up this instant!"

"No!"

"I'm warning you. Open this door!"

There was no answer.

Ryan felt rage as he had never known before. His good sense fled, and with one strong shove, he broke the door off its hinges. Ryan stumbled as his body hit the floor. He looked up to see Patricia's eyes huge, and her mouth slack-jawed in shock.

Well, I warned her. She should have opened the door.

He hated the fear on her face. Never in all their years of marriage had Patricia looked at him with fear. He stepped toward her.

"Don't come near me." She trembled. "You're a monster, and I don't know who you are anymore."

A monster? That description cut him deeper than if she'd used a scalpel. "I'm not a monster. I'm a man fighting for his marriage." He took her hands. "I love you, Patricia. You know that. There's no woman for me but you."

"Breaking down a door is an action of a Neanderthal, not a man in love."

On the inside, Ryan was grateful Patricia's spunk returned. Maybe she realized he wasn't about to hurt her, but he was relieved her face no longer reflected fear. He looked around the room at the bits of wood on the floor. "I'll have this repaired tomorrow," he said.

"If only everything else was that easy to fix," Patricia said. She gathered her sleepwear and returned to their bedroom.

Ryan secured the alarm and turned off the lights before joining her. Patricia had just showered, and she avoided eye contact. Ryan didn't push. At least she was there.

"While I was setting the alarm, I called Pastor Ward," Ryan said. "He's scheduled a meeting with us for tomorrow evening at five, if you're available." His anger had surprised him. Tensions were high in his household, but his behavior had been abhorrent and costly.

Patricia pursed her lips.

Ryan held his breath while she debated.

"I'll be there," she said before diving into her side of the bed.

Ryan nodded. *Thank you, Lord.* He had a long way to go but was glad he had reached out to Pastor Ward.

Once he'd showered, Ryan slid under the sheets. He pulled Patricia next to him. It felt as if he was holding a wooden log. Ryan sorely missed the pliant woman he'd held in his arms on so many occasions.

He whispered a prayer for guidance before falling into a restless sleep. His only consolation was that his wife was by his side.

The next morning, he woke up to a kinked neck, an aching back, and no Patricia. Eying the clock and seeing eight a.m., Ryan didn't have time to waste. He pulled out his tailored black suit, blue shirt, and coordinated tie and dressed in a hurry.

At 9:27 a.m., Ryan sped to the offices of Manchester & Barnes. He held onto the zippered sleeve bag holding all the documents Prim had prepared with meticulous precision.

Though Nigel had warned him about getting too cocky, Ryan felt confident he would prevail against Jackson Higgins. He had the truth on his side. That had to count for something.

Ryan greeted Nigel and gave Jackson a curt nod before taking a seat. He would have addressed the other man if Nigel hadn't pressed a warning hand on his arm. Ryan harrumphed but didn't say a word.

At exactly 9:30 a.m., Kyle entered. "Good morning, gentlemen. The mediator is on her way. She'll be here in ten minutes. In the meantime, we can exchange our evidence as part of the open disclosure agreement."

"We're hoping your client has had time to rethink his position," Nigel said.

Ryan's heart leaped with hope. He could use some good news.

"No, I, uh, I want to continue," Jackson stated.

Ryan was surprised at the younger man's gravelly tone. The Jackson he remembered was energetic and hopeful.

Now he appeared gaunt and pale. He shrugged off any concern. Jackson was after his money. Ryan didn't have time to foster any sympathy.

The mediator, a petite blonde with thin lips, arrived. She took out a manila folder and retrieved an iPod. "I'm Eloise Stevens. I'll be taping our session." She looked at her watch. "I'm hoping we can have this settled before lunch."

Kyle laid on the charm. "I hope so too. We hate to waste the court's time on what may be a trivial misunderstanding." Ryan hoped Eloise would remain immune to Kyle's toothy grin.

He nudged Nigel. "Shouldn't you say something?" he whispered.

"I've got this, but praying wouldn't hurt," Nigel said under his breath.

Ryan bowed his head. *Lord, give Nigel the wisdom to kick this case to the curb.*

Kyle started the proceedings. "Three years ago on October fourth, my client and Ryan Oakes entered into a binding agreement. Jackson agreed to oversee the launching of Spababies. He worked beyond the contracted hours and invested his own ideas in making it a profitable venture. Spababies is a national success and now a worldwide conglomerate. We believe Ryan Oakes knew the profit potential and paid Jackson out of his claim to a billion-dollar industry."

A billion dollars? How could he have known Spababies would take off as it did? Who was he, God? Ryan stewed, but he knew better than to open his mouth. Nigel had warned him enough times.

"Duly noted, Mr. Manchester." Eloise then turned to Nigel. "Mr. Lattimore, the state will hear your position."

Nigel nodded before commencing. "Mr. Oakes entered into an agreement to pay Jackson Higgins the fee Mr.

Higgins asked for. Mr. Oakes recompensed Jackson well for his labor by paying him *double* his fees. Jackson accepted and deposited the check with the note, paid in full. He doesn't have a case. Mr. Higgins is demanding a whopping 60 percent based on the premise that Spababies was his idea."

"We are prepared to submit proof," Kyle said.

"We have records of all Jackson's notes," Nigel said. "We have all his proposals in writing. Spababies was and always will be the brainchild of Ryan Oakes and Michael Ward. We have substantial evidence."

"We have a taped conversation," Kyle said. He sank back into his chair, content to let that information marinate.

Ryan froze. Questions rushed through his mind. Was that legal? He tried to replay in his head many of their conversations and couldn't think of anything he could have said to Jackson that would make the other man feel as if he owed him something.

Ryan loosened his tie.

Kyle must have seen his discomfort and offered Ryan a cup of water. "Do you need to take a break?"

When Ryan looked at him, he saw a snake smiling back at him. Ryan shook his head. Kyle needed salvation.

"Ms. Stevens, I would like to schedule another meeting," Nigel said. "I need time to review this taped conversation and consult with my client."

"Fair enough." Eloise snapped her Coach bag open and took out her iPad. With quick sweeps, she had her calendar open. "We will meet again at nine forty-five in two weeks." She faced Kyle. "Mr. Manchester, please submit a copy of the recording to my office before then." She packed up her case and belongings and departed.

"See you soon," Kyle chuckled.

Jackson scrambled behind him.

Ryan and Nigel walked out of the office into the heat. Ryan squinted against the sun. "That was unexpected."

"It will work out. Let's talk in a couple of days," Nigel assured him with a pat on the back. He pulled out his phone and began rapping orders to someone on the other end.

Ryan entered his Navigator. He rested his head on the steering wheel. If he didn't squash this thing with Jackson, his name would be plastered all over the news. He groaned. It seemed as if since he had given his life to God, his entire life had nosedived. Ryan had put his life into God's hands, so why did he feel as if he was the devil's plaything?

Maybe it was time Ryan played the devil's game *his* way.

He reached over and opened the glove compartment and swished the contents around until he located the small business card. It was Frank's contact information. Ryan grabbed the card. He tapped the card against the steering column.

Jackson wasn't playing nice, and Ryan was tired of being the harmless Christian. He was among wolves, and he wasn't about to bleat with the sheep. Making up his mind, he tightened his resolve. He might have lost his wife. He might have lost his son.

But the devil was not going to get his hands on Ryan's money.

Chapter Twenty-nine

In the privacy of her offices, Patricia admitted she was tired of crying. She had sobbed enough to fill the Hudson River. "Lord, what's happening to my marriage?" she whispered. How had things between her and Ryan soured so quickly that he was breaking down doors?

Mere weeks ago, they were snuggled in each other's arms. Now she couldn't stand for him to touch her.

Seeing it was close to five p.m., she shut down her computer and reached for her purse. She hoped their meeting with Pastor Ward would help, but she felt tried. Tried and tested.

Timothy saw her dragging her feet down the corridor toward the parking lot. He rushed over to her.

Not now, Tim, she thought, but Patricia gave him a welcoming smile.

"Where are you rushing off to?" he asked, lining up his step with hers.

"I'm off to meet my husband and my pastor."

"I won't keep you, then," he said. He stopped and rested a hand on her shoulder.

Patricia met his tender gaze.

"I'm here too. I'll have my phone with me if you need to talk, or text, or . . ."

Patricia felt a light buzz where his hands rested on her shoulder. In a deft move, she sidestepped him to break contact. "Uh, thanks, Tim. I really appreciate that."

With a brisk nod, Patricia hastened her stride and made it inside her vehicle with a relieved sigh.

The devil is using that man to shake me up. Patricia knew it, but she was surprised at how easy her body could betray her. She had to be careful to keep herself under subjection. A verse from James shouted into her spirit, "Resist the devil and he will flee from you."

Yes, that's what she had to do. That's what she would do. After a brief prayer for strength, Patricia navigated her way through the rush-hour crowd to Zion's Hill Baptist.

Ryan and Pastor's cars were in the lot when she arrived.

She exited the vehicle. As she made a step, her heel twisted, and Patricia had to grab the door to keep from falling. She attributed her clumsiness to her crowded mind. Patricia took a tentative step on her foot. She groaned. Her left ankle hurt. Hobbling, she made her way into the building.

Her foot throbbed as she picked her way to Pastor Ward's office with extreme caution. Greeting the two men, she fell into a chair.

"I twisted my ankle in the parking lot," she offered by way of explanation. She lifted her left leg.

Ryan bent to hold her foot. "Honey, I hope you're okay."

"It might be a slight sprain, but it's not broken," she said. For the first time in days, Patricia and Ryan shared a smile. She reached out to touch his forehead.

During all of this, Pastor Ward jumped from his desk and snagged another chair from the hallway so she could prop up her foot. "Should I get you some ice?"

Patricia waved him off. "I'll take care of it once we're done."

"I'll get it." Ryan rushed off in the direction of the kitchen.

Once he returned with a Ziploc bag filled with ice, Patricia placed the cold compress on her left foot. It felt better already.

"We can put this off," Pastor Ward said.

"No," she replied. "It'll take more than a hurt ankle to slow me down. Besides, Ryan and I really need this session."

From the corner of her eye, Patricia saw Ryan straighten. "I broke a door in our house last night."

Pastor Ward's eyebrows hit his hairline. "Let's begin with prayer then. Lord, we invite your presence in at this time . . ."

Patricia listened with half an ear. She adjusted the ice on her ankle as quietly as she could, saying the "Amen" in tune with everyone else when the prayer concluded.

"Okay, Ryan, care to elaborate?" Pastor Ward asked.

"Patricia refuses to sleep with me," Ryan said. "First, she was sleeping in Brian's room, and then she relocated to the guest room. I couldn't take one more night of her sleeping in there. I need her next to me."

Wow, Ryan had made her the bad guy in less than ten seconds!

Pastor Ward gave her a nod. "Why don't you tell me how this all got started?"

Patricia backtracked to the beginning. "I don't sleep in there all the time. I sleep in there sometimes because of his teeth grinding. Ryan doesn't know it, but he does that whenever something is bothering him. I asked him so many times what was wrong, but he wouldn't say. Then, finally, he tells me Karlie might be his daughter." She tilted her head toward Ryan. "And for the record, I'm not the only one refusing intimacy. He's shunned me too."

Pastor Ward nodded. "You said Ryan told you Karlie might be his daughter. How did you feel hearing that?"

Ryan jumped in. "Turns out she already knew. I can't believe she knew all this time, Pastor, and didn't tell me."

"Yes, I knew!" Patricia snarled. "I told you why I didn't say anything. Why are you trying to make me look disgraceful before our pastor? That's not what I'm mad about, and you know it."

Ryan puffed his chest. "I told you why I tried to sabotage Brian and Karlie. I couldn't afford them getting together when I know they're related."

"You could have killed them!" she screamed. "They were dunked into an alligator-infested river. How's that sabotage? That's attempted murder!"

Ryan sailed to his feet. "Are you calling me a murderer?"

By this time, the ice on her leg had started to melt. Patricia curved over to fetch the Ziploc, but Ryan beat her to it. His fingers grazed her leg. Like a jolt, electricity shot through her being. She squirmed but wasn't about to succumb to any attraction. Patricia folded her arms about her chest, cutting her eyes at him.

She glared at Pastor Ward. "Are you going to say anything, or are you content with being a fly on the wall while we bicker?"

Ryan's eyes widened to the size of saucers. "I can't believe you just talked to the man of God like that. You have no respect at all."

Patricia bit her tongue to keep from telling Ryan off. She hated that he was right. She had disrespected Pastor Ward, who was only trying to help. She couldn't believe she had sassed the pastor out.

Patricia lowered her lashes. "I'm sorry for snapping at you, Pastor. I'm just frustrated." She shook her head. "I don't even know how Ryan and I got to this point."

Pastor Ward nodded. "I'm married myself, so I understand." He motioned for Ryan to settle into his chair.

The warmth their pastor exuded made her eyes water. Patricia wiped her face with the back of her hand.

"There's only one person who loves to create division, and that's the devil," Pastor Ward said. "He is your enemy. He's using both of your fears to interfere with your relationship. You both have to decide if you're going to lie back and let the devil win. He's having a party while you're in misery."

"I love Patricia," Ryan said. "I've never loved another woman the way I love her, and there won't be another for me. I'm sorry I slept with Tiffany all those years ago. If I hadn't, then none of this would be happening right now."

Patricia swished her head to face him. "Is that the *real* reason you didn't claim Karlie as your own? That's the dumbest thing I've ever heard. Ryan, that happened over *two* decades ago. I forgave you a long time ago. I'm not even sweating that issue."

Ryan lowered his head. "I couldn't forgive myself. Then, when Anna died, I couldn't bring Karlie into our home."

"I would have welcomed her," Patricia cried. "You don't know how much I wanted Karlie to be yours—*both* of ours. I wanted a daughter to replace the one I lost."

"I take it you lost a child," Pastor Ward said.

Ryan gave Pastor a look because Pastor knew that already. Pastor gave Ryan the eye. Ryan nodded with understanding. Pastor knew Patricia needed to share her pain.

Patricia nodded. She touched her womb. "I lost her at four months."

"I've made a mess of things, haven't I?" Ryan asked. He reached for Patricia's hand. "Honey, I'm so sorry. Please, forgive me."

"I'm sorry too," Patricia said. "You're not the only one who's done wrong. At least you're trying to own up to it." She surprised herself with her choice of words, but Patricia quickly recovered.

"God has forgiven you, Ryan," Pastor Ward said. "Your wife has forgiven you. It's time you forgave yourself."

Ryan's chest heaved as his emotions let loose. Patricia felt compassionate, but it wasn't enough to soften her heart fully. Pastor pushed the tissue box in his direction.

"Patricia, what happened when you told Karlie and Brian?" Pastor Ward asked.

"They were both upset," she said. "I think they're battling . . . feelings for each other."

Pastor Ward's right eyebrow arched. "Oh."

"Yes . . . oh," Patricia said.

"Brian hates me, and Karlie has disappeared," Ryan added. "No one has seen or heard from her for about two weeks now."

"I'm sure Brian is angry, but he doesn't hate you," Pastor Ward said. "Give Karlie time. She'll come around."

"We have to do a paternity test to make sure," Patricia said. "Though we believe in our hearts Karlie is Ryan's daughter."

"That's understandable," Pastor Ward said. He asked Ryan and Patricia to join hands. "Lord, I come before your presence asking for your love, mercy, and grace to be present among us tonight. The devil desires to destroy marriages, but that is not your plan. I ask that you will increase Ryan and Patricia's love for each other. Help them unite and face whatever lies ahead. Strengthen their bond, Lord. Please forgive them for the many ways in which they have failed you, and I ask that you throw it in the sea of forgetfulness, so that they will be even stronger than before. In Jesus' name. Amen."

Then he made both Ryan and Patricia pray. Ryan said, "Lord, thank you for giving me the courage to tell my truth. Thank you for loving me in spite of all my faults. I ask, Lord, that you renew my heart and my mind. Help me to live for you as I should. Amen."

Patricia was next. "Lord, give me more love for my husband. Help me to stand by his side. Forgive him—no, forgive us of our lies and deception. Wash us and make us clean again, Lord. Cover us with your blood. Help me to be the Christian I need to be, all the time to everyone around me. Amen."

As they shouted praises, Patricia felt the pain in her heart recede. Ryan praised God for forgiveness.

When they were done, Ryan said, "We're ready for anything."

Patricia smiled and nodded, but she wasn't as convinced. It would take serious praying and fasting to fix their home.

"You can't rush Brian or Karlie's forgiveness, but you *can* do something about yourselves," Pastor Ward advised. "You both can work on your marriage and build a united front, so when Karlie or Brian wants to talk, you're standing to face them together."

"Together," Patricia repeated, although she was not fully sure.

Pastor Ward gave her a wide smile of encouragement, and a heat rocked her body. She drew in a breath. What in blue blazes was wrong with her that a man only had to touch her or smile at her and she was . . . excited?

Patricia looked away from the brilliance of Pastor Ward's white teeth. Her gaze collided with her husband's piercing eyes. Had Ryan seen her reaction just now? She broke eye contact and shifted.

What was going on with her?

Chapter Thirty

"As much as I've enjoyed having you, I think it's time you called your father," Merle said, entering the family room with two ice-cream sundaes.

"Did you put on extra caramel like I like?" Karlie asked, reaching for the treat.

"Of course. That's what grandmothers do. Spoil you rotten." Merle handed Karlie hers and placed the tray on the cherry coffee table. She picked up her own sundae and spoon.

Karlie smiled, curling her legs under the printed empire sofa. She had been staying with Merle at her home on Edward Street in Baldwin just over a month, yet she could not get used to viewing her as a grandmother. Karlie called her Merle, Ms. Merle, hey—anything but Grandma. She did enjoy their chats. Merle was proving to be a good listener. Karlie had arrived on her doorstep, heartbroken and confused. Merle had nurtured her, and now Karlie felt like herself again.

Merle had not pushed Karlie for information. She had taken care of her. This was the first time Merle had even mentioned her adopted family.

Merle took two bites of her ice cream. "Do you plan on calling Neil?"

"Yes, I do." Karlie sighed. She scooped some more of her sundae. "I also plan on leaving."

"Leaving?"

Karlie nodded. "I can't stay here with you forever."

Merle bit her lip. "I understand. I . . . I hope we won't lose our connection."

"We won't. We're blood. Nothing can change that."

"Are you coming to Bible study with me tonight?"

Karlie scrunched her nose. Her grandmother went to church almost every day. Merle hadn't been kidding when she said she had gotten religion. Karlie tagged along to each of the services, but tonight she needed a break.

"If it's all right with you, I'm going to chill out here," she said, finishing the last of her sundae.

Karlie could use some alone time. Sometimes Merle freaked her out when she stared at her for no reason. "You look so much like Tiffany, I think I'm talking to her," Merle would say. Karlie did bear a strong resemblance to her mother. She was Tiffany's mini-me, but she was very much herself.

Merle gave a tentative nod. She busied herself by gathering their spoons and bowls. When Karlie moved to help, Merle waved her off. "I'm making up for lost time." She moved to the doorway and looked back at Karlie.

"What is it?" Karlie asked.

"Will you be here when I get back?"

"Yes. I wouldn't leave without thanking you." She gave her grandmother a tender smile.

Satisfied with her response, Merle left the room.

Karlie eyed the vacant spot for several minutes. She puttered around the three-bedroom house before settling back into the family room. The plush printed couch had become her favorite sitting spot. The mustard-colored walls soothed her.

Then out of nowhere, a strange feeling assaulted her being. An urgent desire rose from deep within her. Overcome, Karlie opened her mouth and exhaled.

Flashing her hands, Karlie released staccato breaths. She wanted to sing. Needed to, actually. She hadn't felt that churning inside since Ryan tilted her world with his news. She shrieked with excitement, and in a flash, she was on her iPod and on Google. She plugged in some words.

Within seconds, the lyrics to "Just a Closer Walk with Thee" flashed on her screen. Karlie practiced a few notes. She listened to variations of the song on YouTube several times. The first verse in particular resonated with her. Tears rolled down her face.

She pulled up the video camera on her iPod and pressed record. From deep within her soul, Karlie sang the first line: *"I am weak but Thou art strong . . ."* Ooh, her heart thumped. She'd lived these words. Knew what they meant. *"Jesus, keep me from all wrong . . ."*

She thought of Brian, Jamaal, and Ryan's treachery. Karlie held a sob as the words struck her being, and she poured it out in the next line*: "I'll be satisfied as long as I walk, let me walk close to Thee."*

A presence surrounded her. The Holy Spirit was paying her a visit.

Thank you, Jesus.

She sang, *"Just a closer walk with Thee . . . Grant it, Jesus, is my plea . . . Daily walking close to Thee . . . Let it be, dear Lord, let it be . . ."*

Karlie closed her eyes as every word and every note swept her away. She sang the rest of the song knowing she was in God's presence. She repeated the refrain several times. The song was a personal testament between her and God. He had lifted her so that her song drew her unto Him, her comforter.

"Let it be, dear Lord, let it be . . ."

Karlie held the last note until her breath caught. A spirit of rejoicing bubbled up. She lifted her hands and her face toward heaven. "Thank you, Jesus!" She jumped with joy and praised God as she never had before.

With a shiver, she pressed the stop button. She knew without any doubt that she had sung the best she had ever sung in her entire life. Her hands shook, but Karlie knew she needed to hit replay.

No, she had a better idea.

Karlie pressed the video and hit the upload button. She would share her song with everyone. She had to. The screen flashed signaling the video was finished uploading. For one split second, Karlie questioned herself. Then, she hit the publish button and released her pain to the world.

Karlie knew God had just revealed His plan for her life. Her mother had sung and made the world dance, but Tiffany had died before she could use her talents for His glory. God would complete the work in her. Karlie would sing, and the world would praise God.

Basking in His revelation, Karlie shouted, "It's in your hands, Lord! Whatever your will for me, I surrender to you! Use me! Use me for your glory!"

She heard a whisper.

You're ready.

Karlie clapped her hands and whirled like a schoolgirl in the sun. Yes, she was ready. No more hiding. It was time to sing. Face life head-on. "Hold on, world. I'm ready to face whatever you throw my way. Here I come!"

She sang "Take me to the King," "Power in the Name," "Blessed Assurance," and then "His Eye Is on the Sparrow." Finally, her vocal chords pleaded with her to rest. Tired from her tribute to God, Karlie relaxed on the couch. She did not know how long she had been asleep before she felt a hand shaking her out of her slumber.

"Have you been here the whole time I was gone?" Merle asked.

Karlie pranced to her feet. "Grandma! I'm singing again!" She clapped her hands with exultation.

Merle clutched her chest and backed away.

Karlie frowned. "Are you all right?" She placed a hand on her grandmother's forehead.

"You called me Grandma just now," Merle said, releasing her words in small breaths. "It felt good."

Karlie smiled. She caressed Merle's face. The doctors repaired the damage as best as they could, but Merle's face would forever be scarred.

"Let me hear the song," Merle said. "I want to hear the words that made my baby call me Grandma."

"My voice is tired, but I'll do you one better," Karlie said. She led her grandmother over to the computer and pulled up the YouTube video.

Oh my goodness! Her video had 276,000 hits. In what, three hours? That was unreal!

Karlie's heart pounded. "Grandma, so many people clicked my video. Look at all the like buttons." She pressed play.

Yep, there she was. Singing a cappella. Karlie couldn't believe that the voice she was hearing belonged to her.

Merle closed her eyes and swayed her body to the tune. Karlie chewed on her lower lip with extreme nervousness. A couple of times she tried to ask Merle for her opinion, but her grandmother shushed her.

Merle stood in a trancelike position until Karlie's final note flowed through the speakers.

"Grandma?" Karlie asked.

Merle's face beamed. "Honestly, that was magical. You have a gift, child. Actually, let me rephrase that. You're a gift. A gift from God."

Chapter Thirty-one

Brian listened to Karlie's song for the sixth time. Again, dime-sized goose bumps rose on his arms. Karlie's voice was majestic. He had no idea she could sing like that. Neither did any of the over 600,000 people who listened to her on YouTube. People raved how her raw vocals had mesmerized them.

Your voice is transcendent, he texted to Karlie, not expecting a reply. Karlie hadn't responded to his previous fifty-odd text messages.

I can't believe it has 692,000 likes.

Brian nearly dropped the phone when his cell vibrated. He read the screen. Karlie had sent him a text. *She's back.* He quickly pulled up her contact information and pressed the call button.

While the phone rang in his ear, Brian raced into his closet to grab his sneakers and to pull on some jeans. If Karlie answered, he wasn't hanging up until he knew where she was hiding. He had staked out Neil's home. He'd even peeked through Tiffany's old home but saw no sign of Karlie.

His call went to voice mail. Brian redialed. This time she answered.

His breath caught at her voice. Time hadn't done anything to curb his feelings. "It feels like a lifetime," he said. "Where are you?"

"I'm at my grandmother's."

"Merle's? What are you doing in that madwoman's house?" Brian should have considered Merle since Karlie had mentioned her, but in his defense, he did not think Karlie would have spent more than a few hours at her house.

"She's not mad, and Grandma's not that bad," Karlie said.

Brian actually looked at his screen to make sure he saw Karlie's face on it.

"Hello?" he heard through the line.

"I'm here," he said. "I just had to make sure I hadn't gone crazy and that I'm speaking to Karlie Knightly, the daughter of Tiffany Knightly—whom Merle rejected not once, but twice. The first time being when she cruelly chose to believe her rapist husband over her teenage daughter. The second time being when Tiffany was dying of cancer and she refused to open her home to you. Am I speaking to *that* Karlie?"

"Yes. I know the history isn't pretty, but Grandma is sorry for how she treated my mother when she was alive," Karlie said.

What had Merle done to brainwash Karlie in such a short time? And what's with this *Grandma* business? He needed to get over there. "What's her address?"

"This is why I *didn't* want to call," Karlie said. "I don't want you coming here and acting the fool. I'm grown. I came here of my own free will. It's where I wanted to be."

Brian knew that arguing with Karlie might cause her to retreat into her self-imposed cocoon. "You're right, and I'm sorry. Please tell me where you are."

It took a little prodding, but she finally rattled off her location. Brian jumped into his Range Rover, a twenty-first birthday present from his father. He programmed the address into his GPS and took off.

Twenty-five minutes later, he swerved to a smooth stop in front of Merle's home and admired the stucco front. Eyeing the landscaping, he whistled. Karlie had set up her grandmother in style. His mouth popped open at the black Chrysler 500C sitting in the driveway.

For real? Merle is living large off her dead daughter's estate.

Brian bounded out of the vehicle and rushed up the four steps to the entrance of the home. Then he pressed on the doorbell.

Karlie answered the door, and Brian wrapped her in his arms. He hugged her longer than necessary, resisting the urge to swing her in his arms.

"I missed you," he said, peering into her eyes.

She gave him a tender smile that faded.

Brian understood why she tethered her emotions, but he did not like it. Not one bit. He crossed the threshold curious to see the interior. The shiny wooden floors and vaulted ceilings, along with the 60-inch screen in a mauve-color, coordinated living and dining area.

"My grandmother went to bed," Karlie said.

Brian nodded. That was cool by him. He was not eager to see her. "I texted Neil and my mother to let them know your whereabouts."

Her shoulders drooped. "You shouldn't have done that."

"Listen, you have plenty of people worried about you, yet you're hiding out at Grandma's," Brian said. "This isn't the story of Little Red Riding Hood. It's real life. Have you forgotten you have a paternity test you need to take? Not need—*must*. You have to know who you are."

Karlie lifted her chin. "I know who I am. I'm me." She pointed to her chest. "I'm Merle's granddaughter. That's all I need to know."

"The girl singing on YouTube says otherwise. You're bursting with pain. You're trying to hide it under all that praising, but you're only fooling yourself. Karlie, there was real sorrow in your voice. It moved me in ways I can't begin to explain. But you're in denial if you think the song brought you relief. It's just the beginning of your healing. You're ready to face the past."

Her eyes shifted from his. "What would you know about what praising can do? You don't even go to church."

"Shows what you know," Brian said. "I've been going with your folks." He wouldn't add his original motivation had been to see her.

"You . . . You're going to church?" Her eyes were popped open wide. *Sheesh, you'd think he'd said the sun was blue or something.*

"Yes." Brian nodded emphatically. "Maybe it's all that praying you used to do for me. Who knows when God answers prayer."

"What was last week's message?" she asked.

He put his hands on his hips. "Your father preached about the three Hebrew boys who wouldn't bow down to Nebuchadnezzar's image. *Now* do you believe me?"

"I wasn't there to confirm, but, yes, I believe you," she said.

"When I'm there, I enjoy the worship service. I feel a high as if nothing is impossible, but when I leave I still have things to deal with. Like not speaking to my father. Like the pain from this psoriasis." He arched an eyebrow.

"I know I have things to deal with," Karlie said. "But don't sleep on praise. I've seen people healed by praise. Jericho's wall came down on a shout."

Brian squinted. "I hate when you get obtuse. God made psychologists. He made ministers because they minister. Get it? You need to seek help, Karlie."

The fire went out of her. "Did you come here to kill my buzz?"

"No, I came here because I want you to know I'm here. You're ready, and you can face things. Just stop hiding."

Her voice quivered. "Today was the first day I was able to be carefree in God. Just rejoice. All the other days . . . I would be fine until bedtime. Then I'm kept awake by the sound of my thoughts. My heart can't take any more."

Karlie slumped onto the couch. Brian joined her, holding her close to him.

"I don't know how much I can deal with," Karlie said. "I came here to find comfort in my real family, and I've found it. But . . . It's hard. For years, I felt the shame of being a product of rape. My stepfather raped my mother, and here I came. It was tough, but I had Jamaal . . ." She gulped and looked at him. "And you."

Brian rubbed her back as her shoulders heaved from crying. He hated jarring her and spoiling her good time, but Karlie was finally opening up.

Brian found a paper towel in the kitchen and handed it to her. As he watched her wipe her pitiful face, his heart shifted.

"Keep talking, sweetheart," he whispered, kissing the top of her head. "Let it out."

He inhaled at his slip of tongue, but Karlie was too distressed to notice his term of endearment.

"You know what's worse than being a child of rape? Having . . ." She sobbed and wiped her nose. "Having a fa . . . fath . . . father rej . . . reject you because he . . . he . . . didn't wa . . . wa . . ." Her shoulders heaved. "Want me." She raised ravaged eyes to his. "Why didn't he want me?"

Brian shook his head. He wished he knew the answer to that question. He wanted to believe it was more than Ryan's selfishness. "Hush," Brian whispered. "I want you. I want you."

Brian knew he was out of his element. Karlie needed professional help. Only Ryan could answer the question of her heart. Resentment rose. Brian wasn't sure his father was capable of honesty.

Karlie eased onto his lap. Brian comforted her until her tears subsided into small heart-wrenching sniffs. Tears misted his eyes. He tried to fight the anger raging in his system. He hated Ryan Oakes with every fiber of his being. His father needed to have poles hammered into his eyes for causing Karlie such agony. Brian immediately regretted the evil thought, but he swore to make his father pay. He wouldn't leave this earth until that happened.

Chapter Thirty-two

Can someone explain this whole religion thing to me because I am mystified? Ryan studied his reflection in his bathroom mirror.

When he and Patricia had left Pastor Ward's office, he had been hopeful. After that prayer session, surely things would be better . . . he thought. But Ryan didn't know what happened to Patricia during the drive home because when he pulled his car behind hers and stepped out, a different woman exited her vehicle.

She was sullen, uncommunicative, and went to sleep without an explanation. What was the point of praying if she was going to forget everything once they left the pastor's office?

Ryan reached for his electric razor, which he kept charged, to shave his cheeks, but he was so distracted he shaved off half his moustache.

His eyes widened in disbelief. What did he just do? *Maybe it isn't so bad.* Ryan leaned into the mirror to look. *I haven't seen my upper lip in years.* With a light buzz, he shaved off the other side. When he was done, he examined his work. He looked funny. Ryan's hand grazed his upper lip. This "new him" was going to take some getting used to. He would see what Patricia thought.

Ryan entered the room, relieved to see she was still awake.

Patricia's eyes zoomed in on Ryan's face and became bug-eyed. "What did you do?"

Ryan shifted his eyes from hers. "It was an accident."
Please tell me I look good.

Patricia tilted her head back and laughed. She laughed and laughed, while he stood there blinking and blinking.

"I can't believe you're laughing at me. It can't be that bad."

She laughed some more before cupping her mouth. "I'm sorry. I think black men must always have facial hair. You remind me of Don Lemon."

Ryan froze. He knew she wasn't comparing him to that CNN reporter. Patricia knew he couldn't stand him. He stomped into the closet, yanked clothes off the hangers from his otherwise organized closet, and quickly dressed.

Patricia's laughter stung. There was a time when she would have cuddled him and told him how she thought he was cute. Instead, she had laughed at him. He knew it might seem petty, but Patricia's response was big to him. She had always had his back. Always. Now he was a joke. Just like their sham of a marriage. Only he was the only one *not* laughing.

He was a grown man. There was no reason his wife's mirth should rankle him, but it did. He felt self-conscious and naked without the hair on his upper lip.

Before he slammed the front door behind him, he mumbled, "Lord, I know I put myself in this mess, but if you could hurry up and get me out, I'd really appreciate it."

Ryan rubbed his bare upper lip. It will grow back, he assured himself repeatedly as he slipped inside his Navigator. He couldn't resist another peek. Luckily, his cell phone rang to distract him.

"Ryan, this is Frank returning your call. I was caught up in some other business."

Frank. Ryan hunched into his seat. "Thanks for calling."

"Let's meet for coffee," Frank suggested.

Something deep within beckoned Ryan not to take Frank up on his offer. "I was on my way to my office . . ." He thought of his son. His daughter. His wife. None of them were in his corner. He wasn't sure what God was doing because He had him on a spiritual seesaw. His stomach churned.

"If you've changed your mind . . ."

No. Frank's call might be God's doing. Ryan needed help with this court case. "I'll see you in a few minutes," he said, gripping the steering wheel.

The two agreed to meet at a Dunkin' Donuts in twenty minutes. Ryan shifted into drive and arrived in fifteen minutes. Sauntering into the donut joint, he ordered two coffees and a couple of muffins. Then he sat in a booth and waited for Frank.

Frank strolled in behind a young mother and her twin sons. Ryan watched the pudgy man charm the young lady and smiled. Frank made sure to strike up quick conversations with two other patrons before strolling over to Ryan's table.

"Coffee?" Ryan asked.

Frank gave him a brief nod.

"I thought you'd look more . . . *menacing*."

The other man laughed and sank his teeth into a muffin. "I get that all the time." Frank frowned. "Believe me when I tell you, I get the job done."

Ryan shuddered on the inside. Frank had transformed from unassuming to sinister in under two seconds. Maybe he should take Pastor Ward's advice. The walk of a Christian meant faith in God. "Let God fight your battles" was what Pastor Ward sometimes said. But this problem could cost him millions of dollars *and* his reputation. What was a man without his reputation?

Before he could change his mind, Ryan wrote Jackson Higgins's name and phone number on a napkin. "I need him annihilated. I need this case gone."

Frank folded the napkin and tucked it into his shirt pocket. "Consider it done. I'll check in with you in a week."

Ryan felt uneasy but gave Frank an uncertain nod.

Frank leaned into his ear. "This is not for the faint of heart. Be sure. There's no undoing once things get started."

Ryan gulped and held back his shiver. "I'm sure."

"I'll be in touch."

It took Ryan an hour to steady his equilibrium. He wasn't sure what Frank would do, but he knew he wouldn't like it.

He knew he couldn't go into work because there was no way he would be able to concentrate. Ryan drove around aimlessly before calling Brian. No answer. No surprise there. He tried Karlie next.

She picked up on his second ring. Ryan pulled over to the curb to speak to her. "How've you been?"

"I only picked up to let you know I'm ready to do the paternity test."

Her frosty tone intimidated him somewhat. Ryan wasn't sure how to connect with her. "I'm glad, Karlie. I need—no—we *both* need to know."

"Fair enough, but I need you to know that no paternity test is going to change the fact that Neil Jameson is my *real* father."

Her words cut deep. Though Ryan had felt Neil was best for her years ago, hearing Karlie say it jabbed a knife through him. "I wouldn't try to take Neil's place—"

"Good, because you can't," she interrupted.

Ryan counted to five. "I would like us to have a relationship if the results show I'm your father."

"I . . ."

Ryan prayed she would give him a chance.

"Let's do this, get the results, and then . . . We'll see," Karlie said. "I won't make any promises, but that's the best I can do."

Considering his terrible deed, Karlie was being more than generous. "One day at a time," Ryan said. "Thank you for answering my call."

"You're welcome, Mr. Oakes."

Her polite formality was more hurtful than her cool demeanor. "How's Brian?"

"I saw him yesterday for the first time in about a month," Karlie said. "He's okay, I guess."

That told him nothing, but at least Ryan knew his son was alive and well. "Thank you."

"You're welcome." Karlie ended the call.

By the look and sound of things, Ryan had a long bumpy road ahead. Nothing in his life was going right. He slumped over the wheel. His life was so complicated. Life had wrapped itself around his neck and was squeezing the air out of him. Now he understood why some men shot themselves in the head because his brain was moving 300 miles a minute.

Ryan held his head with both hands as despair overwhelmed him. "It's too much." He turned his head and noticed the store sign. He had parked beside a gun shop.

Why not end it now?

What did he have to live for? He cupped the door handle. Maybe he would just browse. Take a look. Ask some questions. He applied pressure to the door so it swung open and placed one foot on the ground.

Then his phone rang.

Chapter Thirty-three

"Could he have closed that door any harder?" Patricia grumbled.

Ryan had slammed the door hard enough to knock it off its hinges. Patricia slipped out of bed and washed up. She dragged herself down the stairs, dreading going into work but knew the twins needed her.

Anna and Alyssa had had another bad night with Alyssa spiking a fever and Anna having another seizure. She hadn't gone in because she half-expected Brian to show up.

On her way home from her counseling session with Pastor Ward the night before, Brian had called her in a rage.

"I hate Ryan," Brian said. "How could he hurt Karlie like this? He needs to pay. I'm telling you, I'll figure out a way to make him regret his actions."

"He's human," Patricia said. "Your father has made a lot of mistakes, but he loves you."

"Well, he has a funny way of showing it," Brian retorted.

Patricia heard a huge sigh.

"I should've known you'd defend him," Brian said. "You're always on his side. The two of you deserve each other. You know what, Mom? You and Dad—Ryan—can go to France and just leave me alone!"

The next sound Patricia heard was the click of the end button. Several times, she pressed her car phone to redial Brian's number. Each time he ignored her call. Frustrated, Patricia banged her hand on the wheel.

"If this man had just kept his pants on, we wouldn't be in this mess!" Patricia raged. Her mouth hung open at her words. What was this? Not even an hour ago, she had been in the pastor's office saying she was over Ryan and Tiffany's affair.

Did she have some residual feelings she needed to tackle? No, Patricia shook her head, pulling next to Ryan in the driveway. Frustration and stress were the reasons she spoke without thinking.

She was furious with herself and Ryan. As she exited the vehicle, Patricia cut her eyes at him, fed up with everything. It took every ounce of strength she possessed to shower and get into bed. Fatigue seeped through her bones, and Patricia fell into a restless sleep.

She replayed her conversation with Brian over and over again. Plus, her biological response to men who weren't her husband still bothered her because . . .

No, she didn't want to go there. She had come too far to pick up the old man and his deeds. Her flesh was warring within, but with God's help she could fight this.

Whatever *it* was.

Two more calls from the hospital—one from the nurse and the other from Tim—also interfered with her sleep and added to her stress.

So when she had awakened earlier to see Ryan's shaven face, Patricia didn't know how to explain her reaction. She had laughed, but she wasn't laughing at him. She had needed and welcomed the release. Unfortunately, she had laughed herself into a headache.

Patricia rubbed her temples. She would try Brian again. When he hung up from her last night, he had sounded determined. Patricia hated the thought of her son and husband at war. She shivered, glad that Brian had no idea of her role in the deception.

She pressed the voice dial. "Brian," she dictated. It rang and rang. He didn't answer. She dropped the phone on the counter. If he didn't answer, she was going up to the city to see him.

It had been a month since Brian had been home. He had called her twice only to let her know he had minor outbreaks. She had her dermatologist fill his prescriptions. Other than that, nothing. Brian's drive out to Long Island to see Karlie without stopping by was telling.

Patricia had just put the coffee on to percolate when her cell phone rang.

"Patricia, you need to come," Tim said. His gravelly voice lacked his usual cheer.

Dread lined her stomach. "No, please, don't say it's the twins."

"Just come." He ended the call.

Patricia ripped the percolator plug from the wall and rushed to jam her feet into sneakers. She didn't know if she would need to do emergency surgery and wanted comfortable footwear.

The Velasquez parents huddled in the corner of the waiting area, clinging to each other when she arrived. "Doctor!" they shouted in unison.

Patricia held up a hand to stall them. She couldn't waste precious minutes to talk with them. "I have to go see the twins, and then I'll come talk to you," she said as she breezed by them.

She saw Tim pacing by the door. "What's going on?"

He grasped her shoulders. "They don't look good. The scans show brain aneurysms."

Patricia clenched her fists. "Don't speak those words as if you're pronouncing their death. You don't know for sure. No one does. It's up to a higher power to decide." She shoved past him and entered the room.

Anna's eyes were open. Patricia checked her pulse and temperature before scanning her chart. She had had two seizures. Patricia clicked her penlight to look into Anna's eyes. There was a small pupillary reaction.

"Prep them for surgery," she said to the full-time nurse on duty. "I'll go update the parents."

Tim stood in the doorway. "Dr. Oakes, I—"

"Not now," Patricia interrupted. "Please," she whispered. "I need to compose myself to speak to the Velasquezes. We're going into surgery. Now."

"That's not a good idea, and you know it," Tim said. "They're not stable and both are too weak for surgery."

Patricia left the room. She wasn't about to listen to his negativity. She entered the waiting room, and the parents rushed over to her.

"Will you be able to help?" Mr. Velasquez cried.

"Can you save my babies?" Mrs. Velasquez wailed. She grabbed Patricia's hand and held it in a death grip.

They were looking at her as if she were God. She couldn't swear on an outcome. Her shoulders dropped. The parent in her wanted to say she could, but the doctor in her couldn't pretend. She couldn't lie and give them false hope.

"Dr. Oakes will need to do some more research," Tim said from somewhere behind her.

Relief seeped through Patricia's spine. Tim approached and gently removed Mrs. Velasquez's hand from hers.

Mr. Velasquez nodded before begging, "Please, Doctors, do what you can."

With a small nod, Patricia turned around leaving Tim to deal with them. She didn't want the Velasquezes to see the tears threatening to fall. She was too emotionally involved to do the surgery. Her chest heaved. Patricia held herself together only long enough to return to her office.

She shut the door behind her before sinking to the floor. "Father God, I need you now. I need your assurance I can do this. Please, stabilize them. Stabilize them so I can help them."

Covering her face with her hands, Patricia wept through her supplication. Two strong arms encircled her and lifted her to her feet. Inhaling Axe body spray, Patricia melted into Tim's arms.

He ran his hands through her hair. She closed her eyes, basking in his strength. How she needed this. To feel secure and safe. Tim whispered words of encouragement in her hair. He pressed a light kiss on her cheek. This was her cue to break contact.

A feathery kiss landed between her eyelid and nose. Patricia took a deep breath and tilted her chin upward. Ever so slowly, she opened her eyes.

Tim pierced her with a gaze filled with longing. "Let me help you. You don't have to go through this alone."

His hypnotic words were enough to awaken dormant urges she had suppressed years ago. These sensations scared her. Though Ryan satisfied her, there was always a part of her that was always . . . thirsty . . . hungry . . . insatiable.

Patricia shook her head. She placed an appropriate distance between them. "I can't. If I do this, there's no going back for me."

"You want me," Tim said. "I know it. I'm in love with you."

Patricia cleared her throat. "I'm sorry I let things get this far. Please leave." Her heart pounded as she hoped he would . . . and wouldn't.

Tim's pager buzzed. "We're not done with this," he said before rushing to answer the call.

For the sake of her sanity, she had to be done with Tim. Patricia strode toward her desk to pull out her Rolodex.

Most of the numbers in there were also in her cell phone, but not this one. She flipped through the small cards until she located the number she desired.

Once she did, Patricia used her office phone to place the call.

"SAA Recovery."

Patricia gulped. She hadn't wanted to make this call, but she had to. Her emotions were spiraling out of control. "I need to see someone."

"Okay," the person on the line said with understanding. "Just wait a moment and I'll set you up with someone."

Patricia tapped her feet while she waited. About a minute later, the operator had given her the names of two women willing to see her that evening. Patricia thanked the clerk and ended the call.

She pocketed the information in her pants and sauntered into the bathroom to look at herself into the mirror.

Patricia opened her mouth and said words she hadn't uttered in almost thirty years: "Hi, my name is Patricia. I'm a brain surgeon, wife, mother, and I'm a recovering sex addict."

Chapter Thirty-four

"Karlie!" Myra screamed.

With the force of a hurricane, the pint-sized woman snatched Karlie in an embrace so tight, Karlie swayed back and forth.

"Where have you been?" she chided, swatting Karlie on the bottom. "I can't believe you didn't answer our calls. Neil's been worried sick. That man hasn't stopped praying. He's been on his knees day and night." Myra paused for a breath.

Karlie smiled at her adoptive mother. She knew from experience she wouldn't be able to provide an answer because Myra wasn't done.

Myra stepped aside. "Come in. I don't know why you rang the doorbell like you're a stranger. You have a key. Addie's going to be so excited to see you. What a great going-back-to-school present."

Karlie held onto her purse while she stood in the foyer.

"Neil!" Myra bellowed. "Addie!"

Karlie heard the back door slam. Neil must have been in his office. Addie's feet scampering down the steps told her she had been in her room.

"Karlie!" Neil exclaimed. He rushed forward and scooped her in his arms. "I've been worried sick." After a tight hug, he released her.

"That's an understatement," Myra chimed in.

"Karlieeee!" Addie squealed and vaulted into Karlie's arms.

Addie had always jumped with abandon because she was sure Karlie would catch her. Karlie wished she had her sister's faith. She needed to fall into God's arms like that. With a laugh, Karlie kissed Addie's cheeks and tickled her until they both fell to the ground. Hearing Addie's infectious laugh, Karlie realized how much she had missed her family.

Myra fussed nearby, wiping at a stray tear.

"I'm sorry," Karlie said. "I shouldn't have stayed away so long and have you all worried about me."

Myra lowered her eyes. "We're glad you're back. We weren't sure . . ."

Karlie understood. She scanned all of them. "You're my family. I just needed some time to process. Ryan's news hit me hard."

"I understand," Neil said. "But you should've come home. I know you texted saying you needed space, but I stopped by your hotel suite. I badgered Brian so much. Where were you?"

Karlie gulped. "I was with Merle."

"Huh?" Myra's mouth hung open.

Neil jutted his chin but said nothing. He turned and stormed toward his office. Karlie hesitated for a second before following him.

"Dad?" she called out before entering his office. "I thought you would've told Mom where I was."

Neil faced the window. "It looks like rain."

Karlie walked over to him and rested her head on his shoulder. "Please don't be upset with me."

"Merle hated your mother. She treated Tiffany like dirt. Tiffany begged her." He held her shoulders until their eyes met. "*Begged*. Begged Merle to take you in so you would have a home before she left this world. Merle rejected you and threw Tiffany out of her home. Tiffany cried so hard, I feared for her mental health."

"I needed to be around someone who . . ." Karlie didn't want to sound insensitive.

"Someone who shared your blood?"

Guilt-ridden, Karlie nodded. "Yes," she said. "I'm sorry if that hurts, but I won't lie about my reasons."

Neil gave a small, sad smile. "You wouldn't be Tiffany's daughter if you did." He patted her head. "I understand your reasoning, and I have to respect your wishes as an adult, but I will tell you to be careful. Be careful of Merle because you never know her motives."

Karlie looked down. She thought of the car she had recently purchased for Merle and the stainless steel appliances she had bought while at Merle's. Merle had not asked Karlie to do these things, but Neil's words of caution made her wonder if Merle was manipulating her. She bit her lip, feeling unsure.

He lifted her chin. "I know we don't share the same blood, but you're every bit my daughter. Nothing will change that. Just as how when we accept Christ, we become His heirs, one of His. It's the same way I feel about you. No pop-up father is going to take my place."

Karlie scrunched her lips when she heard "pop-up father," the perfect segue to another topic she needed to tackle. "I'm going to take the paternity test."

Neil nodded. "You should. For your sanity and mine. You need to know who you are, but it's me you belong to."

Karlie reached out to take his hand in hers. There was nothing like knowing someone had your back without question. "No one will take your place. Ever."

"I saw your video," Neil said changing the subject. "It brought tears to my eyes. You don't need the fanfare and gimmicks, Karlie. You sang from deep in your soul, and it is reaching millions. I'm proud of you. If singing is what you want to do, I'll support you. I do wish you'd reconsider doing the TV show though."

"I know you won't understand, but I want to do the show. With Brian. Though I was more scared than I've ever been in my life, I felt alive. I felt like I was singing my own tune instead of only learning the notes. You know what I mean?"

Neil touched her cheek. "I do. I'm being overprotective, but I've placed you in God's hands, so I have to trust He's got you. What about this whole mess with you and Brian?"

Karlie broke eye contact. She wasn't comfortable talking about her feelings with Neil. He was her dad, after all. "Brian and I are in a complicated spot. I thought it would be me and Jamaal for life but . . ." She shook her head. "I can't say anymore because I'm unsure myself."

"You know Jamaal called me, right?" Neil asked. He arched an eyebrow. "He's hoping you'll give him another chance."

Karlie's nose flared. "Why's Jamaal calling you? He didn't call when he was messing—" She clamped her mouth shut. There was no way she would continue this discussion with her dad. "Can we change the subject? Please?"

Myra poked her head into the room. "I have dinner on the table, and as luck would have it, I've made your favorite dessert."

"Thanks, Mom," Karlie said, savoring the smell of brownies baking in the oven.

Brownies were comfort, love, and home wrapped up into a delicious chocolate morsel. Karlie couldn't wait to sink her teeth into the tasty treat. She pushed thoughts of Jamaal aside to devote time with her family.

"You'll have to wait until after dinner," Myra said, pointing a finger at her.

Karlie laughed. It felt good being around people who knew her. Addie delighted her with all sorts of antics. She enjoyed the barbecue chicken, beef ribs and macaroni and cheese dinner. The ribs were so tender they slid down her throat, and the barbecue sauce tasted like heaven popped into her mouth.

Even with all that, Karlie saved room for a piece of brownie. She took a bite. "Mmmm, this is so good, Mom," she uttered.

Myra bagged a few pieces for Karlie to take back with her. All in all, Karlie's heart rejoiced. It was after ten p.m. when Neil walked her out to her car to see her off.

"Where will you be?" he asked as he flicked a small crumb of brownie off her cheek.

"I'm going to see Jamaal," Karlie said, biting another piece of her brownie.

Neil opened his mouth but must have changed his mind. Karlie was glad, although he would not have been able to talk her out of going across the bridge anyway. She had put Jamaal off long enough. She needed to settle things with him tonight.

Forty minutes later, she swerved into the parking garage of Jamaal's apartment complex. Dressed in her jeans and heels, Karlie strutted with the confidence of a New Yorker used to roaming the city at all hours of the night. At the entrance, she caught the door as Jamaal's roommate exited.

Pharrell's comedic double take brought Bugs Bunny to mind. He pushed his cap further down his head, although those ears couldn't be helped. He muttered, "Jamaal's up there. Although I don't know if—"

"Thank you," Karlie said quickly, and she slipped inside the building. She made her way up to Jamaal's room. With a sharp rap, she stepped back and waited for him to answer.

"It's you," Jamaal said when he opened the door. Shirtless, he fidgeted with the belt on his shorts.

Her woman radar beeped loud and clear. Karlie narrowed her eyes. *Jamaal is nervous.* "Are you going to let me in?"

He immediately closed the door behind him and chuckled nervously. "It's like a hurricane in there. I'm embarrassed at the empty pizza boxes and clothes tossed everywhere . . ." He gazed at her. "Let me grab a shirt and we can go somewhere to talk."

Karlie clutched her stomach. Oh, noway, nohow, was she buying that nonsense spilling out of his mouth. "No. I don't mind the mess. I'm coming inside."

Jamaal blocked the door.

She noticed a tie on the doorknob. Karlie wasn't stupid. She knew that was man code for "woman-inside-don't-come-in." Her chest heaved, and her palms grew sweaty. "Jamaal, get out of my way."

"Karlie," he pleaded. "I can't. It'll ruin everything."

She gritted her teeth. "Move. Out. Of. My. Way."

Jamaal shook his head.

With the strength of a woman betrayed, Karlie swung her hips, and Jamaal tripped over his Tims. She barely spared him a glance and shoved open the door to the studio suite.

Karlie rushed inside. She saw tossed jeans and empty soda cans but no female in sight. But, her radar still beeped. Carefully treading through the clothes, Karlie headed to the bathroom. She pulled the curtains back with a flourish. No one.

Hmm. If I were creeping with another woman's man, where would I slither to hide?

"See, I told you no one is here," Jamaal said from behind her. His frantic, bright eyes told the truth.

Karlie turned up her nose and elbowed him as she went back into the room. "You must think I'm stupid. I *know* there's someone in here."

She wandered over to the closet. *Bingo!* Her heart pounded, but Karlie opened the door. When she saw who stood there quivering in her undies, instant rage flowed like lava through her being and erupted into a wail powerful enough to rattle the apartment building.

"Nikkiiii!!!"

Chapter Thirty-five

"Your call was a lifesaver," Ryan said, pulling Brian into an embrace.

They had agreed to meet up at a nearby park as Brian had spent the night at Karlie's house. It was just before dusk and surprisingly the Baldwin Harbor Park was empty, which was fine by him.

Brian did not return the hug; instead, he shoved Ryan hard. Ryan flailed backward. He would have fallen on his butt, but a bench saved his nasty fall.

Ryan grabbed his son by the shirt. "Don't you *ever* dishonor me by putting your hands on me again! I might be a lousy father, but I command your respect, and you *will* give me that."

Brian pursed his lips and gave a slight nod.

Ryan released him, and Brian slunk into the bench. He couldn't believe Brian had the audacity to put hands on him. Ryan counted to ten, and then sat next to him. "I thought Karlie would be with you."

"No, she went to see her parents." Brian glared at him. "Her *real* parents."

Ryan flinched at the jab. He swiped at his brow. The humidity was no joke. "I'm not trying to take Neil's place. I just need to know if Karlie's mine."

Brian crammed a finger in Ryan's chest. "Why now? Five years went by, and you didn't say anything. Your only motivation was to ruin my life."

Ryan shifted toward Brian. "If you want to leave here with all your fingers, you'd better move your hand."

Brian removed his finger.

"I'm not ruining your life, son. I'm straightening it out. Whatever you think you feel for Karlie must end. I can't have you pining after your sister."

"I didn't know who she was!" Brian jumped to his feet and inhaled deeply to catch his breath. "Have you thought about the damage you've done? Last night, Karlie was crying in my arms trying to figure out why you didn't want her."

Ryan stood so he and Brian were eye to eye. "It's not that I didn't want Karlie. Let's face it. I was a chief contender for the world's worst parent. I was a horrible father to you. I neglected you. I was always working, and I—"

"Enough!" Brian interrupted. "Your excuses are as flimsy as a cheap paper towel."

Ryan lowered his head. There was no talking his way around this mess. "I'm sorry. If I could turn back the clock—"

"But you can't," Brian interrupted. "When I was growing up, I craved your attention. I acted out and did all sorts of schemes for you to notice me. I thought that was painful, but what I went through was a breeze compared to Karlie. Her mother died. Her grandmother rejected her, and now her father didn't have the time or energy to claim her." He held out his hands. "Do you understand her devastation?"

Ryan realized he was worse than mildew scum around the toilet bowl. "I'm beginning to see, son. Before I gave my life to God, I really didn't see the error of my ways."

Brian snorted. "Please don't excuse your bad behavior because you weren't saved before. You knew right from wrong."

Ryan sighed. "If you called me here to crush my head with your foot, it's working. You're contradicting everything I say."

"Are you *really* saved? Or are you *playing* at being saved? I've been watching you, and you seem to think God is there for your convenience."

Now, where did that come from? Ryan wondered.

Brian pierced him with his eyes, and Ryan stepped back under their intensity. For a second, it felt as if God was looking at him. Ryan shook off that feeling.

Ryan was quickly losing patience with what he viewed as a dead-end conversation. His cell phone rang. He saw Frank's name and number pop up. Frank moved fast.

"I'm sorry, but I've got to take this," Ryan said, and he walked away from the park bench.

"Why didn't you tell me Jackson Higgins was telling the truth?" Frank bellowed.

Ryan glanced nervously at his son. Worried that Brian might be listening, Ryan discreetly lowered the volume on his cell phone and walked a few more feet away.

"Will that be a problem?" Ryan whispered. His chest constricted. He needed Frank. Millions of dollars were at stake.

"No, but I like knowing what I'm dealing with. This means I'll have to strong-arm—change tactics. I'll be tossing this phone. We need to meet in person."

Ryan twisted his body to signal to Brian he would be off the phone soon. His son shrugged, but Ryan wasn't fooled. He knew Brian was still angry.

Sweat beads formed across Ryan's bare upper lip. He didn't like the sound of strong-arm tactics. He considered himself a child of God, and God didn't like this kind of ugly. Maybe he should pay Jackson's demands.

"I also learned his wife is sick," Frank said. "Dying. He needs the money."

If this made the news, Ryan worried he'd be the monster who couldn't empathize with a man and his sick wife. Michael Ward's reputation was also on the line. Ryan tensed. He didn't want to alert Michael about this nightmare. It's best he settled it.

Yesterday.

"I need this to go away," Ryan said.

"Give me a couple weeks." Frank ended the call.

Brian could practically smell his father's fear.

From the bits and pieces of conversation he'd overheard, he knew whatever was going on wasn't good. His father looked scared. Brian touched his chin. He had to find out. This might be the opening he needed in his plan for revenge.

"I'm giving up my apartment and coming home," Brian told his father as soon as he ended the call.

Brian knew he had stunned his father.

Ryan blinked rapidly. "Whoa! Where did that come from? Are you on something? My head is spinning. I would love to have you home, of course, but after all you said to me, I would think you'd want to be as far away from me as possible."

"You're right," Brian said. "My coming home has nothing to do with you." Brian didn't trip over his lie. He wanted to know what trouble his father was in and find out how he could use it against him.

"I can't stay at Merle's house, and I want to be near Karlie," Brian added. That was true.

Ryan froze. "You need to leave her alone. There are plenty of other women out there."

Brian folded his arms. "You're not going to dictate my actions. You need to fix yourself because your deeds are way past reprehensible."

"I'm only saying you can have any woman you want," his father said in a much more even-tempered tone.

Brian knew that. It didn't remedy Karlie plaguing his mind, though.

"I'll arrange to close up your apartment and get your things moved into storage," Ryan said. "Are you coming home tonight?"

His father was nothing but efficient. "I'll be home tomorrow. I'm going to check on Karlie. See how her visits went." But first he had to call Nikki, who had been calling him nonstop.

"See you then." Ryan walked off.

By this time, night had fallen and the streetlights were on. Brian watched his father's departure.

Soon, Dad. I'll avenge Karlie, and I'll derive great satisfaction knowing it happened right under your roof.

Chapter Thirty-six

"This Girl Is on Fire" by Alicia Keys was taking on new meaning.

Patricia left her sixth session with Dr. Flowers hissing her teeth. Same old tired jargon. Dr. Flowers had yammered on about reducing stress. How was she to reduce stress when her adult son was back at home and at odds with his father?

Brian and Ryan were engulfed in a war of wills, and she hated being in the middle. Playing peacemaker. This was how it had been for the past two weeks.

After one such battle, Patti had yelled, "Brian, why did you move back here if all you're going to do is cause contention?"

Brian's eyes had widened with hurt. "Do you want me to leave?"

"No, I don't." She shook her head. "But you and your father are driving me nuts. I don't think both of you under the same roof is a good idea."

"Then make *him* leave," Brian glared, engaging her in a stare down.

Patricia stayed out of their way after that. Whenever they argued, she retreated to her room or went in to the hospital to monitor the twins. The good news was that the twins were now healthy enough for surgery, a surgery she felt unprepared for because of the turmoil in her personal life.

Next to praise, sex was the ultimate stress reducer. She loved a good praise session in church, but if she had to choose between the two . . .

She flicked her wrist to glance at her watch. It was about 5:30 p.m. Patricia had bumped up her prayer life. She had increased her scripture reading, but that did nothing to quench the fire raging between her legs.

She jumped into her vehicle and slammed the door. "Think of something else. Think of something else." She slapped her head with her hand several times before plunking her head onto the steering wheel.

Tim's face flashed before her. Though she had diligently avoided him, it didn't stop Patricia from craving a small sampling.

Once she had married Ryan, Patricia had honored her vows. Their marriage had been the kind of obsessive relationship which kept her satisfied and her cravings under wraps.

But things between them were rocky, and Ryan had been distracted. This time she knew what was wrong. He was worried about the paternity test. He and Karlie had met up and given samples. The results would arrive by messenger soon.

She only wished Ryan wouldn't obsess so faithfully about it during their follow-up counseling sessions with Pastor Ward. Like a good Stepford wife, she had said the right words during the sessions, but deep down, Patricia was naughty.

Patricia liked riding on the edge.

She gritted her teeth. She needed something.

Call your husband.

Patricia tapped her feet. That was what she *should* do, but it wasn't what she *wanted* to do. Tim's "I'm in love with you" teased her mind every night.

Her palms shook like a drug addict in need of a fix. She did need her "fix," and she knew just how to get it.

Patricia started up her vehicle and screeched out of the parking lot. She drove at breakneck speed until she arrived outside Tim's waterfront home in Baldwin Bay.

Her chest heaved, and her heartbeat thundered in her ears. She studied the closed front door. If she went inside, there was no turning back. She would be an adulteress, but Ryan would not find out.

It would be her secret.

God knows.

Patricia was fine with that. She knew she would need someone to talk to, and no one could keep a secret better than God.

That did not stop her feet from wobbling as she exited her vehicle and made her way up the path to Tim's door. She spotted the docked boat and admitted she was impressed. She took a moment to appreciate the allure of the water before walking up the three steps to Tim's front door. Patricia noted the numerous sliding glass doors, which she was sure provided a spectacular, uninterrupted view of the bay. Patricia pressed the doorbell. Guilt made her scan the other houses for Peeping Toms. She saw no one.

God, if you're going to stop me, make Tim not be home.

The door swung open.

He was dressed only in a pair of slacks.

Patricia's eyes widened.

Tim flashed a smile and reached for her hand.

Without a backward glance or another selfish, demanding prayer, Patricia stepped inside and shut the door.

Ryan stood inside his front door holding the paternity results. His hands shook, the envelope flapping against his chest. The results inside would change his life forever.

Brian approached him from the kitchen. "Where's Mom?"

Ryan shrugged. He didn't want to delve into Patricia's whereabouts. She had been spending eighteen-hour days at work on the twins' case. However, Ryan suspected Patricia was running away from the tension between him and Brian. Not that he blamed her. He would run too, if he could.

"Are those the results?" Brian crunched into an apple.

Ryan nodded, went into his office, opened a drawer, and found a letter opener. He slid it under the seal to open the envelope and withdrew two sheets of paper. He allowed the envelope to fall to the floor.

"What does it say?" Brian asked.

"Give me a chance to read it." Ryan turned his back on Brian and focused on the words.

I am Karlie's father.

"Well?" Brian asked.

Ryan turned and met Brian's eyes. He tried to cover his disappointment but failed. "I'm, um, I'm—"

"Karlie is my sister?" Brian bellowed, dropping the apple to the floor.

Ryan nodded. "I'm sorry, son."

Steam emanated from Brian's eyes before he snatched his keys off the armoire in the foyer. "I've got to get to Karlie. She's going to need me when she gets this."

"She's with family," Ryan said. He did not want to be alone. He was surprised at how he wanted his son's compassion. A human connection.

"Well, *I'm* her family now," Brian shot back before slamming the front door.

A tear slid down Ryan's cheek. Pain crippled him and sent him to his knees. Crying out, he wailed, "Lord, what have I done?"

Chapter Thirty-seven

Karlie squatted on the living room of her mother's three-bedroom colonial home in Hempstead where she had arranged to have the results delivered by messenger. Neil and Myra wanted to be there with her, but she needed to be with her Mom. Tiffany was gone, but Karlie had good memories in this home. It was where she had had her first kiss and one of the best holidays ever.

She wrapped herself in the Karlie blanket, a gift from Thomas Knightly, the man she had grown up thinking was her father. She had a framed picture of her mother's final live performance in her lap.

She picked up the picture frame and outlined her mother's face. How she wished she could hear Tiffany's voice. "Mom, we're going to learn the truth once and for all."

Karlie opened the envelope. She read the letter and dropped her head. She knew it. Somewhere deep down inside of her, she knew Ryan was her father.

A sharp pain hit her midsection, and Karlie clutched her stomach. "Ryan's my father. God, why? Why him?"

Karlie rocked back and forth but did not cry. She did not know how to feel.

Her cell buzzed. She didn't have to check the caller ID. Brian had learned the results as well. She wondered if Ryan would call.

The wimp probably wouldn't.

Ten minutes later, the doorbell rang.

Slowly, Karlie drifted to the door.

Brian's hand reached out to pull her to him. Karlie collapsed against him like a ragdoll, afraid her legs would betray her. "I came as soon as I heard the results. Neil told me you were here."

Karlie nodded against his chest. "I'm glad you came."

Brian led her by the hand to the couch. He stretched out with his feet hanging off the ends of the couch and pulled Karlie to lie beside him.

Then the tears came.

Her body shook with tremors as pain wracked her. She wept until every last ounce of pain was out of her system. When her tears subsided, Karlie felt cleansed. Brian excused himself to fetch her some tissues from his truck. He returned and wiped her face.

"Thank you." Karlie blew her nose. "*Bro*." She smiled. "It doesn't sound right yet."

Brian wondered if it ever would. "I'm going to make my dad pay for doing this to you. To us."

His words sliced through her foggy brain. Romans 12:17 sprang into her mind: "Recompense no man evil for evil . . ." She knew she couldn't encourage Brian's plan. Karlie shook her head. She adjusted herself on the couch until they faced each other. "I'm angry too. Believe me. But it's not either one of our jobs to make Ryan pay."

"Yes, it is," Brian countered.

"I don't need you to fight for me," Karlie said. "I've got God on my side."

"Don't tell me you're going to *forgive* him."

"I. Have. To."

He shook his head. "I don't understand you, Karlie. My father does the most despicable thing a man could do, and you're willing to let bygones be bygones just like that." He snapped his fingers.

"If only it were that easy," she said with a sad smile. "I've had weeks to prepare for this, but from the time

Ryan dropped the news, I knew." Karlie reached over to touch his cheek briefly. "You knew too. You might not want to admit it, but you knew."

"I didn't *want* to be right, Karlie," he whispered.

"Neither did I," she said. "Brian, you were there for me when I found out about Jamaal's betrayal. I've never cried so hard in my life. But a part of me was crying because I was relieved. Relieved he'd moved on . . . because someone had already captured my heart."

His eyes widened. "Are you saying . . ." Hope glowed in his eyes, and he moved closer.

Karlie allowed the longing to surface from her heart to her face so he could see the emotions she kept banked. Then she blinked, closing the window to her soul. "This moment is the closest thing to a truth you'll ever get from me." Karlie placed a hand over Brian's lips. "Whatever I think I feel ends tonight. When God told me I was ready, I thought it was for me. But it wasn't until I saw your face when I opened the door that I understood what He meant."

"I'm lost," he said, shaking his head.

"I had to be ready to help you."

He creased his forehead. "What are you saying? Help me do what?"

"Help you forgive by forgiving," Karlie said.

"I will never forgive that man," Brian said. "I moved back home to dig and search for evidence."

"What evidence?"

"My father has a court case, and I'm going to help his opponent win. I've been searching his computer files, but so far I haven't found anything. I'm not giving up, though."

"You need to abandon your revenge scheme," Karlie said. "It's not worth it. Ryan's your—*our* blood. He's *our* father. I might not like what he's done, but I don't want to see anything bad happen to him."

"You'd rather see it happen to us?"

"No, I don't," Karlie said. "But I don't want you to do anything. If you care for me, I'm begging you not to do this."

"How can you ask that of me?" Brian asked. "Your request is a devious manipulation of my feelings."

Karlie nodded. "You're right. I need you to promise me you'll let this go." She gulped. "I have. I've been to see a psychologist, and I've been talking with my dad."

"I have no one but you to talk to."

"That's not true," Karlie said. "You have God. He is the Father of all fathers, and He wants to claim you as His son."

Brian chuckled. "Only you would use my most devastating moment to preach to me."

Karlie went to the mantle to retrieve her mother's Bible. Sitting next to him, she began to preach Christ. "You've been a churchgoer. However, it's time you meet the Savior."

"I want Him," Brian said. "I want the God who made you who you are."

Karlie nodded. "This was what God wanted all along for you, Brian. He's the reason I'm in your life. He brought us together for this purpose and at this time."

Brian closed his eyes. "I don't want to feel this hatred and this pain any longer."

Karlie slipped to her knees. "Tonight, I'll take you somewhere you've never been with any other woman. I guarantee no woman has ever taken you this high." She took his hand in hers. "I'll take you to meet the King."

Chapter Thirty-eight

Patricia dabbed at her lipstick and smacked her lips. She twisted in the mirror and shimmied. Dressed in her form-fitting crème dress and gold-specked heels, she knew she looked good. Good enough to eat. With a light swing of her hips, Patricia ran her hands down her body.

She was ready for church.

Today she was going early enough to sit in the front row. Right next to Lady Gina Ward, the pastor's wife. If she played her cards right, she and Gina would have more in common than their salvation.

Patricia hid a sly smile and opened the guestroom door. She stepped out, careful not to make a sound. It didn't matter if she woke Ryan because she didn't have anything to say to him. Not after she had been with Tim.

And not now when she had bigger and better things on her mind, like laying the groundwork for her seduction of Pastor Ward.

She clutched her Dolce & Gabbana purse and made it out of the house without anyone noticing. Before starting up her car, the Holy Spirit spoke to her.

Don't return to your vomit!

Patricia released a sigh of consternation. She knew 2 Peter 2:22: "The dog is turned to his own vomit again; and the sow that was washed to her wallowing in the mire."

She closed her mind to the implication behind the verse, telling herself, *I'm not a dog or a pig. I'm a human being*. The fight with her body was very real.

She had tried and failed. Miserably. So why fight it?

Since she had given in to her temptation two days ago, however, she had grown tired of Tim. He was a vigorous but unimaginative lover. *If I'm going to keep falling off the proverbial wagon, I need to do it with class.* Continuing a fling with Tim would be so . . . cliché. She also worked with him. Too messy. So, after three hot bouts of heavy lovemaking, she fed him the "I can't live with myself and continue betraying my husband" line and cut him off completely.

Luckily for her, Tim didn't push. Maybe because he'd gotten what he wanted. She yawned. She didn't know . . . and she didn't care.

To be successful at adultery, Patricia needed to find someone married with as much to lose as she did. Someone like her hot, look-at-me-flash-my-smile pastor. Pastor Ward heard from God. You couldn't get a much higher connection than that.

A warning hit her spirit.

Touch not the Lord's anointed!

Patricia trembled. *I won't touch him. If my plan works, he'll be touching me.*

Her sassy answer to the Spirit of God should have clued her in on how far off the path she had gone. Patricia pulled down the visor. "You've got this. Maybe after one time with him, you'll be all right again."

She pumped up her courage and headed to Zion's Hill.

Patricia sauntered down the aisle just as the praise and worship leader took the stage. She spotted Gina and Pastor Ward's children, Trey and Epiphany, in the front row, which was generally empty. Today, that was going to change. Patricia ignored the usher who pointed out an empty space three rows back. She strutted to the front row and settled at the end of the row.

From behind her, she heard whisperings, "Who sent her up there?" "She has a lot of nerve" "She isn't family," but Patricia held her head high. The view was better from up front.

Pastor Ward zoned in on her. Patricia could have sworn he hid a smile. Good. His smile indicated a sense of humor.

And perhaps even some genuine interest.

She glanced toward Gina. The First Lady winked at her. Patricia placed a phony smile on her face before turning her focus on worship. Before she knew it, she was caught up in the praise.

Patricia closed her eyes and enjoyed the moment in God's presence. Why couldn't she stay in this euphoria all the time? In church, it was so easy to serve God. To do the right thing. Burdens lightened and nothing seemed insurmountable. But when she left the building, she encountered the *real* world. She remembered her problems were still there keeping her up at night.

Soon the music died down, and the ushers roamed the aisles carrying offering plates. Patricia tapped her purse. It was time to put her insane plan in motion. Gathering her courage, she pulled out two tithing envelopes. One bore Pastor Ward's name written in her bold scrawl.

You're insane.

Before she could think twice, Patricia dropped them both into the velvet pouch. The deed was done. There was no turning back now.

She watched with fascination as the ushers directed everyone to stand and Deacon Broderson blessed the offering. She stifled a giggle because the small item hidden inside the envelope had now been well blessed.

After the ushers took the funds to the back room, Patricia ignored the announcements while watching for the head usher's return. Sure enough, the head usher brought her envelope to Pastor Ward. He tore open the envelope before taking a sip of water.

A millisecond passed before his eyes widened, and Pastor Ward instantly spewed the contents of his mouth onto the floor. Deacon Broderson rushed to offer him a napkin. Pastor Ward blotted his chin and suit before piercing her with his stare.

Patricia squirmed. For the first time she second-guessed putting the tiny pair of panties in the envelope. What was she thinking? Pastor Ward stormed toward the podium. Every part of her shivered with uncertainty. He was going to out her in front of everyone!

But Pastor Ward went right into the Word.

Patricia breathed a sigh of relief. All throughout his message, which she would never be able to recall, she wondered what Pastor Ward would do.

She didn't have long to wonder. As soon as the message ended and the congregation filed out, an usher approached her.

"Pastor Ward needs to see you," he said.

Patricia stepped into the bathroom to freshen up. She reapplied her lip gloss, sprayed some body mist, and did a quick underarm check. Satisfied, she made her way to Pastor's office.

She found Pastor Ward seated behind his desk. He gave her a warm smile.

Patricia smiled, stepped inside, and closed the door.

"Hello, Patricia."

Patricia's eyes widened when she heard Gina's voice.

"First Lady," Patricia said. "I didn't know you'd be here."

Pastor Ward gestured for her to sit. "Well, you've managed to get my attention in the most unusual way."

Patricia saw him reach for the envelope, and her mouth popped open. She watched him drop the scrap of underwear onto his desk.

"I thought it prudent to have my wife with me when I asked you to explain this . . . *gift.*"

Patricia didn't need a mirror to tell her that her cheeks were burning. She swung her gaze between the two, expecting to see anger but instead saw pity.

Patricia's eyes filled with tears. She covered her face.

Gina rose to get her a wad of tissues.

"I'm sorry," Patricia whispered. "I don't know why I did that."

Gina patted her back. "You do know why. You think this is the first time?"

Patricia's head popped up. "Someone's put underwear in the offering plate before?"

Gina shook her head. "No, that would be a first. And *last.*"

Patricia understood the warning. The First Lady was giving her a pass this time. There most likely wouldn't be a next time.

Gina kissed her husband full on the lips and departed leaving them alone—with the door wide open.

Patricia's respect for the shorter woman intensified. If the roles were reversed, she would have been giving someone a beat down.

Pastor Ward asked for her undivided attention and opened with prayer. When he concluded, he asked, "What's going on with you, Sister Oakes?"

"The results came in. Karlie is Ryan's daughter."

Pastor Ward's eyes softened. "I knew there had to be a reason for your behavior. Your action this morning was so out of character."

Patricia wished she could sit there and say the results were to blame, but she knew her secret pain. "No, Pastor. It is more in *tune* with my character. My true nature." Patricia's shoulders slumped.

Pastor arched his eyebrows, waiting on an explanation. Patricia took a deep breath and told Pastor of her sexual addiction and past affairs before Ryan.

"You need to tell your husband," he said. "Ryan loves you enough to forgive. I believe the truth will make your marriage better than before. It won't be easy at first, but no good marriage ever is without struggle." He provided the name of a Christian counselor to help her get back on track.

Properly chastised, Patricia departed. She would see the counselor Pastor Ward recommended, but she had no intentions of following his advice about Ryan. Patricia wasn't telling Ryan anything.

Her cell rang. She saw Timothy's face on the screen and answered.

"Come quickly! Anna had another seizure!"

Chapter Thirty-nine

Jackson Higgins will be taken care of.

Frank had texted Ryan from an unmarked phone with that cryptic message late Friday night. It was now after eleven a.m. Saturday morning, and he was munching on his second bowl of Cheerios.

Ryan shuddered. What did *taken care of* mean? He knew he didn't want Jackson dead, but there were so many other sinister scenarios. Though he had erased the text, the words were seared into his brain.

He jammed his spoon into the bowl. *Stop thinking about that. Think about the millions of dollars. Think about your reputation. Think about anything but Jackson Higgins's sick wife.*

He hadn't been able to. Ryan had stressed over those words all weekend long. He pretended to be asleep when Patricia left for church. Ryan couldn't attend services and clap his hands while knowing that on Monday he was going to ruin an innocent man.

Brian strolled into the kitchen dressed in a charcoal grey suit and dark blue shirt.

"Where are you going?"

"To church."

Ryan arched an eyebrow. "I didn't know you would ever step foot in a church."

Brian stared at him. "What? Did you think I was too much of a heathen to be reached? Well, I've got news for you. Sometimes when you won't go to God, He comes to you."

Ryan nodded at the profound statement. "No, you caught me off guard because I've invited you so many times and you always had a million and one excuses. So I figured I'd leave you alone. Stop asking."

Brian retrieved a bowl from the cupboard and milk from the fridge. Ryan pushed the cereal in his direction. Brian thanked him and prepared his cereal.

"Well, you might have stopped asking, but Karlie never did," Brian said. "Then again, she's for real about God. You can't be around her and not see Him."

Ryan recognized the jab. "I wish you would hate me or love me because this"—he swung his hands between them—"is torture. If you're going to be around me, stop needling me."

Brian dropped his spoon onto the tabletop and hunched over the small round table. "You're a phony. You're *not* a man of God, and I'm going to prove it."

"Wait a minute. Have you been snooping around my stuff?" Ryan narrowed his eyes. He had noticed a few things out of place in his office but dismissed it to paranoia.

"No. I have better things to do with my time." Brian scraped his chair back and stood. "If you'll excuse me, I just lost my appetite."

Ryan held up a hand. "No, son. Please, don't go. I'm sorry I messed up what could be our first decent conversation." He pointed to the chair Brian had vacated. "Please."

"Fine, but one more negative word and I'm gone. I'm not trying to enter God's house upset."

Ryan nodded.

Brian cautiously slid into his chair to resume eating. "So, how come you're not at church?"

There was no way he could tell his son the truth. "I overslept. I think it might be allergies or something."

Brian wrinkled his nose. "Yes, it's the season. I don't remember you being plagued with it, though."

Ryan forced himself not to look like a deer caught in the headlights and tried to keep his voice calm. "True, but it can start at any age and once it does . . ." He stuffed his mouth with the last of his cereal. He figured if he were chewing, he wouldn't need to be talking.

Brian wolfed down his breakfast and glanced at his watch. "I've got to get out of here or I'll miss Neil's sermon." He gathered both of their bowls.

"No, leave them. I'll put them in the dishwasher."

Brian thanked him and rushed off, leaving Ryan alone with his thoughts. He gazed at the empty doorway. Maybe he should visit Neil's church today. The only reason he hadn't visited was because of Karlie. But now that the secret was out . . .

No, he wasn't trying to interfere with Karlie's praise. Besides, Neil might cause a scene.

Ryan slouched. Rubbing his chin, he wondered how he had transformed into the wimpy guy hiding out at home from God when God was everywhere. It was stupid. God's conscience worked inside and outside of church.

The Holy Spirit still urged him to back out of his plans against Jackson, but again, Ryan disobeyed. He placed the dirty dishes in the dishwasher, dressed in the master bedroom, and headed to work. He often worked on Sundays, but this was the first Saturday he had worked in months. He needed to keep busy.

It was his only hope of drowning out the voice of God.

He was knee-deep in taking care of business when the call came. When he said hello, all Ryan heard was, "It's done."

Ryan ended the call.

It's done.

Chapter Forty

Where was Brian? Karlie wondered. Her dad was about to go up. Pastor Johnston had assigned him to do a three-part series, and this was the second week.

He's probably home asleep, she thought. *Stop thinking about him. It's supposed to be about God. Unless his psoriasis is acting up. That could be it too.* She twisted her body to look down the aisle hoping to spot him.

No such luck.

Her fingers itched to text him, but Karlie refused to use her electronic devices in church. They were too distracting. A message or text invariably would pop up and she *had* to answer. Karlie cracked up at the people who spent most of their time posting updates *about* the sermon to social media instead of actually listening *to* the sermon. She preferred a traditional Bible she could hold in her hands.

Her dad took the podium. There was still no sign of Brian. Karlie craned her neck one more time to search for his tall frame, but he was nowhere in sight. She would take copious notes to catch him up later.

It took effort but Karlie forced herself to push thoughts of Brian aside. He was where he was. She needed to concentrate on the Word.

Neil greeted the church. "Today, I'm going to talk to you about a well-known parable, The Sower and the Seed."

Karlie's eyes glazed over. She had lost count of how many sermons she had heard on this same thing. *There was a sower . . . blah blah blah.*

God's Spirit corrected her immediately for her disrespect. Karlie whispered a brief apology to God and tuned in.

Brian slipped beside her, and Karlie breathed a sigh of relief. She made sure there was an appropriate distance between them. Brian rested an arm behind her back. Karlie didn't think anything of it . . . until she saw the last person she expected to see staring right at her.

Jamaal.

Surprise shot through her body. Jabbing Brian in the ribcage, she frantically whispered, "Jamaal. Jamaal is sitting three rows across from us. What's he doing here?"

Brian was not the least bit concerned about Jamaal's probing eyes. Let him look and wonder. Brian did not patronize scum.

He squeezed Karlie's hand to assure her and centered his mind on the sermon. He saw the title and scripture passage on the projector screen.

"In this parable, Jesus spoke about planting seeds on the wayside, on stony ground, among thorns, and on good ground. The Bible tells us each of the places the seed landed represented people. People you know. People I know." Neil walked around the podium to center stage.

"He mentioned four places for four people," Neil said, displaying four fingers. "Of the four people, only one received the Word. The Word took root because it fell on good ground."

Brian leaned forward, instinctively knowing Neil was about to give a crucial point.

"So, in mathematical terms, three out of four people in your life will reject the Sower and the Seed."

Brian's mouth formed an O. *Wow.* He was a math whiz, so he did a computation in his head. An estimated 7.5 billion people lived in the world. Seventy-five percent of that was approximately 5.6 billion. *Are there that many souls going to hell?* He shook his head, stunned at the magnitude of souls lost.

Neil continued to expound on the Word. Brian wrote the scripture on a note and placed it in his Bible. He would have to reread Matthew 13 at some point.

"Jesus taught this parable to reach two kinds of people," Neil said. "You and me. As God's sower of the Word, those who reject salvation can't dishearten me. I still have to keep sowing."

Brian couldn't resist a glance in Karlie's direction. She was *his* sower.

"But Jesus wanted to warn anyone hearing the Word. For the Word to take root, it must be placed in good ground. You can control that. You can ask God to till away all the gunk we keep in our heart so that His Word can take root and grow in us."

People around him shouted, "Hallelujah!" and "All right, now!"

The Word pierced him. He had gunk he needed God to dig out of his heart. When Neil made the altar call, Brian was one of the first people to head up front.

While many prayed and Neil anointed him, Brian asked God, "Please, God, make me into good ground."

At the end of the service, Jamaal approached Brian and Karlie. Brian positioned his body to shield Karlie from him. Or was it the other way around? Whatever. He was making sure there was distance between them.

"Karlie, I knew this was the only place you'd probably see me," Jamaal said.

"Yes, because I have no choice," Karlie replied.

Brian felt her bristling next to him. "What do you want?" Brian asked.

Jamaal reached into his pants pocket to retrieve a stick of gum. "I just thought I'd give you a heads-up. I'm not going to keep quiet about you and Karlie's affair."

He spoke the words casually, as if he were talking about sports or a TV show and not about potentially ruining lives.

"What affair?" Karlie asked. "Brian and I didn't sleep together."

Brian couldn't believe his ears. He gestured for them to move the conversation outside of God's house and into the parking lot. Karlie stood frozen. Brian had to call her twice before she trudged behind him and Jamaal.

"It doesn't matter if you did or not," Jamaal said. "What's important is they will believe you did."

"Why are you doing this?" Brian asked.

Jamaal hesitated for a second. He had the decency to look ashamed. "I need the money."

"No one will care about some stupid picture," Brian said. "It doesn't prove anything." Jamaal had to be bluffing, but on the inside, Brian's heart raced. Salacious gossipers *would* take the picture out of context.

"You can't do that," Karlie said. "Winona is getting ready to release the news that we're brother and sister. That will damage me for good."

Jamaal hunched his shoulders. "Then pay up."

"How far are you sinking? That's extortion." Brian shook his head.

"Not to mention low-down and cruel." Karlie frowned. "We were together six years, and *this* is how you treat me? You broke promises to me *and* to God."

"God has nothing to do with this," Jamaal said.

Brian arched an eyebrow. "You're right about that."

"I *need* the money," Jamaal stated, eyeing Karlie. "I got myself in trouble."

Karlie's eyes softened. She stepped toward him. "What kind of trouble?"

Brian faced her. "Are you falling for this? Karlie, he's manipulating you—pulling at your heartstrings."

Karlie gave him the side eye. "What's going on, Jamaal?"

"Some girl accused me of forcing myself on her," Jamaal said. "She's demanding a huge sum of money, enough to clean out all the money your mother left me. If I don't pay her, she'll report me to the college and the police. This is my scholarship, career, and life on the line. I can't take that chance."

Karlie shook her head. "But if you didn't do anything, then why allow yourself to get blackmailed?"

Jamaal lowered his gaze. He fretted with his shirt and loosened his tie.

"You *did* it, *didn't* you?" Brian asked.

"No, it was consensual, but she's white—and as it turns out, underage," Jamaal said. "Who is going to believe me?"

Karlie stepped back. "You messed around with a *minor?*" She started walking away. "Leave me out of your drama."

Jamaal rushed after her and grabbed her by the shoulders. "I need your help, Karlie. I need you to be my alibi. It would be your word against hers."

"No," Karlie said. "I'm not doing it."

Jamaal grabbed her close to him. "This is my life!"

Brian grabbed Jamaal by the collar. "Get off her," he snarled. "No means no. But you don't understand that or you wouldn't be in this trouble now."

Jamaal shoved Brian, and Brian shoved back. Fortunately, the parking lot was nearly deserted.

"Stop it!" Karlie shouted. "Both of you!" She positioned her body between them. "Stop fighting. I'm tired of you two going at it like boys."

Brian breathed deeply to regain control. He held both hands up and stepped away from Jamaal.

Jamaal wasn't through. He pulled out his phone and swiped the camera icon. Once the picture graced the screen, he said, "I'm going to post this *now* unless you help me."

Brian reached to snatch the phone, but Jamaal side-stepped him and took off running. Brian darted after him. He was going to smash that phone to smithereens.

The men raced into oncoming traffic, bobbing and weaving. Neither saw the Ford F150 truck heading their way.

Chapter Forty-one

Patricia exited the twin's room with bloodshot eyes. She needed to soak her feet. Anna and Alyssa would live to see another day, but their parents had changed their minds about the surgery and Patricia did not agree with their decision.

They would take the girls home and love them. To them, Anna and Alyssa were miracles.

"I'll treasure them until God sees best to . . ." Mrs. Velasquez had been teary-eyed, but she was resolved. "Once they're stable, we're taking them to Disney World or something. It's time for them to have some good memories instead of staring at hospital walls."

Patricia understood their thinking. She reminded herself repeatedly that Anna wasn't *her* daughter Anna. She needed to respect the parents' wishes.

"One good thing is that the seizures should stop," Patricia said. "I've removed the troubling aneurysms successfully and adjusted their meds. Anna and Alyssa will be okay." She didn't know for how long, but they did need quality of life.

"We want to be together," Anna said, hugging her twin.

"We're happy," Alyssa added.

"It's time we start listening to the girls," Mr. Velasquez said. "God made them perfect the way they are. We're the ones who're trying to fix them."

Patricia bit her lip. She felt as if she could "fix" them, but she couldn't interfere with their parents' choice.

The girls would be discharged in a matter of days. She removed her surgical cap and headed to her office.

Tim was waiting for her inside. She clicked the door shut. He held out his arms, and Patricia accepted his embrace. When he pressed his lips to hers, Patricia snapped. She ripped at his shirt and returned his caresses with a vengeance. She moaned under his expert caresses. Yes, she would revel in this. As her pleasure increased, the pain inside her heart dulled.

Moments later, satiated, Patricia lay on the floor. She hid a smile as Tim gathered his belongings. Luckily, he had spare shirts in his office.

Patricia redressed and redid her hair. She had the urge for a strong cup of coffee and marched toward the break room. She pictured the day-old coffee and promptly changed her mind. She decided to go to the Dover Coffee and Gifts shop located in the main lobby. A mocha latte sounded like music to her tired ears.

On her way, Patricia bumped into Karlie zooming inside the building. Jamaal followed closely behind, out of breath.

"Karlie, is everything all right?" Patricia asked.

Karlie's eyes popped wide open. "Brian is here. He was hit by a truck. Where's the emergency room?"

Patricia flailed backward and her insides twisted. "Wh . . . What's happened to Brian?" In horror, she realized that her son had been in danger while she and Tim were . . . She swallowed the rest of that thought.

"The truck was heading toward me, and Brian, he . . . he—he pushed me out of the way," Jamaal said, convulsing into tears. "I would've been dead if it weren't for him."

"Oh my goodness. My son! Brian!" Patricia raced toward the emergency room with Jamaal and Karlie in tow. What a good thing she had walked that way or it could have been hours before she found out about her son's accident. Her cell was in her office. Who could it be but God? Even when she did not deserve it, He had her back. Patricia cupped her mouth, hyperventilating. *Oh, Lord, please let Brian be okay.*

Ryan was already there. She rushed to her husband's side. He enfolded her in a tight hug.

Patricia stepped back. "Did you see him? Have they told you anything?"

Ryan shook his head. "They told me to wait here."

"I'll be back," she said to all three of them.

Patricia swiped her ID card to enter the patient area. She clutched her pounding heart and willed her feet not to give way. Once she approached the nurses' station, she asked, "Where is my son, Brian?"

"Let me check for you." The nurse tapped keys to pull up the information screen while Patricia tapped her feet with impatience.

Seconds agonizingly crawled by until the nurse said, "He's in OR three."

Patricia rushed around the counter to read the screen. Her heart stopped when she saw Tim's name. Tim had her son's life in his hands.

"Tell my husband and the others Brian's upstairs," Patricia said, and she ran toward the elevator.

Patricia scrubbed in to see her son with her own two eyes. Her hands shook, and she prayed, "Lord, please. Please . . ." She sniffed to keep from crying and entered the room.

Tim saw her and waved her out, but Patricia wasn't leaving. He went back to work. "Your son's a fighter, but he's losing too much blood. He's going to need a transfusion."

Patricia clutched her chest. Transfusion. With a numb nod, she left the operating room. By this time, Ryan, Karlie, and Jamaal were in the hallway. Ryan gripped her arm. "Oh Lord. Is he . . . Is he dead?"

"No." Patricia assured him. "He's going to need a blood transfusion, though."

"Where do I go?" Ryan was already rolling up his sleeves.

Her heart plummeted. She looked down at her feet. God, how she prayed this day would never come. Patricia gulped. "You can't help him."

"What do you mean?" Ryan shouted. "I'm A-positive. You're O. So . . ."

"My blood type's A-positive too," Karlie said. "I can give blood."

Tears rolled down Patricia's face. She tried to hold back her sob. "Brian's blood type is B."

Karlie's face paled.

Ryan's head snapped back.

"No!" Ryan roared. He shook his head at her. "That's *not* possible. Even *I* know that. He has to be A, O, or OA. You're a doctor, you know that!"

Patricia stared at Jamaal. "Jamaal, I know you feel you should be here, but this is a time for family. Please go."

Ryan pierced her with a look cold enough to freeze ice. "That's rude. Jamaal and Brian are friends. He *needs* to be here."

"No, it's okay." Jamaal looked at Karlie. "Please call me and let me know he's all right."

Karlie nodded.

"Listen," Patricia said. "I don't have time to give you a biology lesson. Brian needs blood, and I'm the only one able to give it to him."

As Patricia ran down the hall, she knew she was running away from the real issue.

Brian was not Ryan's son.

Chapter Forty-two

Ryan watched Patricia run away from him. He straggled backward until his body hit the wall and he slid to the floor. Patricia's carelessly tossed words had rocked his world.

I'm the only one able . . .

She had made him believe for almost twenty-three years that Brian was his son. Ryan covered his face. He wanted to confront her, but Brian's life was at stake.

"Please, Lord, save my son."

He felt something nudge his foot. Karlie stood in front of him with her hand out. Ryan tilted his chin to look up at his daughter. He placed his hand in hers, and she helped him to his feet. He allowed Karlie to lead him into the waiting area.

They headed for two chairs in the furthest corner in the room and huddled together. Ryan felt her body tremble.

"Brian isn't your son?" Karlie whispered.

Hearing the words aloud sucker punched him. Ryan cringed. "I . . . I don't even know what to think. It's like the person I thought I knew, I didn't really know." He turned to Karlie. "Do you understand what I mean?"

"All too well," she replied, giving him a pointed stare.

Oh, how could he be so thoughtless? Of course Karlie got it. He had done the same thing to her. "I did you wrong, Karlie. I guess God is paying me back for what I did to you."

She shook her head. "You did do me wrong, but God doesn't do payback. Don't even think that way. Rebuke that thought."

Jackson Higgins sprang into Ryan's mind. He may not do payback, but God did enact vengeance—an eye for an eye. Or in this case, a life for a life. Brian was paying the price for Ryan's wickedness.

"I forgive you."

Ryan heard Karlie's soft-spoken words and swung his head around. "What? What did you just say?"

"I said I forgive you," she repeated.

Ryan's shoulders heaved. "No, don't forgive me. I've done too much wrong. I don't want forgiveness." He wanted to be flayed and whipped, even tortured. That was what his punishment should be.

Not the love shining through Karlie's eyes.

"You have my forgiveness, whether you want it or not," Karlie said, patting him on the back. "It took me time, but I had to. I'm God's daughter first, and I'm subjected to His leading."

Tears poured down Ryan's face. What kind of love was this? He looked at the beautiful woman before him and touched her face. "You're perfect. In spite of my flaws and all the wrong I did, you're perfect."

"I'm not perfect, but I'm perfected by God's love," she said. "The Karlie you see is not because of anything I did." Her eyes were now overflowing as well. "It's the God in me. I love others as He loves me. I couldn't be any other way even if I tried." She rose to gather tissues for them.

Ryan still could not believe what he was hearing. "I wish I could be like you, Karlie."

She smiled. "You can be. Anyone who asks God to take over will be filled with His love."

Ryan heard and recognized God speaking through her, yet his heart closed as he closed his eyes. Everything he possessed flashed before his mind. If he told the truth, he would lose it all. His heart hurt at the thought. Ryan knew he wanted God, but he could not let go.

Yes, you can.

Ryan debated, but he did not see how recovery was humanly possible. God continued to pull on his heart, but then Patricia dashed into the room. Her eyes were red, and her face swollen.

"Brian's alive," Patricia said. "He has a ruptured spleen, some shattered ribs and a collapsed lung, but he is alive. Thank God. He's also awake." She turned to Karlie. "Brian has called your name more than once."

A smile broke from within and beamed across her face. "May I go see him?" she asked.

"For a few minutes," Patricia said. "He's still very weak, and he might be asleep by the time you get there. He's on the second floor in ICU."

Ryan watched Karlie gather her belongings and rush out of the room to see Brian. He and Patricia were now alone. Ryan stood. He moved closer to the woman he had loved more than life itself for over twenty years.

His heart chilled. "Who are you? How could you not tell me?"

Patricia's breath caught. "I'm me. I didn't tell you because I didn't know. At first."

"How long have you known?"

"It wasn't until Brian was four years old when he had the meningitis scare that I learned the truth."

Four years old! Fury rose within him. Ryan wrapped his hand around her arm. "You should have told me!"

Patricia's eyes were wide with fear. "Please, Ryan. Don't do this. We love each other. We can work it out. I'm sorry for not having the guts to tell you the truth."

Ryan heard a voice behind him. "Let her go."

Ryan released Patricia's arm to confront the stranger. "Mind your own business. This doesn't concern you."

"Yes, it does," the man said, coming farther into the room. Ryan read the name tag: "Dr. Timothy Newhouse."

"Dr. Newhouse, I suggest you leave me to speak to my wife," Ryan said. "This is a personal matter."

"Tim, please, leave," Patricia said. "I'm all right."

Ryan glanced between the two of them. In a flash of insight, he discerned they were more than mere coworkers. After a meaningful glance her way, Tim left the room.

Ryan met Patricia's eyes. "You . . . and him?" He almost lost his balance as pain whipped his spine. "I don't believe you did this to me!"

Patricia bit her lip. "It was a mistake. I didn't mean for it to happen, but you weren't paying me any attention and I was stressed . . ."

He flailed his hands. "Spare me your sorry excuses." He rested both hands on his hips. "How many men have there been?"

She shook her head. "I don't know. This was before you. I was an addict, but when I met you, I thought I was cured . . ."

Ryan waved off her ramblings. "I don't want to hear it!"

Patricia grabbed his arm. Her lips quivered. "I'm so sorry. Please find it in your heart to forgive me."

Ryan forgot how, moments ago, Karlie had forgiven him. "What you did was beyond forgivable." He shook off her hand. "Get a good attorney because you're going to need it."

"No, let's talk about this later at home." She twisted her hands, "Right now, our son needs us."

"I'll be there for Brian, but as of tonight, you're on your own. As far as I'm concerned I no longer have a home. I'm moving out."

He stormed out of the room as Patricia crumbled to the floor.

***

Two hands gripped her by the shoulders and pulled her to her feet. Patricia raised her tear-streaked face to Tim's.

"I've lost him," Patricia wailed. "Ryan told me he's moving out and filing divorce papers. Divorce. What is that?"

"Shh," Tim whispered. "It's going to be okay."

Patricia leaned into his broad chest. "This is your fault!" she cried. "You tempted me, and now my marriage is over!"

Tim stepped back. "Whoa. You're not putting this on me. Yes, I told you my feelings, but you didn't have to come to my door. You had a choice."

Patricia dipped her head. "You're right. I'm sorry, Tim. I shouldn't have tried to put this on you. This is all me. My problem. Not yours."

"I'd like to think of it as *our* problem," he said.

Patricia smiled. "I don't think you're ready for my drama. I've got to sort things out with God." She covered her face. "Brian's going to hate me."

"One day at a time," Tim said. "Brian's your child. He'll be angry, but he's not going to hate you."

Oh yes, he would. Tim only knew half of the facts. He didn't know the whole truth. He didn't know Brian wasn't Ryan's son. She doubted Tim would look at her with eyes filled with love if he knew that.

Both of their pagers beeped at the same time.

"It's the twins!" Tim shouted. "They've taken a turn for the worse."

Karlie's eyes popped open wide. The nurse on duty had warned her to be prepared, but she could not withhold her shocked breath. There were so many wires hanging from IV poles and contraptions beeping that it overwhelmed her.

"Karlie," Brian croaked.

Hearing her name gave her the courage to step forward. "I'm here."

He struggled to lift his hand.

Karlie rushed to his side. "No. Don't do that. You've broken several bones."

Brian opened his mouth and struggled to speak. Karlie bent her body so he could whisper. "Where's the camera?"

Forgetting about the hours she had spent worrying, Karlie's relief translated into laughter. She laughed until tears rolled down her face. Here he was hooked up to all sorts of equipment, and Brian was worried about her.

"It's smashed to dust," Karlie said. "The truck ran over it."

Brian nodded before closing his eyes and drifting to sleep, his breathing steady.

She rested a tentative hand on his bandaged chest. Like a crescendo, all the emotions she had held at bay burst out of her being. Karlie closed her eyes and uttered a heartfelt praise: "Thank you, Lord, for sparing Brian's life and for bringing him through."

When she opened her tear-filled eyes, she saw Nikki and Charlie hovering by the doorway. Anger as she had never felt before flowed through her. Her eyes took in Nikki's artfully made-up face, her long nails, big earrings, and her twelve-inch extensions. Karlie stormed to the entrance and pushed Nikki hard enough for her to fall to the floor in the hallway.

"You're not welcome here!" Karlie roared.

Nikki bounced to her feet and put up her hands. "You can't tell me what to do."

Karlie pointed her finger in Nikki's face. "Bring it."

Charlie stepped between them, her eyes wide with fright. "Stop it now, both of you. I don't think Brian would want this, and I'm not trying to get kicked out of the hospital because of you."

Nikki's chest heaved. "He would want to see me."

"So would Jamaal." Karlie blocked the door. "But I'm almost positive *Brian* would want to see me more." She slid a scathing glance from Nikki's feet to her face. "Get out of here."

"You're not his woman," Nikki said.

Karlie swung her neck from left to right. "I'm more of his woman than you'll ever be. Now unless you're ready to donate your weave to charity, get out."

With a sneer, Nikki tossed her hair into Karlie's face.

Karlie sputtered for a moment as Nikki turned, then grabbed Nikki's hair and twisted it around her hands. Nikki squealed loud enough to attract the attention of one of the male nurses, who came running.

Charlie yelled, "Stop it!"

"Let her go," the nurse demanded.

Karlie drew deep breaths to calm her temper, but she did not release the death grip she had on Nikki's hair. Nikki's face reddened with pain. Karlie spotted Ryan coming down the hallway.

When Ryan saw the altercation in progress, he broke into a run. "Karlie, release that girl this instant!"

Though she took umbrage at Ryan's "daddy" tone, she let go of Nikki's hair. Karlie blinked. She could not believe what she had just done.

"And you say you're a Christian," Nikki taunted. "*Plllease.*"

Karlie smiled when she saw Nikki massaging her temples as she left with Charlie on her heels. She heard Nikki's sobs all the way to the elevator.

Good riddance.

"Consider this your one and only warning," the nurse said. "Next time I'll call security." With that, the nurse walked away.

"Karlie, violence is not the answer," Ryan said. "Use your words, not your hands."

For some reason, Ryan had a coughing fit after uttering those words.

Following her outburst, Karlie became a model citizen at the hospital. It took Brian three days before he could stay awake long enough to have a sensible conversation, and Karlie never left his side.

She knew she was where she was meant to be. She was not going anywhere.

Chapter Forty-three

"Why are guys looking at me so weird?" Brian opened his eyes to see Ryan and Patricia staring at him. He yawned and pressed the button on his hospital bed to position his bed upright. He eyed the clock. It was almost nine a.m. He must have fallen asleep after eating breakfast. "Did I grow an extra head or something?"

His parents chuckled with distinct awkwardness. They scuttled closer into the room. Brian was grateful to be alive. His near-death experience had brought things into perspective for him. He smiled at his father.

Patricia kissed his cheek before she went over to pull the curtains back and let the sunlight inside his private room. Brian barely noticed the brilliance of the skyline. He was more concerned with the slight tension in the air.

He arched an eyebrow. "What's going on? You're both freaking me out. Am I dying?"

It was a week after his accident and Brian's second day alert. He had spent the majority of his first day awake weaning off the IV and sedation drugs. They had removed most of the gadgets he had been attached to except for the heart and blood pressure monitor. Early this morning, Brian was able to put food in his stomach, and he was happy about that, even if it was a liquid diet.

"No, you're not dying. Your vitals are good, but your body needs time to heal. I thank God for bringing you through surgery, and I'm trusting Him for a complete healing," Patricia said. She wandered over to the meal cart and fiddled with his uneaten Jell-O. Then she walked up on Brian's left side and took his hand. "Your father and I need to speak with you."

Ryan moved on the opposite side of Brian's bed. Brian wrinkled his brows and looked to the left and to the right.

"Brian, there's no easy way to say this, so I have to come out and just say it," Patricia said. "You were in such a bad car accident that you needed to get a transfusion."

His heart rate quickened. "Please don't tell me I got some bad blood or something?"

Patricia squeezed his hand and touched his face. "No, it's nothing that drastic." She had a tender smile on her face. "I love you, son."

"Ha! It is drastic," Ryan butted in. "Your mother donated blood because I *couldn't.*" He cleared his throat. "What Patricia didn't think to tell me until a week ago is that I'm not your biological father."

Brian's eyes bulged. He looked back and forth between the two of them before settling a hard gaze on Ryan. "Is this some kind of a joke? What do you mean you're not my father?"

"I mean Patricia lied to me, to both of us, for the last twenty-three years," Ryan said.

"I didn't lie. I just didn't tell you." Patricia glared at Ryan before looking Brian's way. "Brian, right now, you have to get your strength back. We will talk about this some more once you're better. I told Ryan to wait, but he insisted you needed to know today."

Ryan snapped, "Yes, we needed to tell him because I didn't want Brian coming home and wondering why I wasn't there."

"Wait? What?" Brian's chest heaved. He held his hands up. "Slow down. I'm having a hard time processing all of this. You both are coming at me way too fast." He looked at Ryan. "What do you mean you're not there?"

"I've moved out," Ryan said. "But it doesn't mean you won't see me. I'll be there to check on you. Even though I'm not your father by blood, you are *my* son. It's important that you know that."

Brian shook his head. Ryan was not his father? His vitals monitor beeped with a fury. He knew his blood pressure was wacky. Patricia fiddled with something and soon all was quiet in the room.

"But, you two are inseparable. You can barely keep your hands off each other . . . How did this happen?" Brian's voice escalated with every word.

"We weren't always inseparable," Patricia said. "Remember, your father did sleep with Tiffany, and Karlie is his daughter."

"Why are you bringing Karlie into this?" Brian pointed to his chest. "Can we keep this about me? I don't need a reminder on how Karlie came to be. I need to know—I *want* to know about me. You need to explain and your bringing up Dad's cheating isn't helping your case."

"Yes, Patricia, please explain," Ryan chimed in.

Patricia's eyes slid away from his. "When I met your father, I was sort of in a relationship with this guy."

"What!" Ryan yelled. "You told me you were single! Another lie."

She glared. "Do you want to hear my story, or are you going to keep interrupting?"

"Dad, please give her a chance to talk," Brian said, closing his eyes and resting a hand over his head. "I can't deal with your bickering on top of all this."

Patricia tucked his sheets around him probably to keep herself busy. She released a breath. "I was with someone but the minute I met your father I knew he was the one."

Brian opened his eyes and turned to listen.

"When Ryan introduced himself and we shook hands, I felt a connection. We, um, were together that night, and the next day I broke things off with my boyfriend."

"Why didn't you tell me you had a boyfriend?" Ryan asked.

"Would you have gone out with me?" Patricia arched an eyebrow.

"No, but—"

"There's your answer," she said. "I wanted you. I wasn't thinking past that."

"How did you find out the truth?" Brian asked.

"You were four years old, and I rushed you to the emergency room, thinking you might have meningitis. When they did the blood work, I found out your blood type . . ."

"And you said nothing. Instead, you went on as if everything was all right," Ryan filled in. Brian saw the heat in his eyes. His father bore a look of pure hatred on his face.

Patricia's lips quivered. Tears rolled down her face. "Every day I carried the guilt, and I wanted tell the truth. But I was scared. You would have left us. You were the only father Brian knew, and you loved him. I told myself that's what mattered."

"You should have told *me*," Ryan said.

Brian's composure cracked. His body shook. "Would it have mattered?" Brian whispered. "If you had known, would it have mattered?"

"Honey, I think you need to rest—"

Brian cut her off with a glare. "Mom, I need you to leave. I respect you because you gave birth to me, but I need you to *leave*."

She cupped her mouth and nodded before rushing out of the room.

Brian faced Ryan. "Would it have mattered?" he asked for the third time. His heart pounded as he waited for Ryan's answer.

"No, I wouldn't have left you. I loved you. I still do."

Brian swallowed. "Dad, I know you're hurting, but please don't leave me. I know I haven't been the model son, but I'll change. I'll do whatever you want."

"I don't need you to bargain with me. I love you no matter what you've done. Brian, I'm not leaving *you*. I'm leaving Patricia. Too much has transpired between us."

"It won't be the same without you there," Brian admitted. He gave his father a sad smile.

Ryan touched his cheek. "I'm only a couple of blocks down. I'm not far away."

"I don't think I'll ever see Mom the same." His voice took on a hard edge. "She's not who I thought she was. I thought she loved you, but she's a liar."

"She's your mother, and the Bible said you should honor her. Patricia has some issues . . . She's going to need you by her side."

Brian nodded. *What issues?* He did not ask because he was not sure if he could handle any more truths. "Dad, I feel lost. I feel like I don't know me anymore." He coughed.

"You're still you." Ryan moved around Brian's bed and went to pour him a cup of ice water.

Brian took two sips before returning the cup to his father. "Now I understand how Karlie felt. My heart is ripping out of my chest. I feel like I'm on a crashing plane with no parachute."

Ryan hugged him tight before releasing him. "You're an Oakes. You *will* recover." There was no doubt in Ryan's words. His father sounded sure in Brian's capabilities.

Brian wanted to howl and wail, but he soaked in some of Ryan's optimism. Hearing his father call him an Oakes strengthened him. He swallowed his tears and lifted his chin. "Does Karlie know?"

Ryan nodded and grinned. "Yes, she found out when I did. I wondered when you would get around to realizing you're free to date my daughter."

Chapter Forty-four

It was all a little too convenient for Brian's liking that he was not Ryan's son and was free to be with Karlie. If this were a soap opera, Brian would be applauding with the rest of them, but this was his *life*.

Brian sighed as he looked around the walls of his home and despised his confinement.

If it were not for the long recovery ahead of him, Brian would not be here. His mother had put in for FMLA to care for him, and Brian tolerated her presence. For the past six weeks, he had been the center of her world . . . when she was not secretly entertaining Dr. Tim Newhouse, the physician who had saved his life.

Brian wondered if Patricia thought he was stupid. He heard the nighttime giggles as she sneaked Tim into their home. Brian could not carry on a decent conversation with his mother knowing how she was conducting herself. He did not hate Patricia, but she had broken his heart with her revelation. It wasn't every day a son learned his mother was a recovering sex addict.

He had learned that by accident on one of the days Ryan had stopped in to check on him.

Ryan and Patricia had been embroiled in an argument, and Brian had hobbled out on crutches to beg them to stop.

"I can't stay married to a sex addict!" Ryan had shouted. "I think it's a disgusting excuse for you to sleep around with a clear conscience."

"Please stop fighting," Brian had said, and then Ryan's words registered. *Sex addict?* He looked at his mother with disbelief. Now he knew what Ryan had meant by issues.

"Brian, this isn't what it sounds like," Patricia pleaded.

"Then what is it supposed to sound like?" he asked. "Explain it to me."

Her lips quivered. "Sex addiction is a real problem. It's not an excuse. I thought I was delivered, but then, I was under so much pressure. Your father wasn't the same, and things between us were not the same. I am only using Tim for now. It's a need. I can't help it."

Brian blinked. "Are you *listening* to yourself?"

"You're good at research," Patricia said, wringing her hands. "If you look up the recent studies, you'll see I'm not lying. Look up Sex Addicts Anonymous. I'll be going to meetings again. Honey, I'll be better soon. I promise. It's not the way your father is making it sound. You're a grown-up and maybe this is good you've found out."

Brian had heard enough. He headed back to his room, slamming the door with finality. There was a time when he wished his parents would argue instead of making love all the time. How he wished to have those old days back again. *My parents are at war, and I'm living in a battlefield.*

He only found peace and comfort when he read the Bible. Karlie sent him Neil's taped sermons, and Brian enjoyed the Word.

Neither of his parents attended church anymore. Patricia was busy with her trysts, and Ryan looked haunted by something.

Brian did not care enough to ask.

Thank God for Karlie. She had stood by his side through surgery and came to visit him daily. They shared jokes and laughter, but neither addressed the big question: *What is going to happen next?*

After all the pining of his heart, it would seem logical that Brian would jump to be with Karlie, but he was confused and shaken. He saw the question in Karlie's eyes and was grateful she did not push. Brian knew how he felt about her but had needed to tackle his recovery . . . his parents . . . his soul . . . everything.

Brian heard a knock on his door. Expecting Karlie, he adjusted his clothes and called out, "Come in."

Neil entered.

"Neil?"

"Karlie figured you needed to speak with someone," Neil said. He came into the room and greeted Brian with a brief hug before shaking his hand.

Brian crooked his head toward the chair.

Neil settled in and undid his jacket. It was October, and the temperatures were in the low seventies. "How've you been?"

Where should Brian begin? "My physical recovery is going better than expected. I should be back to myself in two weeks. I can't wait. I'm moving out of here as soon as I can."

Neil nodded. "What about your emotional recovery?"

Brian knew Karlie had filled Neil in on his current situation. "It isn't easy watching your parents fight nonstop. I'm coming to terms with that while trying to cope with the fact that Ryan isn't my father."

"I've had some experience with that, as you know," Neil said. "I can say that it is difficult, but you can get through this. You have Karlie and you have me if you need me."

Brian appreciated the offer. "I have been seeing a therapist."

"That's great. And I know you've been listening to the sermons. Healing takes time. You will get through." Neil tapped his chin. "Now let me address the real reason behind my visit."

Brian sat up. He knew Neil did not come to exchange small talk.

"Karlie's in limbo. How do you feel about her?"

"I love her. Love her like I've never loved anyone," Brian said.

"Have you told her that?" Neil asked. "I know I'm prying, but Karlie means the world to me. I want what's best for her."

Brian nodded. "I do too. I'm not sure I'm that person. My life is . . . complicated. I'm all . . ." He found it hard to believe he was at a loss for words. "I don't deserve her. I'm not worthy of her."

Neil laughed. "Perfect. I'm glad to hear you say that."

Brian squinted his eyes. Had Neil gone crazy? "How's that perfect?"

"A man who feels he isn't worthy of a woman will treasure her. He'll be the best for her and do all he can to keep her."

Wise words. "Karlie is all that's good and pure and I'm . . . I'm . . ." Brian shook his head.

"Karlie isn't perfect. No woman is. But she does have a good heart, and her heart is waiting on you." Neil stood. "I've interfered enough. She'd kill me if she knew I said anything to you. A father can only take so much moping without stepping in."

Brian smiled. "Your secret's safe with me."

"Let's pray," Neil said. "That way, I won't be telling her an untruth."

Brian and Neil held hands. The older man prayed for him with such earnestness that Brian could only open his eyes to stare at him. Here was a man of God. There *were* genuine Christians out there. Knowing that gave him courage.

"I'd be honored to welcome you as a son," Neil said before he left. "You're a fine young man, Brian. God has made you worthy."

Brian's heart expanded at the words. He knew God had used Neil to speak to him. Brian opened the Bible he kept beside him on a nightstand. He saw the note he had written about Matthew 13. *Oh yeah.* He had been meaning to revisit this passage. Brian opened the Bible and flipped through the pages until he located the scripture.

He devoured the parable of The Sower and the Seed. Neil had said each type of ground where the seed fell represented a person. A chill ran up Brian's spine as God opened his eyes.

The first seed fell on the wayside. Jesus said this represented those whom the wicked one snatched away.

Brian saw Jamaal. The devil had captured Jamaal's heart and turned him away from God because of women. Jamaal's flesh had overridden his love for God.

The second seed fell on stony ground. This person heard the Word and received it with joy, but once persecution arose, this person endured it only for a while.

Brian knew this was his mother. Patricia loved rejoicing and praising God, and she still did. But she couldn't endure the sacrifice serving God required.

Ryan was definitely the thorns choked by the need for worldly riches. All Ryan talked about was making money. His conversations with Brian revolved around Brian entering the business with him. Ryan had turned his mind from God, becoming rigid and unforgiving as he pursued wealth.

Brian read about good ground in verse 23: "But he that received seed into the good ground is he that heareth the word, and understandeth it: which also beareth fruit, and bringeth forth, some an hundredfold, some sixty, some thirty."

Or one. Brian smiled. Karlie had been the good seed. She prayed for him, stood by him, and loved him. He knew that without them exchanging the words.

His heart lightened, and Brian closed his eyes.

He heard a knock on his door. "Come in, Karlie," he said, knowing it wouldn't be anyone else.

Karlie poked her head in. "Are you decent?"

I am now. He chuckled. "Yes, why else would I say to come in?"

Karlie moseyed into the room and dropped into the same chair Neil had vacated earlier. "Did my father come see you?"

"Yes," Brian said. "He encouraged me and prayed for me."

She nodded. "My father's the best. He likes you, you know."

"I know," Brian said. It did feel good knowing his future father-in-law approved of him.

Wait.

Brian was getting ahead of himself. He had to ask Karlie first. Though they were both young, Brian knew he wasn't going to be in a long, drawn-out courtship with her.

"I'm moving out," Karlie said. "I'm thinking about moving into my mother's home."

Brian's head shot up. "You can't do that."

"Why not?" she asked. She moved to the edge of the chair.

"Because we're going to find our place together."

She blinked. "I'm not moving in with a man I'm not married to. You'd better get your head checked."

Brian crooked his finger, signaling for her to come closer.

Karlie came over to sit next to him on the bed.

"Karlie Knightly, I am in love with you. Will you marry me?"

Her mouth popped open. "But . . . we're young. You have school, and I'm working on the album. And what about the show? We postponed it until the spring, but—"

Brian silenced her by taking her hand. "I am in love with you. Will you marry me?"

"We haven't even kissed," Karlie whispered. "What if we're imagining these emotions and what we thought was chemistry wasn't, but we were just caught up in a—"

Oh, for the love of . . .

Brian grabbed Karlie and kissed her full on the lips. Fiery heat filled his fingertips. His breathing escalated, and his heart pumped as he poured every ounce of feeling he had into the kiss.

Before he knew it, Karlie was sprawled between his good leg and his bandaged leg. Brian trailed kisses along her ear. He gently undid the clasp holding her luxurious curls at bay. He allowed his fingers to roam through her curls. Her sigh filled him with intense satisfaction.

He found her lips and drank in the taste of them like a man who had been without water for days. When he felt her hand venture into dangerous territory, Brian tore his lips from hers. "No, Karlie. We'll have plenty of time for that on our honeymoon."

Karlie's eyes filled with desire and passion. She licked her lips and moved her face closer to his. Brian suppressed a grin and covered her mouth. He was going to have a greedy bride if she agreed to marry him.

"Still wondering about chemistry?" he teased.

Karlie shook her head. She was out of breath and wore a dazed expression on her face.

Brian watched her chest heave. He was experienced enough to know if he wanted her right here, right now, Karlie would give in, but he would not do that to her. Even if it killed him, Brian would wait for their wedding day.

Karlie abruptly kissed him and rocked her body close to his. It shocked but exulted him because he knew this wasn't Karlie's normal behavior. Brian knew it was going to kill him to wait, but he gently pushed her from him. "No, love. We're going to do this right. I am in love with you. Karlie Knightly, will you marry me?"

"I love you too, Brian," Karlie replied.

Finally. Brian had been waiting for those three words.

She cupped his face with her hands and spread kisses all over it. "Let's get married."

For the first time in forever, Brian smiled. "Forget the show. You're all the adventure I need. Let's plan a wedding instead."

Chapter Forty-five

"His name is Kyle Manchester," Patricia said. This was her second time saying these words. The first had been to Brian who had finally asked who his father was.

Brian had given her a terse nod before saying, "Glad you know his name."

Though Patricia knew why he said it, it stung. Sexual addiction was a real illness, but it had a nasty stigma attached to it. That's why she never told anyone she had it.

Now she stood squaring off with Ryan, who had waylaid her in her office.

"Please tell me I heard you wrong," he said. "Are you saying Brian is Kyle Manchester's son?"

Patricia nodded.

She wrinkled her nose. "I think he's some big-time attorney."

"Will my humiliation know no end?" Ryan shoved divorce documents into her hands. "Kyle Manchester was the leading attorney in the case against me. The one with Jackson Higgins."

Patricia eyes widened. "I didn't know."

"That's because you were too busy squirming under Tim and tripping over some twins to care about me or anyone else."

Patricia felt chilled to the core. "Anna and Alyssa were fighting for their lives. That's important."

"Did they survive?" he asked.

Patricia shook her head. "No. Anna didn't make it. She had a seizure from which she didn't recover. Alyssa hung on, but she passed a few days later."

"I'm sorry, Patricia. I didn't know."

She gave him a sad smile. "I spent weeks with a counselor, and I've learned to accept what was in God's will. Anna and Alyssa are reunited. I'm sure God's got them. I'm sad this is the story of our lives, now, where we don't know what's going on with one another. There was a time when we were each other's breaths."

Ryan pinned her with a gaze. For a moment, time stood still as each revisited pages of their past. *Maybe . . .*

Patricia took a tentative step toward him, but Ryan moved back. "Too much has happened. You've done too much. I've done . . ." He shook his head. "We both have to live with what we've done." Ryan pointed to the papers, which had now fallen forgotten to the floor. "Sign them. Let's be done with it."

Ryan left, leaving Patricia to pick up the pieces of the past.

With each step away from Patricia's office, he said good-bye to the woman he had sworn to love always. By the time, he entered his Navigator, Ryan had managed to push Patricia completely from his mind.

He had another stop to make before flying to New Hampshire for his quickie divorce.

Ryan started up the Navigator and drove a short distance until he pulled in front of the Higgins residence. He straightened his spine.

He exited the vehicle clutching the cashier's check he had for Megan Higgins, Jackson's wife. She had been the one who had discovered Jackson hanging in their bedroom closet.

Jackson's death had made the news. Kyle Manchester had seen to that. Kyle had called Ryan with the news, intimating Ryan was behind Jackson's murder. Kyle had vowed to bring him to justice.

Ryan had denied, denied, denied. After all, Frank had been careful. There was nothing or no one to link Ryan to the murder. *If it had been one.* The coroner had said Jackson committed suicide, and Ryan wasn't about to argue with that.

But if it was suicide, why couldn't Ryan let the matter rest? Guilt rode him. He questioned the wisdom of settling his conscience by offering Megan Higgins money.

Seven million dollars was nothing to sneeze at. He had the certified check to give to Jackson's widow. Since Megan Higgins was on the mend, the money would see her far. Ryan ran up the steps and pressed the doorbell.

He saw the door crack open and looked down at Megan, who was barely five feet tall. She was dark-skinned with jet-black, shoulder-length hair. She lifted warm brown eyes to his face.

Ryan's heart tripped at the sight of her. His mouth went dry. *Oh no. This can't be happening. Not now. Not with her.*

"Megan Higgins?" he croaked. *Please, don't let this be her.*

She scratched her button of a nose before nodding. "I'm Megan." She covered her pink lips with her finger. "The baby's sleeping."

Then Megan smiled. It was a bright, big smile that revealed the prettiest set of teeth he had ever seen. Ryan's breath caught. Sensations rocked him. Ryan had only felt this once before in his life. He had fallen in love with Patricia at first sight. Many doubted it, but Ryan knew from personal experience that instant love like that *was* possible. He resisted the urge to drop to his knees and ask for Megan's hand in marriage.

"I'm Ryan Oakes," he said.

"I know who you are," she replied, appraising him from head to toe. "You're better looking on TV than in person."

He stuck out his hand because he needed to make physical contact.

She placed her small hand in his, and then raised trusting eyes to look at him.

He almost jumped out of his skin. Ryan snatched his hand away. "I'm surprised you're talking to me."

She blessed him with a knowing grin. "I'm willing to bet everything I have that you came here with a check for me."

Ryan realized that underneath those long lashes was a cunning, sharp, savvy woman. "How do you know that?"

Her laugh was a melody to his ears. Ryan could listen to her laugh all day. "Jackson said you would. He said if he died, you'd come with money. Blood money to ease your guilt."

Ryan's eyes widened. "Well, you and Jackson were wrong. I came to—"

"Please leave," she said. "I don't want your money. Keep your millions and wallow in it. It won't bring Jackson back."

"How about my heart? Can I give you that?"

Ryan could have slit his tongue at his corny words. Who said that to a virtual stranger? *Apparently buffoons like I do.*

Megan's eyes narrowed to slits. "Leave now, Mr. Oakes, before I change my mind and call the cops."

Ryan's heart spoke. He held his hand out to her. "Marry me."

"You're insane," Megan said, before slipping behind the door and slamming it in Ryan's face.

Ryan walked away moaning. God had gotten him good. There was no way Megan would want the man she believed responsible for killing her husband. He tapped his chin. *Or could she?* Megan had said he was good looking. Granted it was a backhanded compliment, but it was a start.

Ryan hadn't gotten where he was without being a risk taker. He made up his mind. He would marry Megan Higgins. Two weeks should be enough time for her to see things his way.

Ryan whistled all the way to the Lincoln. Once inside, he tore the check into small pieces. Megan didn't need his money. She needed him. He would use all the resources at his disposal to make sure that happened.

He smiled.

Megan Higgins would be his.

His bride.

By any means necessary.

Reading Guide Questions

1. *My Soul Then Sings* is a tale of many secrets. Consider how the secrets unfolded between Ryan and Patricia. Was their marriage really built on love? Is there a chance for recovery?

2. Ryan struggled with his secret for years and came clean only because of the circumstances. Do you think there are some secrets not worth telling? Tell why or why not.

3. Brian and Karlie were best friends dating other people. Do you think it is possible for men and women to be just friends? Tell why or why not.

4. Jamaal's faith wavered as he got older and his body craved intercourse. How can you counsel young couples battling lust and strong sexual temptation?

5. Karlie debated if she should give in to Jamaal to keep him from cheating on her. However, her love for God and her principles won over her fleshly desires. What counsel can you give other young women who are in this situation? Can you hold onto God and your man if he is pressuring you for sex? If he loved you, would he pressure you?

6. Karlie and Brian were friends for years before their love developed. Describe the importance of friendship in a relationship. Which is more important for a foundation for marriage: friendship or attraction?

7. Many of the characters had difficulty maintaining their faith when faced with life's struggles. They often sought their own solutions. What practical advice can you give to keep our faith rooted and grounded in God?

8. Patricia admitted she was a sex addict. Do you believe this is a real addiction or just an excuse to sleep around? Tell why or why not.

9. Should Ryan have stuck by Patricia's side after her admission, or does he have a legitimate reason to divorce his wife? In your opinion, are there ever good grounds for divorce in Christian marriages?

10. Patricia made a pass at Pastor Ward—oh yeah, let's talk about that move. Discuss Pastor Ward's actions following her bold behavior. Did you believe her reasons or was she lying to justify her actions? Do we sometimes develop inappropriate crushes on our ministers because of our pain? What suggestions can you give ministers to keep them from women's advances?

11. Read the parable of the Sower and the Seed. Do you see Brian's interpretation of the scripture? Is there hope for seeds that fall on places other than on good ground?

12. Brian was the seed that fell on good ground. Discuss his transformation from the beginning of the story to when he opened his heart to Christ. What role did Karlie play in his path to Christ?

13. Brian had psoriasis, a debilitating disease. He did not receive healing for this, but God healed his heart. What scripture or words of encouragement can we give Brian as a new believer to prepare him for when his next outbreak occurs?

About the Author

Michelle Lindo-Rice enjoys crafting women's fiction with themes centered around the four "F" words: Faith, Friendship, Family, and Forgiveness. Her first published work, *Sing A New Song,* was a Black Expressions-featured selection. *My Steps Are Ordered* made the African American Literature Book Club bestselling list for the months of May/June and July/August 2014. *My Steps Are Ordered* was also #1 in UBAWA's 2014 Top 100 list. *The Fall of the Prodigal* made #2 on Black Christian Reads Fiction List for March 2015. Michelle is proud to be a nominee for the 2015 Christian Fiction Author award by the African Americans on the Move Book Club.

When she is not writing, Michelle enjoys singing, reading and spending time with her two teenaged sons.

For more information about her other books or to leave an encouraging word, you can reach Michelle online at Facebook, LinkedIn, Twitter @mlindorice, Pinterest, and Google+. To learn more about her books, please join her mailing list at www.michellelindorice.com.

UC HIS GLORY BOOK CLUB!

www.uchisglorybookclub.net

UC His Glory Book Club is the spirit-inspired brain-child of Joylynn Ross, Author and Acquisitions Editor of Urban Christian, and Kendra Norman-Bellamy, Author for Urban Christian. This is an online book club that hosts authors of Urban Christian. We welcome as members all men and women who have a passion for reading Christian-based fiction.

UC His Glory Book Club pledges our commitment to provide support, positive feedback, encouragement, and a forum whereby members can openly discuss and review the literary works of Urban Christian authors.

There is no membership fee associated with UC His Glory Book Club; however, we do ask that you support the authors through purchasing, encouraging, providing book reviews, and of course, your prayers. We also ask that you respect our beliefs and follow the guidelines of the book club. We hope to receive your valuable input, opinions, and reviews that build up, rather than tear down our authors.

What We Believe:

—We believe that Jesus is the Christ, Son of the Living God.

—We believe the Bible is the true, living Word of God.

—We believe all Urban Christian authors should use their God-given writing abilities to honor God and share the message of the written word God has given to each of them uniquely.

—We believe in supporting Urban Christian authors in their literary endeavors by reading, purchasing, and sharing their titles with our online community.

—We believe that in everything we do in our literary arena should be done in a manner that will lead to God being glorified and honored.

We look forward to the online fellowship with you.

Please visit us often at:

www.uchisglorybookclub.net.

Many Blessings to You!

Shelia E. Lipsey,
President, UC His Glory Book Club